10677499

THE LAST FOUR DIGITS

THE LAST FOUR DIGITS

…We had brought cartons of Chinese food, but I was so wound up I couldn't eat. Michael could eat, no problem. Hours passed. Around midnight, we took turns trying to sleep, but I couldn't. Michael could sleep, no problem. Around four in the morning, he woke up after about three hours of sleep.

"Tell you what, spygirl," he said, "I didn't think when we finally spent the night together it would be like this."

Just then, an SUV turned into the row and crept along with its lights off. It was a black Cadillac Escalade with tinted windows.

"Looks like your boyfriend's car."

Eye roll. But it did look like Santiago's SUV. I wondered briefly if he had lied about finding the Dostoyevsky novel on his desk. It could've been in his glove box because he was the one delivering them to warn people off. But bottom line, I didn't feel that Santiago was Dostoyevsky. Mexican mafia, maybe, but Russian mafia, *nyet.*

"Half of southern California drives that car," I said.

The Escalade stopped midway down the row. The driver's window buzzed down and a flashlight beamed out at one of the storage units. The Escalade inched forward and the beam flashed on the next one, and the next. It stopped in front of our unit. The flashlight went off, then the rear window slid down.

"This is it," Michael whispered.

It suddenly hit me that what we were doing was insane. We had no backup. Worse, nobody knew we were there, not even Molly. If these people were Russian mafia, they would have AK-47s. They would gun us down without the least hesitation…

THE LAST FOUR DIGITS

BY

JULIE LEO

This book is a work of fiction. All names, characters, locations, and events are products of the author's imagination or used fictitiously.

THE LAST FOUR DIGITS. Copyright © 2015 by Julie Leo
Cover Art © 2015 Trace Edward Zaber
Cover Beach Photograph © 2015 Dawn Lyons
2nd Edition: April 2016

All rights reserved. No portion of this book may be transmitted, reproduced, or stored, in any form or by any means, without written permission from the author, with the exception of brief excerpts for the purpose of review. For information: julieleo.com

First Amber Quill Press Edition: March 2015
Published in the United States of America

For David, Kasia, and Sebastian

ACKNOWLEDGEMENTS

I am deeply thankful to several people for helping me bring this book to life. I wrote it in England while living in a little village just outside Glastonbury. In the UK, fellow writers David Parish-Whittaker, Caroline Winstone, and Shirley Borokhov encouraged me and kept me going. Nina Harris showed me great kindness, and my son Sebastian shared the adventure. In the US, those who aided and abetted were my initial publisher, Amber Quill Press, especially Trace Edward Zaber and E.J. Gilmer, my writers group, the Penny Dreadfuls, fellow writer Mark Barsotti, the sparkling Debbie Morrish, my daughter, Kasia, and most importantly, David, my very own handsome prince who supports and inspires me every day.
Many thanks to you all.

CHAPTER 1

I was on my way to meet a new client, the first one in nearly a month. Jack Stone, movie star, 2004's Sexiest Man Alive, had been found dead behind the wheel of his red Ferrari a month ago, an apparent suicide. His upper body had slumped into the passenger seat, the right hand clenched in a fist, the left hand holding up four fingers in front of his face for all eternity. One of Stone's exes, the second of four wives, wanted me to look into his death. I'd done some work for Jack a couple of years earlier, and his ex found my business card in his desk drawer. She had the idea he was murdered, but the police weren't even considering that possibility. So, she would pay me to consider it; I take cash, check, plastic, or Paypal. One time I took poker chips.

The 10 Freeway into Santa Monica was backed up and barely moving, so I decided to put a coat of clear polish on my nails. I cranked the air conditioning up a notch and opened the sunroof all the way to minimize brain damage. It was a typically hot LA day; the brown air outside wasn't moving any more than the cars. I was stuck in the fast lane with my ramp two more exits away. At a dead stop, I painted my right hand, no problem. The left didn't go so well. Traffic started to move, so I let off the brake and the car rolled forward, picking up speed. The bottle tipped and polished my lap instead. Instinctively, and echoing a theme that plays out again and again in my romantic life, I opened my legs and hit the brakes simultaneously.

The car lurched to a halt. Luckily, the car behind didn't rear-end me, but the rest of the nail polish spilled over the steering wheel and pooled between my legs in a curved shape that looked like a fang. This, at a time when I was looking for a sign from the universe about whether I should give up barely scraping by in the private eye biz and go back to practicing law. Yes, I had once been a promising criminal defense attorney, but now the first of the month was one week away, and I had exactly twelve dollars to put toward the rent. That was if I could convince Sunnyside Property Management to take bitcoin.

A bee flew in the sunroof and landed on my left leg, probably drawn by the strong odor of nail polish wafting up from my lap. I took aim to flick it, but my left hand wasn't dry yet. As I blew on it frantically, the bee slid its stinger into my bare left thigh. I flicked the bee and it landed in the nail polish, which sucked it in like a mini-La Brea tar pit.

"Die!" I said through clenched teeth—part searing pain, part evil rictus. I honestly thought things couldn't get any worse at that point. So naïve.

With the traffic stopped, I figured I could quickly scrape the whole mess off the car seat with a folded shopping bag. I had kicked the door open and maneuvered myself above the spill, bag in hand, bum out the door, skirt grazing my knees, when a police siren made a short double whoop as it sped up the gravel shoulder next to me. It stopped behind my car door, lights flashing. At that moment, the legendary Santa Ana winds decided to kick up a little air, and my skirt along with it, revealing the green satin bikini beneath it.

"Shoot!" I shoved my skirt down, quickly jumped back into my position around the spill, and shut the door so the police car could get around. But the cop car pulled up next to me and stopped again. As its window slid down, I wondered if I could get a ticket for getting out of my car on the freeway.

"Well, if it isn't my favorite spygirl. Thought I recognized those legs." It was LAPD's finest—and by finest I mean hottest—cop, Detective Michael Escobar. He was my best contact at LAPD Homicide. "Contact" sounds so cold, but "friend" would be too strong a word. Michael was more of a nemesis. No, not that, either. In truth, he'd been a big help to me, and it would have been tough to get by without him. If he just had a reasonably sized ego, we would have gotten on fine. Michael was alone in the car and had to lean way over to flash me his actor-quality smile. "Do you need to be somewhere? I can give you a police escort."

"No, thanks," I said, hoping he'd been playing with the radio or something during that gust. "Wouldn't that be a misuse of taxpayers' money or something?" True, I was already running late thanks to traffic. But my thigh was swollen and itching like mad, and for all I knew, my face could be next. I didn't want Michael to see me when I turned into a puffer fish. The traffic started moving again. "Looks like we're moving now, anyway."

He rolled along next to me. "You sure? Come on...live a little."

"I'm living just fine, thank you!" I scratched the thigh just a little, which, of course, made it worse, and I was quickly out of control, scratching with abandon.

"I don't think so. You need to get out more. I can tell. Let's grab a drink later."

"I do not need to get out more," I cried. The traffic crawled along, and Michael obviously planned to stay by my side for the duration, taunting me.

Michael grinned happily. "Look, your face went red just thinking about going out with me, and you kind of sighed just then, too."

All true, because I was swelling up and scratching myself silly. I had to get rid of Michael fast. "Okay. Actually, I'll take you up on that escort offer. I need to take La Cienega."

"Follow me. And by the way, green looks great on you!" Michael said and pulled forward.

No, I wasn't wearing any other green, just the lingerie. He turned on his flashing lights and whoop-whooped me down the shoulder and then parted the sea of cars, which was starting to break up anyway, to get me onto my exit ramp. He shot me a wave and a huge grin as we parted ways, and I wondered if I would ever hear the end of this.

I stopped for an ice pack and some calamine lotion on the way to my meeting, scheduled for two o'clock. Around two-twenty I arrived, limping, reeking of nail polish, and with a giant stain in my lap, at ex-number-two's home. Her place was a modest third-floor condo in a complex off Pico called The Tides. It had the high ceilings, the white carpet, and the granite-and-steel kitchen, but it by no means screamed "movie star ex's home." I figured she must've been with Stone before he made it big.

She was less attractive than the Southern lilt on the phone had led me to expect—a square-jawed blonde, chunky with a few pounds that didn't fit her, the telltale sign of stressed binge eating. She wore pink sweatpants, a white T-shirt, and no jewelry, not even earrings. The same sweet, slightly hoarse voice greeted me, though, and a Southern Comfort smile to go with it.

"You have a lovely home, Ms. Stone," I said, as she motioned me inside.

"Gross," she said, giving me a handshake a personal trainer could envy.

"Sorry?" I assumed she was commenting on my scent, Eau de Hard As Nails.

"It's Gross now. I haven't used Stone for years. But anyway, call me Linda. I love your hair, by the way. I'd kill for wavy red hair like that."

"Thanks. I just pay for mine," I said, impressed that she graciously took in my obvious limp, reek, and stain without comment. I took the seat she offered on a loveseat before a cozy gas-flame fireplace. She sat across from me on a matching sofa and poured us both strong coffee in tiny cups. I took mine black. She smothered hers with sugar, then drowned it in milk.

"You and Jack must've had a pretty painless divorce to stay friends as you did," I said.

"Oh, sure 'nough. A little thing like a divorce couldn't bust up a friendship like ours. We were just too immature to be married, that's all. Never should've done it."

"Rumor has it Jack and his current wife, Leilani, were headed for divorce court, too," I said, though really I'd heard no such rumor. I made it up to see what she would say. In fact, though Jack mostly managed to keep his family out of the tabloids, they had painted a picture of his current marriage as a real-life fairy tale and left it at that.

"I'm afraid that one's true," she said.

"So, do you think it was still immaturity on his part at age fifty?"

Linda dropped a single laugh. "Oh, probably. Jack was still a boy at heart. That was part of his charm." Her chin tipped up. "If anything, he'd grown younger."

"Certainly the women had," I said and laughed at my own little joke.

Linda sipped her coffee.

"You don't think he might've killed himself over the failing relationship?" I asked.

"No, Mrs. Vega. Jack would *never* have killed himself." She leveled her eyes at me like she was aiming a gun. "He was murdered."

"Do you suspect anyone in particular? And it's Ms., by the way. But call me Lola." As always, I cringed as I said this. Who sees their newborn baby girl and thinks, Oh, let's call her Lola? Not short for anything. Did my parents look at my scrunched red face and see the fiery glamour of a Copacabana showgirl? Or was it Lolita, the fictional child-woman hottie that sprang to mind when they gazed at my chubby cheeks? Most likely they had simply been drinking on their way to the christening.

But if Linda found my name hilarious, she politely held back her laughter. "That's a tough call, Lola. Plenty of people were envious of Jack, and I'm sure plenty will gain from his death, too. He was a generous man. There might be some clue in his will…only nobody can find it. But it's out there somewhere. Or was, at least. Jack always kept a will."

"Do you know if he had a pre-nuptial agreement?" I asked.

"He didn't believe in them. Leilani would've come out of that divorce set for life, like the rest of us exes. I tried to talk him into a pre-nup, several of his friends did, but he wouldn't go for it. He said you have to always affirm faith in love." She shrugged, then shook her head with a smile and leaned back. "Jack was the most romantic man I've ever known in my life."

"Really? Jack Stone? But he was so macho." My personal acquaintance with Jack was a short-lived business relationship, but close proximity to that perfect six-foot-two body strutting in jeans and cowboy boots had only reinforced his man-of-action screen image for me.

Linda giggled. "Funny, isn't it? He did those action films, but he wasn't really like that at all. I mean, he was strong, yes, but so soft-hearted. You must've heard the stories about him and his sister, for instance? What kind of man goes to lengths like that?"

I nodded. This was familiar territory because the work I had done for Stone two years back had to do with his sister. Her name was

Jessica, and she definitely had been murdered. There's no question about murder where there's a neck garroted from behind, apart from, Who did it? Stone had hired just about every PI in LA in search of her killer, each one for exactly three days. If we didn't turn up anything new in that time, we were gone. I, like most of the others, hadn't made it past the three days.

"Don't you think suicide is kind of a romantic thing?" I asked.

"Maybe, in a tragic way," Linda said.

"He did make some pretty dark films, didn't he?"

"But he was playing characters. They weren't him."

"He was drawn to those parts, though. He chose all his parts, right?"

She shrugged. "True."

"By the way, how did you happen to come across my card?"

"It was in Jack's desk."

She'd said that much on the phone. I said nothing, only downed the rest of my coffee. People don't like silence, so they usually fill it up with talk. I was hoping she'd explain what she was doing in Jack's desk, but she didn't, even though the question hung in the air like a lead chandelier. I also imagined the fat stack of business cards that must have been in Stone's desk and thought, Why me? But I decided to let it go for the moment. A high profile case would make all my problems go away. If I could solve it.

"More coffee?" Linda asked.

"No, thanks. I want to get on this. Do you happen to have a photo of Jack I can have?"

"Sure." She rose and walked over to one of two bookshelves, neither of which contained a single book. Taking a file folder from one, she hesitated, then turned to me again. "Lola, I know it won't last, but I'd like to keep the tabloids away from this for as long as possible."

"Of course," I said, rising to leave. The tabloids had been all over Jack's death when it happened a month ago, but the initial feeding frenzy had died down for now, waiting for new information to come along and chum the waters. If none did, eventually they would make something up.

From the manila folder, Linda pulled out a signed eight-by-ten headshot of a somewhat younger Jack Stone and brought it to me. "I still have a stack of them from back when I took care of his fan mail.

Oh! I almost forgot your money." She giggled.

"Don't worry," I said. "I wouldn't have."

Without further giggles, she picked up a check from her dining room table and gave me that, too. I checked the amount. It was spot on.

"Could you also give me Jack's—I mean, Leilani's—address and phone number again?"

"Sure 'nough." Linda scribbled the information on the back of the headshot with a ballpoint pen and handed it off to me.

"Okay, Linda," I said, grabbing my bag, "I'll let you know what I come up with." I glanced at the picture. Jack Stone's boyish, crooked smile and dark, deep-set eyes looked out at me from the photo. The eyes twinkled with life. He looked like a happy man, but the photo was a decade old. At the bottom, hand-scrawled in heavy black marker, were the words: Keep Stayin' Alive! Jack Stone.

"Personally, I never much cared for *Stayin' Alive*," I said, to check her reaction.

"Are you kidding?" Linda said, as she walked me out. "That was my favorite movie!"

Back at my car, the hardened puddle of nail polish on the seat had expanded and congealed into a final shape. It now looked to me like a big, curvy, Sherlock Holmes pipe, smoking a honeybee. I chiseled out the bee with my car key, flicked it to the asphalt, and climbed carefully into the driver's seat.

I pulled out my cell and sat staring at it. I would need to touch base at some point with Michael Escobar about this. I thought about running into him earlier. I often bumped into him when I was in some kind of sticky situation, and I didn't like it one bit. It didn't do much for my confidence. Michael had enough confidence for two people, although, to be fair, he definitely had the habanero-hot looks to back it up. An image popped into my mind of Michael, who was big on water sports, lying on the beach atop a giant green chili pepper, white cheese melting over his brown skin, sizzling in the sun. In my daydream, his hands rested behind his head, exposing the soft undersides of those sculpted arms, and the cheese slid off, achingly slowly revealing his Speedo-clad body. I shook the vision from my head, took a deep breath, and decided to put off calling Michael to another time.

Instead, I put in a call to Jack Stone's attorney over in Century

City—J.M. Klein of Bishop, Sigorsky, and Klein. The assistant assured me Klein would get back to me quickly. This usually proved to be true; only the alpha attorneys would make a fellow attorney wait for a callback the way they did with clients. There was no telling with Klein, though, because he was a definite alpha.

In the meantime, I decided to check public records to see if either of the Stones had filed any divorce-related papers recently. Driving downtown, I went over in my mind every word Linda had said. One thing alone kept bugging me: Why on Earth would she rather be called Gross than Stone?

CHAPTER 2

Down at the LA County Courthouse, I found no divorce or separation papers filed for marriage number four. I had asked the clerk a question and was about to leave when she noticed the headshot of Jack Stone topping my clutch of papers on the counter. She was about twenty years old and wore huge beaded earrings. Like many people in customer service jobs, she was unperturbed by the long queue of people behind me awaiting her attention.

"Oh, Jack Stone," she said, spiking the white border of the photo with a long silver fingernail. "*Such* a hottie! I can't believe he killed himself, can you?" Her face scrunched into a pained expression.

"I really can't, no," I said and meant it.

"Did you ever hear him on the *Clay Parker Show*?" she asked.

"Uh-uh. Never heard of it."

"You've never heard of Clay Parker? He's the late-night talk radio guy on KFX-AM. I listen to him every night until I fall asleep. Jack Stone used to call the show. I was actually listening the very first time he called in. And you know, you're thinking, there's no way it's really him…but it really was him."

"When was that?" I asked her, but quietly, so the placid crowd behind me wouldn't turn into a mob.

"About six months ago."

"What did he talk about?"

She scrunched her eyes up again. "Oh, the poor thing! He called about his sister. They were *extremely* close and then she was murdered." Her eyes grew wide. "He was contacting her spirit through a medium, trying to find out who killed her. It was *so* sad!" She clutched the sides of her computer monitor, toppling a tiny stuffed koala perched on it.

"Did she tell him who did it?" I asked.

"No. She said a lot of stuff, but never that."

That didn't surprise me. "How did he sound? Was he, you know, heartbroken?"

"Oh, *God,* yes!" She almost cried.

"Can we keep this moving?" a guy behind me said at last.

I tilted my head and did a peripheral take on him. He was thick and surly-looking. His face said he would eat a child if it would jump him one spot closer to the front of the line.

The clerk flashed him a cool look and me a weak smile.

"Love your earrings by the way," I said, waving goodbye.

Like I'd always said, leads are like men...you never know when one might pop up.

*   *   *

I headed over to KFX to talk to the station manager about Clay Parker, the pop culture high priest of weird. His guests were people who talked about the paranormal: ghosts, UFOs, exorcisms, and the like, and the audience called in with questions and comments. The station manager was happy to let me explore the archives of Parker's show, so long as I didn't remove anything from the premises.

Thanks to the clerk, it didn't take me long to zero in on Stone. He had been taking a lot of heat in the media and on the Internet ever since it got out that he was trying to contact his sister's ghost. The tabloids were putting out every bizarre story imaginable about him. The first night he called in there was no special guest on the show, so people could call in and talk about anything. A lot of callers wanted to talk about Jack Stone. Apparently, Jack was a late-night listener, further evidence that his marriage bed had gathered some frost, and he didn't like what he was hearing. Someone else might have turned the radio off, but not Jack Stone. But he sounded more angry than heartbroken. I fast-forwarded several times until I heard Jack's voice, then backed up to a little before that.

"You're on the air," Parker said.

"This is Dark Mark from Minneapolis. That rumor about Jack Stone contacting his dead sister is probably true. My brother has an

10

occult bookstore in LA, and he says Jack Stone is a regular customer. He's totally into the occult and based on the books he buys, he most likely belongs to a witch coven."

"Um, okay, well, there you have it. Thank you. Next caller, good evening."

"Is this Clay?"

"Probably. That's who you called, right?"

"Okay. You sound different. Anyway, yeah, I'm actually in a coven with Jack Stone, and I can tell you that he really is into talking to his dead sister. We help him, and he talks to her about once a week."

"Really! So, even rigor mortis doesn't stop women talking. Is it difficult to contact her?"

"For witches, it's no more difficult than making a phone call."

"I see. Hmm…that actually sounds kind of boring."

"Well, yeah, if it weren't for the blood sacrifice we do beforehand, it probably would be."

"Oh, now that's interesting. What do you sacrifice?"

"Well, last week it was my landlord's cat. Ha! That'll teach him to lean on a Satanist for the rent."

"Okay, thanks for the info. Goodbye, caller. If you're a Satanist, shouldn't you be able to pay the rent? I'd get a more upscale demon. Next caller, you've got the *Clay Parker Show*."

"That guy was full of it. First of all, witches and Satanists are two completely different things. Witches don't even believe in Satan. Second, you don't contact the dead through covens and sacrifices. Nobody would do that. It simply isn't necessary. That would be like using a fire hose to put out a cigarette."

"Okay, so how do you do it?"

"Usually, you have a medium make contact and the ghost will speak through them."

"Do you do this yourself, sir?"

"No, I don't, but I have an aunt who does it."

"And how much money does your aunt charge for her services?"

"I don't know. For Jack Stone, I'm sure she'd make him a sweet deal. Man, she loves that guy."

"Okay, thank you, caller. Hello, you're on the air."

"Yeah, this is Jack Stone. I just want to say I'm sick of hearing this <bleep>. Excuse my French. But none of these people have a clue what they're talking about. There's no coven or sacrifices or any of that."

"You really do sound like Jack Stone."

"I *am* Jack Stone. And I'm sick of hearing this stuff."

"Okay, so why don't you set the record straight for us, then. Here's your chance."

Silence.

"Caller? Uh, Mr. Stone?"

"I'm here. Look…have you ever lost someone you love?"

"Yes, I have."

"Then you know how it is. Well, take that feeling, that wrenching grief and guilt that gnaw at your gut and won't let you sleep at night, and put on top of it…that the person you love was murdered by a worthless scumbag. Can you even imagine how that feels?"

"Yes, I can. I'd want someone to pay."

"Exactly! I wanted to see if, from the other side, she could tell me who killed her."

"What about the police?"

"Ha! Don't make me laugh! The police couldn't find a Jew at a Bar Mitzvah. That's where I got the idea in the first place—they wanted to bring in a medium. They never had any solid leads from day one. They got hundreds of phone tips, but none of them ever amounted to anything."

"I see."

"Too bad their medium didn't. She got nowhere, but I decided to find someone else and keep trying. As long as there's a chance Jess might be able to say who he was."

"He?"

"Well, it was someone with some strength, at least hand strength. I don't want to get all into it, but she was strangled. From behind. That's already well known. Anyway, I put the word out I was looking for a medium to contact someone who had passed over. I got a few names, tried out a couple people. Finally, I hit on one, let's call her Mrs. O, who told me some things nobody but Jess would've known."

"Like what, for instance? Her high school prom date, that kind of thing?"

"Look, I don't want to get into that either because some nut might take that and use it. You know, when you're famous, people just do some unbelievable <bleep>. Well, you probably do know. Don't people do some unbelievable <bleep>?"

"Oh, they do indeed. Very true."

"So you know what I'm talking about, then. Anyway, mediums have probably been around as long as people have been burying their dead. Some very respected people have contacted the other side— Thomas Edison and Arthur Conan Doyle to name a couple. And I'm sure a lot more people believe in it than admit it because they're afraid of getting laughed at."

"Can you actually see the ghost of your sister?"

"No, I haven't actually seen her."

"Do you hear her voice?"

"No, no disembodied voice, either. Just messages from Jess that the medium tells me. She's kind of like a translator. I can smell Jess's cigarette smoke, though."

"Really?"

"Yeah, my sister had a major smoking habit, and I swear, the minute she's there I know because I can smell the smoke."

"So there's smoking in heaven?"

"I didn't mean that; she just always reeked of cigarettes, her clothes and her hair."

"So, has she told you who killed her?"

"No. At least, not yet. Anyway, I should go. Probably shouldn't have called."

"No, I'm glad you did call. This has been very interesting, and you explained it well. I hope you'll keep us posted and let us know if she does tell you who done it. Or anything else."

"Yeah, sure. You have a good night."

"And you as well, Mr. Stone. Well, there you have it, listeners, the explanation from the man himself, Jack Stone. I'm just happy to know he listens to the show!"

———

I had to get down the freeway before rush hour, or put my already fragile sanity at risk, so I left the rest of the archives for another day. I put in a call to Linda. She didn't answer, so I left a message. I hoped she could answer one question: Exactly who was the mysterious Mrs. O?

CHAPTER 3

"A girl's best friend is her mother," to quote my mama. But in my case, truer words were never spoken. My mama was my refuge from the storm called life, plus she was as sharp as a shot of Cuervo. She often helped me with my cases. I went straight to my mama's house in Glendale, where I was expected for dinner in a couple of hours. If I didn't solve this case, I would soon be dining there every night. I found her in the den assembling gift baskets for her new home-based business, Sweet Greets. Six months in, it had not made her a millionaire yet. She didn't need the money anyway. It kept her busy and kept her mind off my papa, who had passed away nine months ago.

"Hi, *Mami.*" I kissed her on the cheek. She clutched my shoulder with the stem of a chocolate baby rattle in her hand. It snapped in half.

"Darn," she said. "Oh well, I have more. Isn't that cute? It actually rattles, see?" She waved the two ends at me like maracas.

"Yeah, cute," I said, kicking off my shoes, looking at my feet and wiggling the toes. I was actually thinking how cute my feet were, but she would never know. "Can I use your computer to do a quick search?" I asked.

"Well, of course you can! Why would you even ask?"

I got up and went down a short hallway to the office. As soon as I figured I was out of earshot, I said, "Because I'd do anything to avoid coming close to the subject of babies, that's why. I'm surprised you haven't figured that out."

"Don't worry. I figured that out long ago," *Mami* cried from the den.

Oh, she was sharp.

I shut the office door, took a seat at the desk, and wiggled the mouse to wake the computer. Normally, this was the kind of thing I tried to get my mama to do, but I had now stuck myself with it. I opened a new tab and considered how to search for a medium. Psychic? Clairvoyant? Opportunist? I typed "mediums los angeles" in the search box.

A band of graphics across the top of the screen showed photos featuring either psychics or their buildings, usually with a neon palm or eye in the window, or pictures of crystal balls or angels. Below the graphics were tons of text listings. I clicked on a few websites. On several of them, animations blinked like Fourth of July displays alongside blurbs about tarot cards or offers to put me in touch with angels. Some of the names started with "Mrs." followed by a first or last name, but none of them started with O.

Then I remembered that Stone spent a lot of time at a large adobe house he owned on sixty acres in Santa Fe. What if the mysterious Mrs. O wasn't in LA at all, but in New Mexico? She could be almost anywhere. It was too big a task; I'd have to find the medium some other way. I killed the tab and shoved the mouse away with a vengeance.

I stood up and poked about the room, full of my papa's things. He'd had a law office downtown, but this was his home office. It still looked exactly as it had when he was alive. *Mami* hadn't touched it, and she wouldn't let anyone else touch it, either. Every surface held framed photos of three generations of the family, individually and in combinations.

I picked up a framed photo of *Papi* and myself on the day I graduated from law school. I was so happy that day. It was my papa who had made me want to study law, but the practice of law made me want to do something else. That and the secret I'd never told anyone: ever since reading my first Raymond Chandler novel back in eighth grade, I'd wanted to be a private detective. *Papi* never got over it. If only he had stuck around a little longer, maybe someday I could've convinced him quitting law was the right move for me.

So far, I was still trying to convince myself. It's not all glamour.

Three years on my own as a private eye and I still couldn't afford an office. I worked out of my apartment, which was fine since so much of my work was on the computer anyway, but a lot of clients expected me to have an office. I might be taken more seriously if I had one. When I'd practiced law, I had a nice office. And lots of money. Back then, my shoes were Jimmy Choos; three years on, I was buying Carlos Santanas and I liked them fine. Fortunately, my old clothes still fit me. But all my savings had evaporated. *Papi's* eyes came back to me from the day I'd told him my news. They'd filled with disbelief and tears. Then he turned away from me.

"Lolita!" *Mami's* muffled voice carried through the dense wooden door. "Will you come help me with dinner?"

"Okay," I said, too quietly for even her to hear.

I'm sure my face looked like that of a sullen eight-year-old as I walked into the kitchen. It didn't make me any less glum to find Tony DiMarco standing next to *Mami,* a bright blue blazer slung over one shoulder, making small talk as she chopped carrots. They turned to me in unison. My mouth opened, but no words came out.

"There she is!" Tony grinned and swept toward me like a ballroom dancer. In one smooth motion, he swung his blazer off the shoulder and over an arm in order to greet me with a warm hug. "Hi, sweetie!" He pressed me to his mint green shirt, and the lush scent of his A&F Fierce cologne filled my head and soothed my mood.

"*Mami* didn't tell me you were coming," I said, flashing her a mid-embrace kill look from safely behind his back. Lately, she had been trying to match-make us by "accidentally" running into Tony and inviting him over for dinner. The two of us together didn't look like a crazy idea to *Mami.* Tony and I had clerked together one summer during law school. He was a nice guy, funny, good looking, and had a great future ahead of him as an entertainment lawyer. Too bad he was gay. Even more too bad, he seemed to be the only person on Earth who didn't know he was gay. Except for *Mami.*

"We just ran into each other this afternoon, and I said, come on over for dinner," *Mami* said and continued chirping away, telling the whole story.

Tony released me and looked into my eyes. "I think this is our third date," he said under his breath, smiling at me like a used car salesman.

I pulled away. "I don't think this counts as dating."

"Sure it does." His porcelain veneers beamed from his classically handsome square jaw.

I made a wide circle around him to pour a glass of water from the refrigerator door. "Want some?" Water. I meant water.

"Mmm, sure," Tony said, bouncing his eyebrows up and down.

I couldn't help rolling my eyes. He might be fooling himself, but he wasn't fooling me. My friend Mia had gone out with Tony for two months before she got fed up with him ogling other people. Male people. True, he did the occasional double take of a woman, but would then invariably comment on her outfit. I poured him some water, wondering if it was possible he truly had not figured himself out yet.

"Dinner's ready," *Mami* chimed.

During dinner, Tony kept us laughing with stories about clients and would-be clients of the law firm where he worked. Nothing privileged, of course. An actor who supposedly did his own stunts wanted to silence a stuntman who'd Tweeted a selfie after he was almost blown up on the set of the actor's new movie. A well known actress wanted to sue the caterer of her dog's wedding because the canine hors d'oeuvres tasted, in her opinion, like dog food.

At one point, I felt Tony's hand nudge my thigh, and I poised to jam my fork into it should it roam any farther into my lap. But he only took my hand into his under the table and gave it a squeeze, a sweet secret for both of us to share. Tony was going to make some man a wonderful husband one day.

*   *   *

I drove home around ten o'clock, alone. All I could think about was how many Tony DiMarcos *Mami* would try to fix me up with if I actually lived there, and how I could not let that happen. Or would it be night after night of Tony himself, until I gave up? She meant well; she only wanted to see me as happy as she'd been with *Papi*. But *Papi* was one of a kind. It wasn't every day a man came along with his combination of character, looks, and loyalty.

Soon after leaving my mama's, an annoying set of headlights came up behind me, glaring painfully in my eyes. Flipping the rearview mirror up didn't help much because they shone in my wing mirror as well. The car stayed behind me all the way to my place in Burbank. I only lost them when I turned into the parking lot.

Mami had given me armloads of stuff to take home, so I spent several minutes twisted around toward the backseat, organizing things into two bags so I could carry everything up in one trip. Eventually, I got out of the car and opened the back door to get the bags out. I hooked a shopping bag with a handle on one arm and cradled a grocery bag, then pushed the car door shut with my free hand.

I looked up. Across the car, on the passenger side, another car sat right next to mine, perpendicular to it so it faced straight toward me. I caught the briefest glimpse of a light-colored sedan before the car's headlights came on.

Blinding light hit me straight in the eyes. I would have dropped the brown bag, but I grew dizzy and fell forward against the car door, pinning it. I put my free arm up in front of my face to shield my eyes. Someone came up behind me and pressed me tight against the side of the car. A hand went over my mouth before I could scream. My assailant was male for sure, a head taller than me and much heavier than my size eight frame.

He wrenched my arm from my eyes and twisted it behind my back with one hand. My eyes slammed shut from white pain as the lights hit them again. I went limp, afraid my arm would break, though I sensed that if he'd meant to hurt me, he would have twisted it more. The smell of his leather glove under my nose was suffocating. I had no plan. One of my arms was sandwiched between the bag and the car; the other twisted behind my back. I froze.

Warm breath grazed my neck. The man pushed my hair aside and whispered in my ear, "Back off, chickie. It's good for stayin' alive. You got that? *Stayin'. Alive.*"

I stopped breathing. I'd swear my heart stopped beating. Linda and I had just been discussing the film *Stayin' Alive* that morning.

He pushed my head over gently, so my face went forward into the grocery bag. I might have panicked then, but he shushed me, and I felt his weight lift off me, so I stayed put. He slid away from me. When I picked my head up and opened my eyes, the blinding headlights still had me pinned. I squinted, desperately trying to glimpse my assailant. I heard a car door open and shut, then the car took off fast. It didn't make a sound.

CHAPTER 4

I stood staring after the car for several minutes before I could move, or see for that matter. Had Linda sent someone over to strong-arm me? Why would she? She could just fire me. She could have simply not hired me in the first place. Maybe somebody had bugged Linda's place. Could it be only a coincidence that my attacker had used that phrase, and even emphasized it? He didn't mug me or anything, only delivered his message and tried to scare me off. And called me "chickie," which was a misdemeanor as far as I was concerned. No, my gut said this had to do with the Stone case. And my gut was most often right.

Collecting myself and my slightly squashed things, I glanced up at my front door. It was on the second floor of a three-story motel-style building. A woman with gleaming blonde hair leaned back on her elbows against the handrail in front of my place, smoking a cigarette. I couldn't see her face, but the figure didn't strike me as Linda.

By the time I got to my front door about a minute later, the woman was gone. The smell of her cigarette lingered. She must have gone down the stairs at the other end of the walkway. I looked over the handrail, but saw nobody below. No one would come from another floor to smoke alone on this one. There were three other units on this floor, but she didn't look like any of my neighbors. I figured she must be someone's guest, but after what had just happened in the parking lot, I felt pretty creeped out about her, too.

I went inside and locked the door behind me. My cell phone

chimed. I rushed into the kitchen to put my stuff down, struggling to remove the shopping bag handle that had gouged the Grand Canyon into my wrist. I caught the phone call on the last ring.

"Yes?" I snapped. It had been a stressful evening.

I heard wavering sounds and a slow, garbled voice, like someone practicing Shakespeare underwater. Not one word was intelligible.

"Hello?" I said.

It cut out.

I hit a button and looked at my log to see where the call had originated. It said Restricted. I hit End. Whoever it was, they didn't call back.

*   *   *

The next morning, I made a few phone calls and then went straight to the bank to deposit the check Linda had given me. I wanted to get it into my account before she had time to have second thoughts. As I was parking, Stone's attorney, J.M. Klein, called me back. I hit the answer button and propped the phone in the crook of my neck as well as I could. I drawled a long hello, whipped the car in too fast and slammed on the brakes, sending the phone plummeting into my lap. No problem; Klein's voice boomed.

"Ms. Vega," Klein said, "are you with Lyons, Lyons, and Harris?" He had done a little checking, but not much.

"Not anymore, no. I was with them for a couple of years, but I work for myself now." I turned off the engine and turned down the volume as I brought the phone to my ear.

"Are you still doing criminal?"

"No, sir. Investigation. I'm not practicing law right now."

"I see."

What seemed like a full minute, but was probably five seconds, of dead silence ensued.

"What can I do for you, Ms. Vega?" Klein finally said.

"I wonder if you would answer a couple of basic questions about the Jack Stone estate."

"You have a client with an interest in the estate?"

"Yes."

"An ex-wife, no doubt."

I hesitated a beat, not wanting to reveal my client unless I had to. "Possibly."

"Okay, I understand. Well, here's what I can tell you. Jack Stone always kept a will, which I drew up for him. Oh, he changed it over the years, specifically with each new marriage, but he always kept it up. When he married the fourth time, he wrote up a holographic will on his own. He came to me and had me look it over, and it was fine. You're familiar with holographic wills?"

"A handwritten will, not necessarily witnessed."

"Exactly. And legal in California. He copied most of the material provisions from previous ones I'd drawn up and added in the changes he wanted. Had some notion that a handwritten will was more personal, more befitting a final act, or some such. He ought to have locked it in his vault at home, and that should have been that. But when it came time to put it to use, the will wasn't in the vault. There were no copies, and he'd had me destroy the previous will. So, the estate is in probate now, and unless that will turns up, the current Mrs. Stone will inherit the entire estate. Now, she knows what was in his will. She can choose to honor his wishes or not. It's up to her."

"They didn't have a pre-nup?"

"Nope. Not that I know of, anyway."

"One last thing, Mr. Klein. Were you preparing divorce papers for Stone?" Klein wouldn't answer that directly, and I knew it.

He said, "I had not gotten any papers filed on his behalf," which I took to mean he had been preparing papers, but had not filed them by the time of Jack's death. Now, they never would be filed.

"Well, thanks very much for your trouble, Mr. Klein. I do appreciate it."

"Not at all. Keep in touch."

I wondered what he meant by that. It sounded like he expected some kind of estate litigation, and he was probably right.

I went into the bank and pulled out Linda's check to deposit. I hadn't looked at the check apart from making sure the amount was right. I looked it over for the first time as I stood filling out the deposit slip. It was pre-printed with the amount I had specified when we spoke on the phone. Even more interesting, it wasn't Linda's check.

The check was drawn on a numbered account from a bank in Singapore. I pulled out my phone and called Linda again. I had already tried her earlier that morning without reaching her. This time I got her machine yet again, the phone number announced by a synthesized male voice. I was nervous about depositing the check. I knew that sometimes bad checks were used to steal bank account information and empty an unsuspecting victim's account. But I needed the money to pay the rent, so I crossed my fingers and took it to the teller. Then I went straight over to Linda's. She had some explaining to do.

It was around eleven when I got to Linda's. I rang the bell, knocked, and called her name, but there was no answer. I tried the door. That never works, but this time it did, which was weird because nobody in LA goes out and leaves their door unlocked. I walked in slowly, calling Linda's name. No answer. I took a quick look around outside to see if anyone might notice me, saw no one, and shut the door behind me. Then I locked the deadbolt so if anybody came I'd have time to hide.

Her living room looked just as it had the day before, except the gas fire log wasn't lit. I walked across the room toward the hall when voices rose outside. I froze. If Linda walked through that door, I'd have some explaining to do. The voices grew louder, and footsteps were coming my way. I ducked behind the loveseat just as they reached the door. But whoever it was walked on past, and the chatter faded. I stood up, shook it off, and went down the hallway calling softly for Linda.

There was a full bathroom on one side, decorated in blue and sparkling clean, with two untouched hand towels monogrammed with the letter L. The end of the hall forked into two bedrooms. The one next to the bathroom was large, and apparently Linda used it as a crafts room because it was full of stuffed badgers. They were different sizes, but apart from that, all were identical. There were small, medium, and large badgers. An extra-large, five-foot-tall badger stood on its hind legs in one corner of the room, and another giant one peeked out from the closet. They looked like they might come to life at any minute. I didn't hang around.

The other room was Linda's bedroom. It, too, was decorated in blue and white, and a single badger sat on the bed. The room was immaculate. I walked into the huge, dark walk-in closet. There were few clothes, all hung perfectly, as though they had just come back from the dry cleaner, but the plastic had been taken off.

I thought I heard a noise in the living room. I froze, but heard no further sounds. After waiting a long time, I finally decided it was nothing but someone outside.

I went through the closet into a large ensuite bathroom. Sunshine poured in through a window. There were no bottles, no makeup, no toothpaste or brush on the counter. I opened the cabinet and the drawers. There were no prescription bottles, cotton balls, nail files or bottles of polish. Not so much as a Q-tip. Nothing. I went back to the closet. A single pair of generic black pumps sat on the floor. If I wasn't convinced before, that did it. No woman can get by with only one pair of shoes. Linda was gone. And given I just met with her yesterday, she had moved out in a hurry. I looked in the drawers by her bed, hoping for travel notes. They were empty, too.

I went back up the hall to check out the kitchen. Linda's answering machine was sitting on the counter. Its red light was blinking, indicating unheard messages. I pushed the play button and absently opened the fridge. There was a single can of Diet Coke sitting on a shelf. I took it out, opened it, and drank. Meanwhile, the answering machine played the three messages I had left Linda. There was one last message.

"Mission accomplished," a man's voice said. Click.

The voice was soft, almost a whisper. It could've been the man who had whispered in my ear the previous night. I sucked on the Diet Coke and listened to it a couple more times, but I couldn't be sure. I erased all the messages and reset the machine. Time to go.

Walking into the living room, I almost dropped my Coke on the perfect white carpet. The fireplace was lit. I think my heart stopped for a second, but I got it together and rushed, very quietly, to the front door. There I found the most disturbing thing of all.

The deadbolt was unlocked.

No wonder the door had been unlocked when I arrived. Someone had been in there with me, and I was willing to bet it wasn't Linda. She would have spoken to me, if only to ask what I was doing in her place. I got myself out of there, shutting the door softly behind me. As I slipped through the door, I smelled the faintest trace of cigarette smoke.

CHAPTER 5

I went to my favorite place for lunch: *chez moi,* meaning home. It's the only place I find truly affordable, and the food is great. My brain was tied up in knots. If there was no Linda, did that mean I was off the case? She had paid me a good chunk of money up front. It didn't seem right to put the brakes on just yet. Maybe she moved to a new place and forgot to mention it. Anyway, it was my curiosity that had gotten me into the private eye game, and it was curiosity that kept me in it and happy to get out of bed every morning.

I decided I was still on the case.

I needed to get the hard facts from LAPD. If only the facts would be the only hard part. It was time to put in a call to my favorite homicide cop, Detective Escobar. I made myself a power burrito for endurance, then picked up the phone and called Michael.

"Well, my favorite spygirl," he said. "What's up?"

"I'm looking into Jack Stone," I said.

"Jack Stone? He's not as good-looking as me. And anyway, he's dead."

I could feel him grinning through the phone.

"So I've heard," I said. "What's the scoop on that?"

"Text me a picture of yourself and I'll tell you."

"Michael!"

"Michael!" He imitated me in a stupid voice, like a kid on a playground.

"You're like a ten-year-old," I said, taking a bite of my burrito. I figured I could take bites between sentences, and once he really got going, I could munch at will.

"I'm just messing with you," he said. "Jack Stone, movie star, found slumped in the driver's seat of his favorite car, a red Ferrari Enzo, in his four-car garage in Malibu. Cause of death: carbon monoxide poisoning. A suicide note was on the passenger side floor."

He finished talking sooner than I'd expected, and I still had a mouth full of burrito. I struggled silently.

"You still there?" Michael asked.

I swallowed. "I'm here, yeah. Just messing with you. Um...who found him?"

"His wife, the lovely Leilani." I could almost hear him salivating. I'd never met her, but being a movie star's wife, she'd be hot. "By the time she found him, he'd already been dead for eight to ten hours. Leilani thought Jack was in San Diego. She came home from a party around two A.M., went to put her car in the garage, and there he was. She called nine-one-one."

"So, no garden hose, no duct tape?"

"No, but they don't always do that. It may have been an impulsive decision. Or maybe he was worried about scratching the paint on his beloved car."

Both of those sounded like Jack. "There's no question in your mind it was suicide?"

"Nope, looks pretty standard. Unless something turns up. Why, you got something?"

"No. Just someone's suspicion. You know his will is missing."

"Yeah, but that doesn't mean anything by itself. One interesting thing—his right hand was clenched in a fist, and the left hand was holding up four fingers."

"Four fingers? Like, saluting? Jack was never in the armed forces."

"It looked more like counting. The fingers were splayed, thumb was crooked."

"His wives, probably," I said. "Or, maybe he was waving goodbye—to his killer."

"Suspicion isn't evidence, spygirl. You'll have to do better than that."

"They do an autopsy?"

"Yeah. Typical tailpiper, tox screen showed significant alcohol, a couple sleeping pills, not enough to inspire any more than a nap. You want to hear the funny part?"

"There's a funny part?"

"Ironic funny. His license plate said: A-L-I-V-E-1. Get it? A Live One."

That chilled me, after what had happened in the parking lot. I said, "Not 'a live one.' It's 'alive one,' from *Stayin' Alive*. That was the film that made him a star."

"Oh yeah, I know that movie," Michael said. "He's a rookie racecar driver, right? And somebody fixes the race, but he won't go along with it, so he has a horrible crash and his face is all burned off. He has to wear a mask. So then he goes back to his hometown and finds his girlfriend has married his best friend."

"Why shouldn't she?" I said. "He left without even telling anyone. No goodbye, nothing. If his old football coach hadn't seen him on TV, they wouldn't even have known he was alive."

"But he only did that because he wanted to make something of himself…to show her what he was worth," Michael said, maybe a little too passionately.

Awkward silence. I tried to lighten things up. "He was better off without her anyway. If he'd been stuck with her back in Mishawaka, he never would've gone to work for the CIA and gotten a brand new face and identity."

"He was better off without her because she didn't love him!" Michael got even more worked up. He did that a lot.

"How can you say that when later, after the best friend died, she fell for him all over again with his new face, and she didn't even know it was him!" I was a little worked up myself, but only because what Michael was saying was outrageous.

"Oh, hang on a sec," he said.

I could hear him talking to someone while holding his hand unevenly over the mouthpiece of the phone. I took the opportunity to down the last chunk of my burrito.

Michael came back on the line. "Hey, sorry about that. What are you doing right now?"

I was picking a piece of tomato skin out of my teeth. "Right now?"

"Yeah. You want to get together for lunch?"

"Oh darn, I just ate. Listen, one more thing before I let you go—"

"I don't have to go," he said.

"Well, I do. What did the suicide note say?"

"Well now, that information is on a need-to-know basis. What'll you give me for it?"

"*Give* you for it?"

"Oh, come on. You can't work all the time. Why don't you come out for a quick drink with me after work?"

I said nothing. I buried my face in my free hand and shook my head. The man simply would not get the message.

"Come on," he said. "I'd have to look at it again anyway. I don't remember what it said, and I can't do it right now. I'm on my way out."

"You just said you didn't have to go."

"I lied. Come on; meet me for one drink. In broad daylight. Say, five-thirty at Chaya Venice?" He knew I loved Chaya. I had let it slip once a few weeks ago.

"Okay. But don't forget the note!" I gave him points for not mentioning the color green.

CHAPTER 6

I figured it was time I paid a visit to Leilani Stone. I put together a professional look, a little black and white Michael Kors suit, easy on the bling, and drove up Pacific Coast Highway to Malibu right after lunch. The traffic wasn't bad. The ocean was a beautiful robin's egg blue, twinkling with sunlight. I felt happy just looking at it.

I kept thinking about what Michael had said. It did sound like a pretty straightforward suicide, but one thing was bugging me. A four-car garage is pretty big. It would take a while to fill up with fumes. Maybe I was just grabbing at straws, but something about it felt wrong.

I pulled up to the gate of Jack and Leilani Stone's mansion overlooking the ocean. The metal bars formed a pair of dolphins leaping up from waves toward each other, their bottlenoses touching to form a heart. I buzzed the intercom.

"Yes?" A woman's voice came back at me, muffled.

"Lola Vega for Mrs. Stone, please."

"Are you expected?"

"Yes." It was worth a shot.

"Just a minute, please."

The next thing I knew, the gates were opening. I got back in my car and drove on through. But I had that bad feeling again, like I had at Linda's place. I pulled up in front of the house along a circular driveway of fine gravel. A huge fountain in the center of it featured dolphins at play. The house was pink, Spanish-style, with a red tile roof. It was the size of an airport terminal. The sweep of the front double doors alone would be bigger than my bedroom. I rang the doorbell.

An attractive, horsy girl with light brown hair, pulled into a ponytail, opened the door. She must have been in her mid-twenties, but she looked childlike standing in the enormous doorway. A little princess in her castle. I almost said, Is your mother home? But I didn't.

"Hello," I said, smiling.

"Come in, please," she said. Her words were striking because they gave a completely different impression of her from the visual one. Her voice was mature and even, and her presence commanding for one so young. The phrase "good breeding" came to mind. She wore a thin white turtleneck shirt, small, jeweled earrings, khakis, and soft leather slip-on shoes like bedroom slippers.

Inside, the house had a catalpa tree in the center of a large tile-floored atrium flanked by potted flowering plants of various bright colors, their soft perfumes filling the air. Behind the catalpa, a sweeping staircase rose and split off in two directions at the upper level.

"Would you mind leaving your shoes out here?" she said, sweeping a hand to one side where some shoes lay, both men's and women's, I noted. I slipped off my pumps. The tile floor was cool through my nylons, which I wore with a red satin garter belt, just to feel good. I never skimped on lingerie. Lingerie choices were crucial to my well-being and inner peace.

She led me into a reception room off the atrium. Thankfully, it was carpeted. Sweet flute music played quietly and a faint scent of sandalwood incense permeated the room.

"Please make yourself comfortable," she said. "I'll just tell her you're here."

"Oh! I thought you were Mrs. Stone," I said, feeling stupid.

"I'm her assistant, Jennifer." A thin smile appeared and disappeared quickly. "Would you like some coffee or tea?"

"Coffee would be nice. Thanks. Black is fine." I sat on a crimson sofa that was surprisingly soft and deep. I had to work hard to remain upright and finally perched at the edge.

Jennifer went out one side of the room just as Leilani Stone came in another. She had a pretty face and a generous backside. She wore an orange low-riding skirt, like a big open blossom, over cowboy boots. Her sandy hair tumbled over a tight black off-the-shoulder top, above which dangling earrings hung from three piercings in each ear. She appeared to be in her mid to late twenties and had an air of serenity about her. She walked over to me showing a lot of teeth in approximation of a smile, holding out her hand to shake. I stood up again.

"Hellooo, Lola," she said, in a singsong way. "I'm Leilani." We shook hands for an instant. Her grip was like the brush of a feather.

"Lovely to meet you," I said.

We both sat. I parked myself at the edge again. Her earrings tinkling, she pulled the voluminous skirt out of the way and kicked off her cowboy boots. Then she tucked her socked feet up under herself on the other end of the sofa and reclined into its cloying embrace.

"Thank you for seeing me," I said. "I was a huge fan of your husband, by the way. Please accept my condolences for your loss."

"Oh, thanks. That's very kind of you. I've accepted it; he chose to go down a path where I can't follow." The toothy grill never left her face. She didn't seem at all broken up about Jack's death. "Relax, sit back. You look ready to sprint out the door."

I smiled and leaned into the sofa, which felt extremely awkward. My skirt was too short to pick my feet up as Leilani had.

Jennifer came in with coffee and tea, slid a crystal dolphin figurine to one side to set the tray down on the table, and left without a word. I started on my coffee.

"I always drink green tea," Leilani said, pouring herself some. "So, I imagine you have a lot of questions."

"Um, yes, I do," I said.

"Have you ever had a channeling session before?" she asked.

"Channeling?" I said, at a loss for words of my own.

She looked at me funny. "You *are* my three o'clock appointment?" she asked, sipping her steaming tea carefully.

"Oh. No, sorry, I'm not." I put the coffee down like a thief caught stealing. "I'm looking into your husband's death."

The serenity fled from her face. "What?" she asked, her tone harsh. She set her tea back down on the tray.

"I understand your husband worked with a medium," I said.

The doorbell rang. Leilani didn't seem to notice it.

"Why are you asking about that? Are you with the police?"

"No, actually, I'm working for a private party," I said.

Her face went bright red. "And who would that be?"

"I'd rather not say. I only have a couple of quick questions."

"You're a reporter?" Then she screamed in my face. "Get out of my house!" Her hands were in tight fists, one of them jutting toward the door, a finger pointing.

I protested, but she didn't hear me deny being a reporter. I escaped from the smothering sofa as fast as I could and made for the door.

"Get out!" she screamed again, standing up. She snatched the dolphin figurine off the table and took aim at me.

As I reached the door, Jennifer appeared in the doorway with a shoeless woman. They both stared at Leilani in disbelief.

"Excuse me," I said, slipping past them and out the door. I heard the glass dolphin shatter against the wall behind me and then more screams, other voices. I only hoped she hadn't hit her perfectly innocent three o'clock appointment.

I slid across the tiled atrium like an ice skater, grabbed my shoes, ran outside and bounced across the gravel to my car. I threw the shoes on the seat and raced out of there. Waiting for the gate to slide open was agony. As I flew down the PCH, I was glad to be meeting Michael for a drink; in fact, I planned to get there early. I could use a stiff one after Leilani's brand of hospitality.

CHAPTER 7

I went straight to Venice and sat at the bar at Chaya. Half an hour early for meeting Michael, I ordered a tangerine margarita, drank it way too fast, and then ordered another one. By the time Michael showed up, I was feeling a little more relaxed. Okay, a lot more.

I could see why Michael had the ego. Oh yes, he was hot. He had the smoldering dark eyes, the wry smile, and the brains to back them up. All that and a sleek, strong, swimmer's body. I'll admit I'd have liked to see him in the Speedo. But in spite of his finer attributes, he was way too much of a player to get involved with. At least, that was my impression from the way he talked. And it seemed safe to assume with those looks, he'd be successful with women. Plus everyone had heard how one of the beat cops, Valerie Farrell, had to be transferred last year due to complications of a bad break-up with Michael. I didn't know the details, but at some point they would surely make their way to me.

Michael sauntered into the bar in his usual way. He gave me the look that was supposed to melt me. My immediate thought was, no matter what, to be careful not to drink too much. This would be tough because I had already drunk too much.

"Hello, beautiful," he said.

"Hi, Michael," I said, shining a big, lubricated smile his way.

"You started without me." He looked at me closely, sizing up how much I had drunk already. "Everything okay?"

"Yeah! Great! Absolutely!" Perhaps I may have been a little too enthusiastic.

He took a seat next to me and ordered a beer. "You want another one?" he asked.

I looked at my half-full glass. "Sure!" I said. This time I ordered the Sweet Tart margarita. I thought the change might slow me down.

When we got our drinks, Michael said, "Come on…let's grab a table."

I sucked down the end of one drink and picked up the other. I had slid my shoes off as I sat there and stepped back into them as I stood up.

Michael stood looking down at my feet, getting an eyeful of my nylons, shredded from running across the gravel at Leilani's place. "What have you been doing, *muchacha?*"

"Don't ask," was all I said.

He frowned at me.

"Okay, I'll tell you later." I took a big gulp of my drink because it was so full it would be hard to walk without spilling it.

He herded me over to a table in a corner of the bar.

"Why, Detective Escobar, are you trying to get me alone in a dark corner?" I laughed. I should not have ordered that third drink.

He smiled. "I just thought we should get away from people so we can talk without being overheard."

"Oh." We found a booth. I plummeted into my seat.

Michael sat across from me. "You sure you want to talk about this right now?" he asked.

"Sure, I'm sure!" I pushed the drink away from me so I would pick it up less often. I took a deep breath in and out, and put myself in as sober a frame of mind as possible.

Michael lowered his voice and leaned in. "As I mentioned, Stone was in the driver's seat, the suicide note on the passenger side floor." He closed his eyes to visualize the note. "It said: 'They say where there's away, there's a will. I have few true loves and no true friends. Not even a Rosebud. All I've got is regret for the many mistakes I have made all my life and can live with no longer. I seem only to hurt the people I love most. My family will be better off without me. Now, only my fans will miss me. I love them as they have loved me, and that will have to be enough. Goodbye.'"

"That's so sad," I said. Tears of the slightly drunk variety welled in my eyes.

"It is," Michael said, nodding. "It really is. That's Rosebud with a capital 'R' in there, like in the movie, *Citizen Kane*. A little strange, but maybe not for an actor."

"Hmm. In the film, Rosebud was a sled. It represented…what? Good memories long gone?" I reached for the rim of my glass, took a finger-full of sugar, plunged it into my mouth and out with a small slurp. "Innocence lost, maybe?" I pulled the drink to me with one finger and took two big gulps of it.

"Something like that," he said. "The handwriting matched; the paper was his."

"Why do you think he said that part about,Where there's a way, there's a will?"

"That his will was to die, I guess, and he'd make it happen. He got it switched around, though. Actually, he also had 'away' as one word, but he was obviously distraught."

"What about the nine-one-one call?" I asked.

"The call came in from Leilani at 2:13 A.M. Said she'd just come home and found the body. She reported it as suicide; she'd read the note. Told the guy what it said over the phone."

"Verbatim?"

"Paraphrased."

"Could I listen to the call?"

"I'll get you a transcript."

"Was she distraught?"

"Suitably so. Your client one of the exes?" he asked.

"You know I'm not going to tell you who my client is," I said.

"Yeah. Well, get her to pay you more. You need to buy some new stockings."

"Oh, God!" I rolled my eyes and buried my face in my hand. I felt like a loser, like some pulp fiction version of a private eye, the kind who finds trouble at every turn.

He ran one finger along my arm. "Come on. Tell *Papi* what happened."

I broke down in tears. It was a combination of things—the Leilani incident, the parking lot guy, the margaritas. But mostly it was because *Papi* used to actually say that to me. And I missed him so much.

"Hey, what's this?" Michael came over on my side of the booth, sat next to me, and put his arm around me.

"I'm a walking disaster," I said, and buried my face in his

shoulder.

"That's not true! Come on. Tell me what happened." He pulled back, looked me in the eye, and unfolded a cocktail napkin and handed it to me. "Here, blow your nose."

I was annoyed with him telling me what to do, but at the same time, impressed. If Michael had wanted to take advantage of me, this would be the time to start something. But he behaved like a friend.

So I honked into the napkin and told him everything. I told him about the parking lot assault, the weird phone call, my client's sudden disappearance, even about the fireplace lighting itself, which I'd never have mentioned had I not been just the slightest bit tipsy. Everything. I topped it all off with Leilani's freak-out at the mansion.

"Maybe Leilani killed him, with a temper like that," he said, a grave look on his face.

"I can't really blame her for being upset," I said. "First she thought I was her client, then some sleazy reporter. I never got a chance to explain who I was."

"Even so, she could've put you in the hospital."

"She's just lost her husband; maybe she's still really broken up about it."

"Yeah? According to the team that talked to her, she said they were about to get divorced anyway. Which is one reason the whole suicide thing kind of makes sense. Anyway, the misunderstanding wasn't your fault. It was that assistant's fault in the first place."

"True." Sort of.

"And then she just jumped to the conclusion you were a reporter and never gave you a chance to explain. She sounds like a real dragon lady to me."

That made me laugh. And Michael was right. Most of it was not my fault. He had managed to make me feel a hundred percent better.

We stayed and had some dinner in the restaurant. We spoke no more about the Stone case, but talked a lot about our families. Michael told hilarious stories of his childhood. I couldn't help thinking what a cute little boy he must have been, mostly because it wasn't much of a stretch.

Then he drove me home. I had mostly sobered up by then, but he insisted on driving me home anyway because of the parking lot incident. He said he would come by in the morning and take me to my car.

When we got there, Michael walked me to the door. I was sure he was about to make a move. He waited outside while I went in, flipped the lights on, and looked around to see that everything was okay. Then he left. No move. Still, as I watched him out the window walking back to his car, I had the distinct feeling we'd just been on a date.

CHAPTER 8

The next day was Saturday. Armed with a cup of steamy coffee and its wakening aroma, I stumbled to my computer. I felt like something dug up by the roots. Half a cup in, I Googled "Linda Stone." There were some old articles about Jack Stone that made reference to a wife named Linda. She had indeed been with him after he made it big. There were a couple more Linda Stones, but I felt sure they were not her. One was on a high school basketball team in Redondo. Another was about to retire from a large, well-known corporation.

Then I tried "Linda Gross," and there she was. When I clicked the link to her website, there was a head shot of her, smiling out of the photo with her square jaw and blonde hair beside a caption that read:

Linda Gross, real estate broker, residential and commercial, greater Los Angeles area. Let me find your next home or office!

I picked up the phone and hit star-sixty-seven to hide my number, then called the office number on her web page. I got an assistant.

"Are you handling those condos off Pico, The Tides?" I asked her.

"Yes, we have a unit there for sale. I can have an agent call you back with information or arrange a showing for you," she said.

"Can you tell me which unit it is? I don't like to be at ground level," I said.

"It's a third floor unit, number three-eleven, if you'd like to drive by."

"Thanks, I'll do that. Oh, one more thing. Can you tell me how long it's been on the market?"

"An agent could look that up for you. Let me have someone call you."

"Ballpark? More than a week?"

"Oh, it's been more than a week, for sure. May I have someone call you?"

"Um…I'll call back. I have to go." I hung up and called Michael. It was eight-thirty. I was afraid it might be too early to call, but he was up.

"Can't wait to see me, huh?" he said.

I told him I had some semi-urgent things to do and needed my car. He said he would come right over. I hung up the phone, realized I wasn't even dressed yet, and bolted for the shower.

*   *   *

Michael took me to my car. He kept looking over at me and grinning. He seemed to think we'd had a date, too, but it wasn't like he had scored with me or something. I couldn't figure him out.

"You look like you ate a canary," I said.

"Oh, baby," he said, "I'm not touching that one."

"You know, if you're trying to mess with my mind, I wasn't that drunk last night. I do remember it. I know nothing happened."

"Nothing?"

"Nothing!"

"You're hurting my feelings now," he said. "I thought we made a connection."

I turned away and looked out the window. Truthfully, I thought we had, too. And some small part of me was disappointed he was acting like his usual player self again.

When we got to my car, I barely looked at him as I thanked him for driving me over and took off. I've been known to get a little obsessive about things, and by then I was obsessing about Linda Gross. I had to find her.

Either she had put her place up for sale and left in a hurry, and just happened to be a real estate broker, or else she'd never lived in that condo at all, and it was simply one of her company's listings she had pretended was her home. I suspected the latter. If that was the case, why the pretense, and where did she live? And why had she suddenly made herself scarce? I had a bad feeling about all this. I was afraid Linda could be in serious trouble somewhere.

I got in my car and went straight over to The Tides and up to number three-eleven, where I had met with Linda. There was a lockbox hanging on the doorknob. It hadn't been there before; Linda must have taken it off to use the condo.

Maybe when I came back the next day, Linda was already there, inside. Why else would the door have been unlocked and the lockbox off? Maybe she had been in the kitchen when I went down the hall, came out and lit the fireplace, and left through the front door before I did. She could always let herself back in later; she had the key from the lockbox.

I tried the doorknob again. It was locked this time, but as I jiggled the lockbox, it fell open. Whoever had closed it last hadn't shut it completely. I took the key out and let myself in, then put the key back. Once inside, I locked the bolt behind me as before.

There was a nasty smell in the place of stale cigarettes with an undertone of mildew. I flashed on the badgers with some distress; maybe there had been some sort of flooding.

I went in the kitchen to see if there were any new phone messages. The light wasn't blinking. I rewound it anyway and hit play, in case it had been listened to recently, but not erased. It was blank.

There was a neon green Post-it pad by the phone that I was sure hadn't been there before. It had a handwritten address on it. The address was in San Diego, but had no name with it. Beneath it were four more numbers: 4535. The end of a phone number, maybe? The last four digits of a social security number? I peeled off the note and stuck it in my purse.

I went down the hall to look for clues to who had been there. I checked on the badgers; they were fine. Neither bedroom looked like anything in it had been touched.

The walk-in closet off the master bedroom looked the same as before, but the bathroom door was now closed, which left the closet dim. I walked across to the bathroom door. My foot kicked something hard. I spotted a small shape on the floor, bent down and picked it up. It was cold, solid, and heavy. I knew what it was. I dropped it and flipped on the wall switch by the bathroom door so I could see clearly. It was a gun.

I opened the bathroom door and walked in. I could no more stop myself from opening that door than I could stop myself from eating the last truffle in a box of chocolates. The bathtub was straight in front of me, its curtain closed. When I pulled back the shower curtain, it became instantly clear that at least two people had been in the condo since my last visit, one of whom was Linda. Because Linda, fully clothed, was curled up in the bathtub, dead from a gunshot.

CHAPTER 9

The bathroom had been starkly empty only yesterday morning, so Linda and her killer must have been here sometime in the last twenty-four hours. She had taken a single shot to the heart. I pressed two fingers lightly to her neck to see if there was a pulse. There was none. Though her skin felt icy cold, it was still soft. She couldn't have been dead for long.

Blood was spattered over the bathtub, tub enclosure, faucet, and shower curtain, but none on the bathroom floor. Either Linda had been about to take a shower with her clothes on or her killer was a very tidy person. A thin paperback novel lay next to her in the tub: *The Gambler*, by Dostoyevsky. It appeared she'd been surprised while reading and ordered into the tub for her execution.

Someone probably had heard the gunshot, yet as was typical in LA, no one had called the police. I went out to the kitchen and called Michael; Santa Monica was his territory. He sounded concerned, and I heard his chair skid across the floor before he hung up the phone. He told me to go out to my car and wait there in case the killer came back. I did. I kept an eye on the place, but nothing further happened.

Michael pulled up ten minutes later. He ducked into my car, and his physical presence instantly flooded me with a sense of relief. When he pulled me toward him and gave my hair a peck, I didn't object. As we sat together to wait for the rest of the crew to arrive, I told him every detail I could think of, including that I had picked up the gun.

He looked at me sideways. "Lola, you know better."

"It was dark! I couldn't see what it was," I said.

"So you picked it up."

It did sound really stupid when he said it like that. "You had to be there," I said.

He took my hands in both of his like he was warming them. "That's okay; don't worry. We'll figure it out. Everything will be okay."

"Thanks," I said and smiled. My next thought was I was looking in his eyes a little too long, then I realized with horror that, while having the thought, it must be even longer.

Thankfully, tires squealed into the parking lot to save me. I jerked my hands abruptly out of Michael's grasp. The fingerprint guys pulled up, and the coroner was right behind them.

"Okay, Lola, go home," he said. "I'll call you when I have anything. Oh, and hang onto this for me." He pulled a folded transcript of Leilani's nine-one-one call from the inside pocket of his jacket and handed it to me. Then he got out of my car, and I took off for home.

I read through the transcript at red lights. It was just as Michael had described it. The nine-one-one operator kept Leilani on the phone until police arrived at her place. Leilani reported a suicide and talked about the note a little. There was nothing suspicious in any of it.

Back at home, I felt wrung out. My sole desire in life at that moment was to take a nice hot bath and relax. I took my cell phone out of my purse to turn the ringer off, and there was the green Post-it note. After finding Linda dead, I'd forgotten all about it. I typed the address into my phone's GPS and as the map and red route line materialized, so did my second wind. I decided to forget about the bath. San Diego was at least a two-hour drive, more if I hit traffic.

I threw some things in a tote bag in case of an overnighter, rolled up a quick burrito, and twenty minutes later was on the road. At Oceanside, I cut over to the coast road to get an eyeful of ocean. Nothing calms my mind like the sight of pure blue Pacific surf breaking on a stretch of sun-baked golden sand. Gaze at it for a while, and all your troubles seem to wash away. The Pacific was as beautiful as ever, but my mind remained restless. Mostly I pondered the wild goose chase I might be on. The address might belong to the owner of the condo, some relative of Linda's, or another branch of her real estate office. It could be anything at all, like a sushi restaurant or a dry cleaner. The curiosity was killing me.

It was two-forty when I got to San Diego, and a few minutes more to downtown off the 5. The address was at the corner of Grape Street and India, a few blocks from both the airport and the harbor. A sculpted metal arch over India Street proclaimed the area "Little Italy." The building was a squat orange rectangle, probably a former gas station, with a broken overhead sign almost as big as the building. My quest was over. Two quests, really. The sign had a big picture of an eye.

It read: Mrs. O'Reilly, Spiritual Medium.

CHAPTER 10

Mrs. O'Reilly's place had more parking lot than building, and the lot was almost full. The two spaces nearest the door were reserved for her business. A big sign, hand-painted in red so the drips looked like blood, was posted in front of the two parking spaces. It read:

———

Parking for Mrs. O'Reilly's only!
Do not park here for even 5 minutes
if you are not going to see Mrs. O'Reilly.
You do NOT want to mess with me.
If you do, I will put a curse on you,
and being toad is far worse than being towed.
Have a nice day!

———

I parked in one of the reserved spaces. The other one was already taken. I assumed the other car belonged to Mrs. O'Reilly herself because it was orange with eyes painted all over it. I went up to the door and rang the doorbell. It was one of those electronic ones that play the first couple bars of a tune. The tune was the seventies Eagles' song, "Witchy Woman."

I waited. All I could think was, Why would someone with Jack Stone's money, who could pay for the top medium in the world, even some super-expensive one with a TV show, want an eyeball-toting, gas station medium like this one?

Nothing happened, so I rang the bell again and got another chorus of the song: DUH…DUH…Duh-Duh-DUH, DUH-Duh-Duh-Duh, Duh-Duh-Duh, Duh-Duh-DUUHH. Again, no one came to the door. I figured she must be out, but just as I turned to walk away, the door whooshed open behind me.

There at the threshold stood a striking African-American woman. She was slim, with a pretty face that could have been forty or fifty. She wore a long green skirt, a crimson top with a gauzy leopard-print blouse over it, and several jangling gold bracelets and earrings. Her dark hair was natural and full, with a bunch of ends twisted together so that it looked like a big puffy spider was sitting on top of her head. She greeted me with an intense gaze.

"Come in," she said. "I've been expecting you."

"I don't have an appointment," I said, not wanting a re-run of the Leilani incident.

"I know," she said.

Oh, of course. She "knew" I was coming. I introduced myself.

"Do you take Visa, Mrs. O'Reilly?" I asked, looking around. I'd wondered what took her so long to get to the door. The whole place was the size of my bedroom, with a kitchen area and a closet-sized bathroom off to one side. The reason for the delay was clear, although furnishings were minimal: a dinette set, a red futon sofa bed open to the bed position, a small TV. There were huge piles of books and papers all over the room to be navigated. They grew up from the floor like stalagmites, forming a sort of labyrinth with pathways cleared among kitchen, bed, and door.

"You bet I take Visa," Mrs. O'Reilly said. She wound her way over to the dinette table and cleared off five or six empty Chinese food boxes by tossing them from where she stood over to the kitchen counter. She overshot all but one, and the others landed on the kitchen floor. She waved them off; they were out of the way.

"Everyone just calls me Mrs. O," she said. "Come on and have a seat. I'll tell you why you're here."

I sat down. I had seen the TV show mediums. I expected her to begin fishing around for clues by dropping some common name or first letter of a name.

"Just relax, honey. Open up to me. As much as you can, that is. I see you have some trust issues."

True. She'd read my body language there. My legs were crossed, and I was hugging my purse to my chest like a shield. I knew exactly how these readings worked. Anyway, who doesn't have trust issues these days?

She reached over and took both my hands in hers. Her hands felt cool. She took a deep breath in and exhaled. Then her eyes popped open wide. She stared intently at a place just behind my left shoulder.

"You recently lost your father," she said.

That was a lucky guess.

"Less than a year ago," she said.

Not bad. I was impressed.

"He's here," she said. "Hello, Hector!" She waved at the space behind me.

That one was a little spooky. A common enough name, Hector, but it also happened to be my papa's, so it was still spooky.

"Your father wants you to know he's very proud of you," Mrs. O said.

I'd heard this on TV more than once. It was one of the classic lines.

Then she said, "He says he now knows it doesn't matter whether you're an attorney or whatever; do what you want to do and be happy."

I was floored. The whole room seemed to tilt and slide. Reality didn't slip away; it bolted from the room. Somebody must have tipped her off I was coming, but who? It had to be somebody who knew about my papa, but I couldn't think of anyone; certainly Linda wouldn't have known of such a personal matter. I said nothing. I'd been struck dumb.

"Girl, you are popular," Mrs. O said. "Here comes somebody else for you! Ooh, and it's somebody I know, too. Jackie, how you doing, baby?" She paused and cocked her head to one side, as though listening. "What's that, baby?"

She had to be referring to Jack Stone. This was a good thing because I'd been pondering how to bring up the subject of Stone and his death, but nothing felt right. But she did it for me, and with that, I also could be certain she was the medium Stone had been seeing.

"Jack says you're wondering why he came to me. Ha!" She found this very amusing and broke up laughing. "He says to tell you, 'Mrs. O is the real deal.' His words, not mine. He says he paid me and got answers, maybe to different questions than the ones he asked, but good answers. Ha! He says he paid you and got nothing for it." She cracked up laughing again.

It was true; I hadn't been able to turn up anything on Jessica's murder the police hadn't already found out. Her death appeared to be the end result of a one-night stand, and the more random a killing is, the tougher it is to solve. I was quickly off the case, but to be fair, nobody else did any better. The police never even made an arrest.

That reminded me… "Oh," I said, "ask him if he knows now who killed his sister."

"You hear that, Jackie?" she said. "How 'bout it?" She paused, listening. "Uh-huh. He says he knows, but he doesn't want to say."

"He doesn't want to say? Why the hell not?" I said, getting the tiniest bit upset. I can have a little bit of a temper sometimes, especially when people are just plain annoying or idiotic.

"He says he's done with all that now. He says the other side is far away from most of the stuff you think is important when you're alive, so enough already." She broke off, and her eyes came back to focus on mine. "Oops, he's gone. Did he say anything interesting? I never can remember much afterward, except who showed up," she said and pinched her eyes.

"No, not really. I had a lot more questions for him," I said.

"I know," she said. "It's okay; we'll call this one a freebie. They do get temperamental, but there's nothing you can do about it. One thing I do know…you got to roll with things. Maybe I can answer some of your questions."

"Oh, I'm sure you can. That'd be great. How long were you working with Jack?" I asked. My cell rang, but I reached into my purse and turned the ringer off without looking at it.

"Mmmm, since about a year and a half ago, just before he married Leilani."

"Do you know Leilani, too?"

"Yeah, he brought her down a couple of times."

"Is she a good channel, do you know?"

"It's channel*er*, and yeah, she's okay. You know what she does, exactly?"

"Not exactly."

"Channels dolphins," she said, with a perfectly straight face.

"Dolphins?" Was she kidding me?

"Live dolphins and spirit ones. Takes groups to Hawaii for big group readings and channeling workshops, too."

"Seriously? How does she understand what the dolphins are telling her?"

"Oh, no problem! The spiritual world transcends earthly limitations," she said, "including species. There's no language per se; messages from spirit come straight into the mind, whole. It's a little hard to explain. Have you ever just been struck by a complete thought—bam!—out of nowhere, and you just knew it was right?"

I thought about this. The truth was, this happened to me often, and when it did, I always followed it up. Some of these were personal insights; others were professional hunches. They told me what direction to take, and they almost never failed. I took them to be intuition, born of scattered elements coming together into a noticeable pattern.

"Sure, intuition. Couldn't get by without it."

"Amen to that," Mrs. O said. "Well, those flashes of genius are messages from spirits. You may not know who yours are coming from, but they're phone calls from the other side."

The mention of a phone call reminded me of the Post-It note. "By the way, does the number four-five-three-five mean anything to you?"

She thought about it. "No, why?"

"No big deal," I said. "I thought it might be the end of your phone number. Do you happen to know what hotel Jack Stone stayed in when he came down here to see you?" I was pretty sure he didn't stay at her place. He would have had to sleep on the only six-by-three-foot patch of uncovered space in the place—under the dining room table.

"Jackie had a little yacht over in the harbor. Well, still does. I guess nothing's going to change until his estate is settled. He stayed there. He loved that little boat! He used to talk about her all the time. Probably still does."

"Is anyone taking care of the boat now?" I asked.

"Couldn't tell you. He had a diver scraping the hull every month, but no paid crew. Maybe he went there to be alone."

"Can you tell me which boat it is?"

"Sure. Her name is *Alouette*. She's not in a slip; she's on a mooring ball in the bay right across from the airport, number A-2. The first row of moorings from the dock is A, second one down the line. You take a little blue launch called *Rosebud* to get over there. She's tied to the dock with no lock on her. It's not far...take you three minutes. I have a key if you want to go look around. Jackie left it with me in case he lost his. You could even stay there tonight. It's nice. You sleep like a baby on a boat."

Rosebud. All I could think was: Why would Jack write in his suicide note that he didn't have a *Rosebud* when he did?

CHAPTER 11

I left Mrs. O's place with a promise to come back the next day, got my bag out of the car, and walked down to the harbor. She said I could leave my car at her place. It was only four or five blocks. As I approached the harbor, I saw a restored three-masted tall ship anchored there, the *Star of India*. I could see why Jack would keep a boat here...the place would suit his romantic sensibilities.

I skirted the harbor until I came to the very first row of moored boats. A nearby dock had a crowd of dinghies tethered to it. I walked down the metal ramp. The whole dock scraped and whined loudly from the constant motion of rolling waves moving it up and down. The motion made me uncomfortable, but I remembered Mrs. O's voice in my head saying, One thing I do know...you got to roll with things. I laughed thinking of her. In that short time, she had completely endeared herself to me.

There it was—the only blue dinghy, the name *Rosebud* painted on its nose in yellow. *Rosebud* had definitely seen better days. She was old and chipped, and the seat sagged when I sat down. But I cast off and motored over to the boat hitched to the second mooring ball. When I got there, I tied *Rosebud* to the back. I couldn't help but think of her as a pony. Not a sled.

Stone's "little" boat was a forty-six foot Hunter sailboat. I climbed aboard and, using Mrs. O's key, went down into the cabin to look around. Everything seemed all right. The place was small, but luxurious, done up in polished oak with brass fittings. It had two double staterooms, two heads, a galley with the works, and a comfy lounge with satellite TV. It would make a nice place to stay for the night. I went topside to watch the sun go down.

The sky streaked with pink and darkened, and eventually the moon came up over the San Diego skyline. I enjoyed the soft rocking motion of the water, but soon got chilly and went below. I didn't think Jack Stone would mind me spending the night on his boat. In life, he was the kind of man who liked to spread his good fortune around. I went into the forward stateroom and fell asleep in Jack's big captain's bed. I wondered if his ghost was there, too, watching me sleep.

*   *   *

The next morning, I awoke to loud, sharp knocking on the cabin door. I had been dreaming that I was in the movie, *Stayin' Alive*. In the dream, I was Jack Stone's character's girlfriend, the one who had married the best friend who later died. Fate had thrown Jack's character and mine together a second time, and I was falling for him all over again, in spite of his new identity. When I reached up to touch his face, he pulled it off. It was only a mask, but it looked exactly the same as his face.

He held it up next to him and said, "I'm not the man you think I am. I have two faces."

I gasped. Both faces were right in front of me, but I couldn't tell them apart. I kept thinking that because he had gotten a new face with his new identity, he really he had three faces, a mask over a mask.

That was when the knocking woke me up.

At first, I thought somebody had fired a gun, it was so loud and sudden. I wasn't used to such a high bed and fell off. I scrambled to throw some clothes on, bleary and squinting like a ten-day-old puppy. The insistent double-time knocking seemed to remotely control my pounding heart. I made it to the cabin door in about four minutes, threw it open and screamed, "What do you want?"

I think I scared him. The man at the door recoiled violently. He was in his late sixties, wearing sloppy clothes, and his bright white hair hurt my eyes. On top of that, there was the blinding daylight of a lovely sunny day beyond his stooped shoulders. It all added up to a crushing headache for me.

When he recovered, the man said, "I'm sorry, little lady. I thought you might be some kind of robber. I seen *Rosebud* there and thought maybe something fishy was going on. We neighbors got to look out for each other. No harm intended."

That piqued my interest. "What's so fishy about seeing *Rosebud*?" I asked.

"She been missin' a long time. Don't look like you was having her fixed up. Now I get a good look at you, you don't even look like Jackie's lady friend. You a friend of his?"

"Yes. It's all right; I'm an associate of his. My name is Lola. *Rosebud* was at the dock when I got here last night. How long do you think she was missing?"

"Been more 'n a month now. Jackie was real upset about it."

That would explain the reference to having no *Rosebud* in the suicide note.

He thrust his hand forward. "I'm Barnaby, by the way, Barnaby Watts. I live on the boat right next door, *Unchained Melody*."

I gave his hand a shake. "Barnaby, would you come in and have some coffee with me?"

"Sure, don't mind if I do," he said.

"Good, you can show me where it is," I said. "And did I hear you call me 'little lady' before?" I hadn't thought anyone really said that. It was right up there with "chickie."

Barnaby and I made coffee and shared it out on the deck in the fresh morning air. I broke the news to him about Jack. Barnaby only saw Jack on the weekends when he came down from LA to sail two or three times a month and apparently didn't read or listen to news. He had no idea anything had happened to Jack. He looked shattered.

"Jack Stone was a good guy," Barnaby said. "He was exactly like that guy he played in *Stayin' Alive*. Exactly, A real hero-type guy."

"Barnaby, who was that lady friend of Jack's you mentioned?"

"Mmm, I'm no good with names."

"What did she look like?"

"Oh, taller than you, slim little thing, light hair. Had a real fine way of talking."

Jennifer. "Does the name Jennifer ring a bell?" I asked.

"That's it. Jennifer. Don't know her last name, though."

"Neither do I," I said, "but I plan to find out. Was she... I mean, just how friendly were they?"

He smiled. "They were kissing friendly. Jack had me over for drinks sometimes, so I seen them real friendly now and then."

So, Jack and Jennifer were having an affair, right under Leilani's nose. That sounded to me like a motive for murder.

CHAPTER 12

I tried to think of how Leilani could have killed Jack. Michael had said some sleeping pills showed up on the tox screen; maybe she drugged him, put him in the car, and started it. But Jack was a big guy. There was no way she could've dragged him around in passed-out mode. I let it mull. Sometimes I just let things roll around my brain for a while and see how they shake out later...kind of a mental martini.

It was time to head over to Mrs. O's, so I said goodbye to Barnaby and took *Rosebud* back to the dock, where I tied her up soundly. Then I walked from the harbor up to Mrs. O's. She was excited to see me again. She cooked us toast and eggs for breakfast, and we ate them off paper plates, doused in hot sauce.

"I love hot food," she said.

"Me, too," I agreed.

"You should call me Molly, since we're going to be traveling together for a while and all. It's just friendlier."

"Molly O'Reilly? Seriously?"

"A good Irish name."

"I'll say."

"Got the second sight and the luck of the Irish, too," she said. "That's both good luck and bad, but plenty of it!"

"What was that about traveling?"

"Oh, Lola," she said, "I just remembered. Jackie came to me last night in a dream."

"Really? Me, too."

"What happened in yours?"

So I told her mine first, about the mask and what Jack had said about having two faces.

"In mine," she said, "Jackie told me the same thing he used to say when he was alive: 'I didn't get where I am today by not taking risks.' Must've said that a hundred times."

"What do you think it all means?" I asked her.

"I think the dreams mean just what they said, that our Jackie had two faces, and that he was not averse to risk-taking. You finished with those eggs?"

She snatched the plate away without waiting for an answer or even looking at it. I had a bite left, but didn't protest. All I could think about was where Jack was today. Dead.

"Let me pack a few things and we'll get going," she said.

"Where are we going?" I asked.

"You got to get back up to LA, and I'm not sure why, but I'm supposed to go with you."

I shrugged. "Okay, if you say so, Mrs. O." I wouldn't mind company.

"Molly," she said.

"Right. Molly."

I sucked down another cup of coffee while she packed, then we put our bags in the trunk of my car. Instead of hopping right onto the freeway, I drove down to Grape Street to skirt the harbor one more time before leaving town. We sat at a red light gazing out at the boats.

I said, "Don't the sailboats look so nice, all lined up, just bobbing in the water so peacefully? It really puts your mind at ease just looking at them, doesn't it?"

"Yeah, that's real nice," Molly said.

Both of us were smiling oh-so contentedly.

The next instant, an explosion boomed out on the water. A huge fireball flared and spit flaming debris in all directions.

"That's the *Alouette!*" Molly cried.

The fireball settled down to spikes of orange flame rushing over the boat like the pitchforks of an angry mob. They engulfed the hull and snaked along the mast and boom. Clouds of black smoke rippled in the sky.

"We have to get down to the dock," I said.

A car horn sounded, jarring my attention from the orange fire on the bay to the green light in front of me. I started forward, then wrenched the car over into the far left lane, cutting someone off and causing further honking. I pulled an illegal U-turn and pulled up in front of the dock gate for some illegal parking. We sprinted down the ramp, shoes scraping metal, metal scraping brain. I mentally retraced my steps from that morning to be sure I hadn't left the stove on after making coffee. I definitely had not. We watched Jack's beautiful sailboat burn. The mast broke in half and fell flaming onto the deck, joining the bonfire there. Orange and black filled the world.

The Coast Guard station happened to be right across from the moorings, a loud siren blaring from it. Coast Guardsmen were scrambling to get the fireboat over to the *Alouette* so the other boats wouldn't catch fire. It was so close, they probably thought it was a terrorist act directed at them, but I knew it wasn't. I figured, either someone knew I was on that boat and meant to kill me, or there was something on the boat they didn't want discovered.

"Hell of a marshmallow roast," Molly said.

I snickered involuntarily and then put my arm around Molly's shoulders, gave her a little squeeze, and turned to go. "It's great you can be so philosophical at times like this," I said.

"You got to roll with things," she said.

"You got to," I agreed.

Then something hit me. "Hey, wait a second!" I whirled around.

Rosebud was gone again.

Whoever planted that bomb might have used *Rosebud* to get to the sailboat. Had the bomber left *Rosebud* tied up to the *Alouette*? And if so, how had he or she gotten away without blowing up along with the boats? I couldn't see the dinghy out there, but there was too much smoke to see much of anything. I had a feeling *Rosebud* might yet turn up somewhere with some evidence. For the moment, since I was probably the last known person on the *Alouette* before she blew, I had a sudden desire not to be seen hanging around the dock.

"Come on; let's get out of here," I said.

CHAPTER 13

We hit the road; this time I drove straight to the freeway. I wanted to get far away from San Diego. It gave me a bad feeling in the pit of my stomach to think that explosion might have been intended for me, and that whether it was or not, I had nearly been fish food.

Once we were out of the city, around Carlsbad, I stopped for coffee at an old-style diner. We grabbed a booth. I checked the time on my cell phone, found the ringer off, and turned it on. My nerves were jangled, but Molly seemed to be fine. She ordered a chocolate milk shake and a Home Run breakfast.

"We already ate breakfast, remember?" I said, when the waitress brought Molly her food.

"Stress always gives me an appetite," she said. "I don't fight it. I just go with it."

"I can't eat when I'm stressed out," I said. "Molly"—I leaned in—"you realize, I could've been on that boat."

She shook her head. "No, you couldn't have. Because if you had been, it would've been your time to die. And it obviously wasn't your time or you'd be dead." She drowned her eggs and sausage in hot sauce, her home fries in ketchup.

"I don't know if I believe that. But even if it's true, whoever planted the bomb may have *meant* to blow me up," I said.

Her forehead contorted into hieroglyphs of utter disbelief. "Were you one of the unpopular kids in high school or something? Oh no, maybe they're buying toilet paper to roll my house tonight! You think people got nothing better to do than to sit around plotting against you? Hey, maybe somebody's stealing my car right now. You don't see me worrying about it."

I recalled her orange car with the eyes painted all over it. "Believe me, Molly. Nobody is stealing your car," I said. Feeling grumpy, I decided to keep quiet. I didn't tell her about the guy who had grabbed me in the parking lot. She'd probably just say I imagined it.

We got back on the road soon after that. Around San Clemente, my cell phone rang. It was *Mami*. I didn't have a Bluetooth, but figured I'd keep it short, so I put the phone on speaker and set it in a cup holder.

"Where have you been?" I detected an edge in her voice.

"I went down to San Diego to check out a lead," I said, irritably. "Why, what's up?"

"The police are looking for you," *Mami* said, a bottled hysteria beginning to fizz.

"Was it a Michael Escobar?" I asked. *Mami* was normally as sharp as a tack, but I thought she must have forgotten about Michael. I was sure I must've mentioned him before.

"No! Not that Michael you talk about all the time—"

"I don't talk about him all the time!"

"Lolita, they think you killed a woman!" *Mami* let go and burst into tears.

"What?" I swerved horribly, but corrected. I was never any good at talking on the phone and driving at the same time, much less when the talk is upsetting.

Molly nonchalantly gripped the road rage handle and smiled. "Yahoo," she said, quietly. "Here we go again."

"I've been calling and calling you," *Mami* said, sniffling. "I didn't know where you were or if something had happened to you!"

"Oh, I'm sorry. I turned off my ringer yesterday, and I must've forgotten to turn it back on."

She cried louder. I looked at Molly, who raised her eyebrows in alarm.

"Listen, *Mami*…we're on our way up there. We'll be at your house in about forty minutes. Let's talk then, okay? I have to go. I'm driving. See you soon." I picked up the phone.

"We?" she said. But my finger was already hitting the button. I dropped the phone back into the cup holder.

"Did you get that? The police are after me!"

Molly laughed. "It's your dream come true—somebody's out to get you!"

"Why do I even talk to her?" I asked the heavens.

"Who's this guy you can't stop talking about?"

"That is *not* true," I said.

"Miii-chael?" She drew out the syllables and wiggled her eyebrows.

"Which of us is stuck in high school?" I asked.

"Your mama said it. And mothers know these things, even when we don't know them ourselves."

"Oh, puh-lease! He's a homicide cop. We work together. End of story."

"What, is he ugly?"

"No, not at all! He's very good looking." Speedo-burrito Michael flashed in my head again. I shook him away.

"Then what? Does he have a tiny little—"

"Molly, please! No! I mean, I wouldn't know. He's just a guy who's really full of himself."

"Good. Probably not," she said. "Then again, you never know; there is such a thing as overcompensation. What color are his eyes?"

"Brown. Why?"

"Oh, I just wanted to see if you knew." She flashed me a knowing smile.

"His eyes are just really dark. It's not like I gaze into them!" Not intentionally, anyway.

"Okay, so just what's wrong with him?"

"He's like an eight-year-old! Like the way he says 'Lei-la-ni,' all drawn out, like he's tasting her name as he says it. I mean, what is that?" I hadn't actually seen him say it, but an image of Michael's mouth forming the name in slow motion popped into my mind.

"Maybe he was just trying to get a reaction out of you."

I'd been creeping toward the left lane, and a car honked to correct me.

I sighed. "We'd better change the subject before I kill someone." I hated to admit it, but he certainly did get a reaction out of me. I kept my mouth shut about Michael Escobar for the rest of the drive and tried hard not to think about him, his mouth, or his Speedo.

We drove straight to my mama's house in Glendale. She hustled us inside, glancing around to see if anyone was watching the house. She shut the front door and collapsed against me. New grey hairs sparkled on her head. I hated upsetting her, especially while losing *Papi* was still so fresh.

I poured myself a glass of my papa's Scotch, the closest thing I could find to the margarita I was craving. *Mami* was horrified.

"It's three o'clock in the afternoon," she said, her hand on her heart.

"It's okay. It's legal now to drink in the afternoon, even when you're not at a party. Molly? Want one?"

Molly shrugged. "Okay."

"*Mami,* what did they tell you? Did they call or come over here?" I asked her.

"I got a phone call. From a Detective Whittaker in homicide. He said they want to talk to you about a woman who was murdered, Linda Gross."

"And they said they think I killed her?"

"Well, no, not in so many words, but I can tell that's what they think," she said.

I relaxed and laughed. "Oh, *Mami,* it's all right. I'm the person who reported the murder; that's why they're looking for me. Why would they think I killed her?" I snorted.

"Detective Whittaker said your fingerprints were found at the place where it happened," she said.

"Of course they were! I wouldn't have found her if I hadn't been there." I suddenly remembered how long my phone had been off. "Oh! I should check my messages."

I hit a button on my phone. The display showed twenty-seven missed calls. "Looks like I missed a couple calls." I hit my voice mail. "I have nineteen voicemails."

"About a dozen of those are from me," *Mami* said. "They all say the same thing—where are you? So you might as well just erase them."

"Okay. That leaves about seven." I listened to voicemails for the next few minutes and finished my Scotch, keeping my face impressively blank for a person experiencing the mental equivalent of a category five hurricane.

"The other messages were from Michael," I said, clicking off. "They were a lot like yours, *Mami,* only less hysterical. He wants me to call him."

"So call him!"

I walked over and poured myself another Scotch, keeping my back to her so she wouldn't see my hands shake. "I don't know..." I said.

"What do you mean you don't know?" *Mami* said.

"She thinks maybe Michael's out to get her, and in more ways than one," Molly said.

"What if it's true," I said to *Mami,* ignoring Molly, "and he just wants to arrest me? He sounded so serious on the voicemail, not like himself at all."

"Call him," *Mami* said. "He's your friend."

"You know what this means, don't you?" I turned to Molly, ignoring *Mami.* "I'm going to have to find Linda's killer myself."

CHAPTER 14

It was time to make dinner. Three cooks in the kitchen, two of them tipsy, could be a recipe for disaster, but it worked out. Molly and *Mami* hit it off well, and *Mami* insisted we both stay the night at her place. She thought the police might arrest me if we went to mine. It sounded like a good idea to me.

Some time after dinner, my cell phone rang. The number was unfamiliar, so I let it go to voicemail and then listened to the message:

"Hello, Ms. Vega. This is Leilani Stone. I'm calling to apologize to you for the other day. I realize now that it was all a big misunderstanding and no fault of yours. I behaved just awfully and, well, I hope you'll forgive me. I've been under a lot of stress lately, as I'm sure you can imagine. I really haven't been myself. If you still want to talk, I'd be happy to speak with you. If you're still interested, please contact my assistant, Jennifer."

She left Jennifer's number. I listened to it again and wrote the number down, then saved the message. This was a big surprise, and it couldn't have come at a better time.

"Maybe you're bringing me some of your luck, Molly," I said and related the message. Exactly why Molly was in LA with me, spending the night at my mama's house, I could not have said, but I enjoyed her company. "Maybe you're my fairy godmother," I said.

"Sure, why not!" Molly said. "Sounds like a full time job."

"All you have to do is make all my wishes come true."

"You don't need me for that; you need you."

"But you can help me."

"Okay," she said.

"A get-out-of-jail-free card might come in handy, too," I said, under my breath, as I left the room to call the number Leilani had left.

Jennifer was also apologetic. She gave me an appointment with Leilani the following morning. I was walking back to join the others when my cell phone rang again. The display showed Restricted, so I let it go to voicemail, too. But when I listened to the message, it was hopelessly garbled. I couldn't make out a single word.

I went to bed early, tuckered out from driving and stress and Scotch. Molly and *Mami* sat in the dim parchment light of the kitchen, talking late into the night.

*   *   *

The next morning I slept late, despite having gone to bed early. When I got up, Molly and *Mami* were in the kitchen and had already eaten. They shuffled around getting me coffee and breakfast. It was like having two mothers.

After breakfast, Molly and I went over to Leilani's. Our appointment was for eleven o'clock. Jennifer led us into a different reception room from the last time I'd been there. She looked as neat as before and wore the same soft, soundless slippers. A button pinned to her lapel bore a picture of an elephant and read: Circuses are no fun for me!

In a few seconds, Leilani swooped in like the breeze of an opened door. "He-e-llooo," she sang, just like last time. "Ms. Vega, thank you so much for coming. And...Mrs. O? This is a surprise! How nice to see you again." It sounded genuine. She gave Molly a hug. Then she hugged me, too, and reiterated her apology.

"Please, call me Lola," I said.

"It's such a nice day, why don't we talk out in the garden? The children are out there playing. I hope you don't mind."

Mind? The garden was a paradise. Rows of tall date palms lined each side of the property. There was another dolphin fountain set in the center of a large swimming pool surrounded by weeping birches, and roses and lilies of all colors.

Two beautiful children were splashing in the pool below the dolphins, a girl and a boy. Jack and Leilani had adopted the girl,

Sienna, from Cambodia at age five, right after they married. Harley, the boy, was adopted about six months later from Sudan at age three. A little farther off, diving and then shooting up with an orange ring, was Ozzy. Fifteen years old, he was Jack's biological child with an Australian model he'd had a short-term relationship with. All three swam and played as happily as otters under the watchful eye of their nanny. Their laughter and squeals blended musically with the cascading waters of the fountain. The family dog, an adorable Fox Terrier named Asta, frolicked on dry land close by, completing a near-perfect picture of domestic bliss. The only thing missing from this pretty picture was Jack.

"Your home is so lovely," I said to Leilani, as we took seats at an umbrellaed table.

"Just like my place," Molly said under her breath, as she leaned back to take in the full grandeur of the palms.

"Thank you, Lola," Leilani said. A tray held a pitcher of iced tea and some glasses. Crescents of ice tinkled gently as Leilani poured.

I backed my chair away from the table so I would be out of easy range if she decided to hurl the pitcher at me.

"A police detective was here yesterday," Leilani said. "He told me about Linda. He also told me about you being a private detective, not a journalist. I hope you understand; the tabloid reporters have put us through hell the last couple of years. They'd stop at nothing to get photos of Jack, or me and the kids, or personal information of any kind. After a while, you can get a little crazy. You start to imagine people are after you all the time."

"Oh, she knows exactly what that's like," Molly said.

I ignored Molly. "I do understand. There's been so much going on with your family. Who was the detective you spoke with?"

"His name was Escobar. He's in homicide. He didn't give me details, but I take it Linda was murdered. I guess it's going to be like Jessica all over again. The questions will be asked, the leads will be followed, but in the end nothing will happen. They'll just get away with it. Apparently, people get away with murder all the time." Tears brimmed in Leilani's eyes. "I was no fan of Linda, but nobody deserves to be murdered."

"You and Linda didn't get along?" I asked.

"We got along okay, until she started driving Jack crazy."

"Oh? What's that about?" I asked. "I had the impression she and

64

Jack were still good friends."

"They were for a long time. And then Linda started calling all the time. Eventually, Jack didn't want to talk to her anymore. He almost never took her calls, but that just made things worse. She started harassing him, calling late at night, hitting redial until we had to turn off the phone. She left some really nasty messages sometimes, too. I said we should call the police, but Jack said she would give up eventually."

"Did she?"

"Never. Not until Jack died did the phone calls finally stop." Leilani wiped away a tear with her hand, but she felt angry, not sad. I'd learned to read between the invisible lines. I could tell her brow would have been furrowed if not for extreme Botox, and her mouth was spread almost in a smile. Those with overdone Botox or fillers in the folds between nose and mouth, like Leilani, came closest to smiling when they were raging angry.

"What did Linda want, do you know?" I asked.

"Jack said she wanted money. That's what they always want, all the ex-wives and ex-girlfriends. No surprise there."

"Did Jack give her any money?"

"He did, of course. That's the kind of guy he was," Leilani said. "But she still kept after him for more. She must have been desperate."

"Would you mind if I had a look at Jack's bank statements, so I can check his against hers and see what matches up?" I asked.

"Sure, I don't mind. Just his regular bank account? You don't need his investment accounts, do you?"

"Anything would be helpful."

"I'll have Jennifer make copies." Leilani hit a button on her cell and called Jennifer. She told her to get Jack's bank and brokerage statements together and bring them out to us.

"Thanks, I really appreciate it. Did Jack happen to tell you why Linda needed money so badly?"

"He didn't have to. I could guess," she said. "Back when everyone was still friendly, Linda started hanging out with Jack's third wife, Irena. Irena's into dog racing, and she got Linda into it, too. Only Linda has—I mean had—a little gambling problem. Irena told me about it. She quit taking Linda to the dog races, but it was too late. Linda was already in too deep. She sold her home around that time, probably because of all the money she lost gambling."

"That's sad," I said. It hit me that possibly Linda hadn't been reading the novel I found beside her in the bathtub.

"It is," Leilani said. I knew her eyebrows would have risen sympathetically, if only they could.

"I'm surprised the police didn't take Jack's bank records yesterday," I said.

"Oh, that detective didn't ask me for a thing," Leilani said. "He didn't ask me a single question about Jack, or Linda, or Ozzy."

"Ozzy? Why would he ask about him?"

"Well, I guess he wouldn't, being from homicide, but the police had been here just the day before about Oz, so at first that's why I thought he was here." She rolled her eyes. "Ozzy took the Ferrari out for a spin again, and they picked him up for reckless driving. He loves that car as much as his father did, but he's not ready to drive that much car. He's not even legal yet. He only has a learner's permit."

"Oh. But then what did Detective Escobar want?" I asked.

"He informed me that Linda was dead, but mostly he just talked about you," Leilani said. "He wanted to know if I'd seen or heard from you again and said to call him if I did."

I felt a sinking sensation in my stomach. He was obviously looking for me. But did Michael just want to talk, or did he plan to arrest me?

CHAPTER 15

Until I figured out if the police wanted to arrest me, I planned to lie low.

"Did he say why he was looking for me?" I asked Leilani, as casually as possible.

"No."

Good. At least he hadn't told Leilani I was a suspect, even if I was.

"But he seemed to know all about our meeting the other day." Leilani flushed pink. "I thought you sent him over to set me straight on things."

"No, I didn't, but I did tell him about that day," I said. "I'm mainly interested in Linda's death right now, but I wonder if I could ask you a few questions about Jack's?"

"Sure," she said, no hesitation.

"Would you mind telling me the whole story of how you found him?"

"Well, I thought he'd gone down to San Diego. He went there most weekends. The kids and I had a typical Saturday: sleep late, yoga, errands, swimming. Then I dropped them at their friends' houses to spend the night, and I went to a party."

"Where was the party?"

"Here in Malibu," she said. "I came home pretty early, around two in the morning. I went to open the garage door to put my car in and saw Jack's car still in there, the one he usually drove down. And then I realized…he was in there."

"The car wasn't running?"

"No. I guess it had run out of gas by the time I got there."

"You said you went to open the door; don't you have a remote for it?"

"We had just extended that garage, that one used to be a three-car—Jack had so many cars, but the Ferrari was his favorite—and while they were working on it we had the power shut off, so I had to walk over and pull the door up."

"What time was it the first time you opened it, when you left for the party?"

"I didn't open it before. Jack would take my car out every morning and park it in the driveway because he knew I didn't like to bother with the door. He was a very thoughtful guy."

"Leilani, I don't mean to be insensitive, but if Jack was such a great guy, why were you divorcing him?"

She shrugged. "Things change," she said. "We weren't connecting anymore. He was hardly ever here to even try. He'd been through divorces before—I certainly never imagined he would take his own life, but I guess he'd just had enough. I guess he was ready to leave this plane of existence and move on." She looked up to the sky as if Jack might be floating there, which according to Molly, he could be.

"Okay. Just one more thing. How can I find Irena? I'd like to talk with her. Maybe she can shed some light on Linda's situation."

"Irena is a performer with the Murmansk Circus. She's a trapeze artist. In fact, her family is all circus people. They're in the three-ring circus from the time they're children."

"Oh, right." I remembered her from my three days working for Jack Stone. They were married at the time, soon to be divorced.

"Sounds a lot like my family," Molly said.

"They're circus people?" Leilani asked.

"No," Molly said.

"Anyway"—Leilani turned back to me—"they have a big compound out east toward the desert, near Sunspot City. I've never known Irena to answer a telephone, not my calls, anyway, but if you just head for Sunspot City, anyone out there can point you to it."

"Great, thanks," I said.

Jennifer came out from the house and walked across the patio. She set a thick brown envelope on the table before me.

"That was quick," I said.

"Jenn is amazing!" Leilani said, but she seemed to be talking to Jennifer because she gazed warmly into her eyes. Jennifer took a step back so her hip was touching Leilani's shoulder and stroked Leilani's hair. Leilani responded by putting her arm around Jennifer's backside, pulling her close against her cheek, and giving her a little squeeze.

Molly nearly choked on her iced tea, but recovered. I guess ghost-Jack had never mentioned that Leilani and Jennifer were an item. I was surprised, too. I knew from Barnaby that Jennifer was having a fling with Jack, but apparently she was involved with both Jack and Leilani. A somewhat crowded page from the *Kama Sutra* popped into my mind. To gather my thoughts, I looked down at Jennifer's shoes.

"I love your shoes," I said, because nothing better came to mind. "The leather looks so soft."

"Thank you," Jennifer said, a smug smile on her face, "but actually, they're pleather. Fake leather. I don't wear animals."

"Nice," I said. "It looks just like leather."

"Jennifer is very active in the fight for animal rights," Leilani said, beaming with pride for Jennifer. "She'll stop at nothing in defense of animals, or any part of the environment."

The landline rang in the house.

"Please excuse me," Jennifer said and loped back across the patio, graceful as a doe.

"We won't take up any more of your time." I stood to go and clutched the envelope. "I'll get on these; please call me if you think of anything at all that might be of interest."

"Sure," she said, rising from her seat to walk us back to the house.

"Oh, don't bother. I'm sure we can find our way out," I said. "And fewer ants will be stepped on that way!" I laughed; she didn't.

As we drove in silence down the driveway and out the gate, I was pondering Jennifer, and I knew Molly was, too.

Finally, Molly said, "There's a lot more to Jennifer than meets the eye."

"I'll say." I kept going back to Jennifer's silent shoes. Then a thought hit me. I decided to level with Molly so I could toss my idea around with her. "Molly, I just thought of something! You know how you think I imagine people are out to get me? Well, a couple of nights ago, a guy in a black trench coat grabbed me in a parking lot and warned me off this case."

"Whoa—seriously?" she said.

"Seriously. And he was able to sneak up on me like that because his car didn't make any noise. So, it must have been either an electric car or a hybrid. And what kind of people drive those kinds of cars?"

"Environmentalists!" Molly said.

"Exactly. Maybe Jennifer saw me leave Linda's that night and put two and two together. She could've known I was a PI because I was on the Jessica Stone case. What if Jennifer was in on blackmailing Jack? Maybe she had me warned away because she thought I was getting too close. Or maybe she thought Linda was double-crossing her. I remember seeing a blonde woman outside my apartment smoking a cigarette."

"I don't know," Molly said. "Do environmentalists smoke? That's air pollution. And a lot of people drive hybrid cars nowadays."

"I'm sure there must be environmentalists who smoke. They probably roll their own. And Jennifer had been on Jack's boat with him. She knew the boat, and she had opportunity anytime she was down there with Jack. Maybe she plants bombs all the time. Maybe she goes around blowing things up for radical environmental groups. I'm going to check her out."

My cell phone rang, and we both jumped. I picked it up to look at it, but it slipped from my grasp to the floor of the car. Molly and I both scrambled for it, but kept fumbling it and knocking it away. I figured it was probably *Mami,* and I didn't wish to worry her any more than I already had. When I managed to get a grip on the phone, it was on the last ring. I answered quickly…and immediately wished I hadn't. It was Detective Michael Escobar.

CHAPTER 16

"Michael. Hi." I tried to sound normal, but my voice quavered.

"Where are you?" He sounded annoyed.

"Actually, I'm driving right now. I'll have to call you back."

"Don't hang up, Lola! Where have you been?"

"Why? You didn't tell me not to leave town, Sheriff."

"No, but I didn't think you were going to, either. Maybe I should have."

"Well, too late. I've already left town and come back."

"Lola, listen to me. We need to talk to you about Linda Gross. I didn't know you were going to disappear! I'd have put a tail on you."

"Don't be silly. I've already got a tail."

"Lola, this isn't funny! I've got Whittaker breathing down my neck, telling me to get you in here ASAP."

"Okay, be straight with me. Do they want to arrest me?"

"You are, at this moment, a person of interest, but no arrest is imminent."

"Oh, thank God! I've been so worried." My whole body relaxed.

"It doesn't look good, though. You're the last person we know of who saw Linda alive. The only prints they turned up in her whole place are her own and yours. And the only prints on the gun are yours."

I rolled my eyes and groaned.

"Apparently, you also called her office that morning and got The Tides address under false pretenses," he said.

"But I star-sixty-sevened that call!"

"That only hides your number from the person you're calling. The phone company still has a record of the call."

"I just wanted to see if it was one of their listings. I already had the address; that's where I had the meeting with her, remember?"

"There's no record Linda met with you or paid you anything. There was no appointment in her computer or cell phone, no one at her office knew about it, and there's no check to you in her bank statement. Don't tell me she paid you cash?"

"Ugh! She gave me a check from a numbered bank account. I don't know whose account it is. That's one of the things I've been trying to find out. Wait a second! You have Linda's bank statements? Then you can answer this question: Did Linda start making large cash deposits and withdrawals somewhere around a year ago that stopped just after Jack Stone's death?"

"I'm supposed to be asking you the questions, remember?"

"Michael, please. This is important. Because I think Linda was blackmailing Jack Stone, and I think Linda's bank records will prove it."

"Well, come on in, and maybe I'll let you take a peek."

"Michael, for God's sake, I'm a murder suspect."

"Person of interest. And it'll look better if you come in voluntarily."

"You don't actually think I did this, do you?"

There was a lengthy moment of silence suitable for a funeral. Finally, I heard a small rustling sound.

"Okay," he said finally, "yes, she did make deposits and withdrawals like you describe. You're right on the money. Does that make you feel better?"

I breathed again. "Yes, definitely!"

"Okay. So come see me. I know you miss me," he said.

"Um, I can't come in right now, but I will soon."

"Lola, come on!"

"Soon. Very soon, I promise. Look, obviously somebody is setting me up. If I come in now, Linda's murder is going to get hung on me."

"So, you think the police can't handle it, but you can."

"This is too important. I can't be sitting around getting drilled with questions I don't have the answers to anyway while the trail goes cold. Two days."

"Twenty-four hours!"

The fact was he couldn't compel me to come in without arresting me. But my taking off like that did look bad and might make them more inclined to arrest me as soon as I raised my head. Unfortunately, the longer I stayed away, the more likely it became they'd do it anyway.

"Michael," I softened my voice, "tell me you know I didn't do this."

Michael's voice softened, too. "The fact is, Lola, you've never let me get to know you all that well. But from what I do know of you, no, I don't think you did it."

Ouch. But it was certainly true. "Um, thanks, sort of. Okay, twenty-four hours." I tossed the phone on the back seat, willing it not to ring again for a long, long time.

CHAPTER 17

Sunspot City: cheapest place to live in southern California that isn't an urban slum. It's more of a landfill. Scorching hot sun sucking the life out of anything that moves, doublewide trailers heavy with retirees, nineteen-sixties boat-sized cars, and trash, mostly fast-food cups and containers, blowing across parched, hard flatland dotted with spiky brown scrub.

We blew into town in my 2006 VW GTI, the only small car—also the only car from the current century—to be seen for miles. The only thing on the horizon taller than a trailer was a gigantic billboard. It showed an elephant decked out in glitter on one side, standing next to a dancing bear wearing a sequined hat and vest, waving both its paws. On the other side of the picture a scantily clad, sparkling woman seated on a swinging bar was leaning backward, her arm sweeping the air in a grand flourish. The sign read: Come see Ivan, World-Famous Dancing Bear! Famous Murmansk Acrobats! Trapeze, Clown, Elephant, and much, much more! Come to World-Famous Three-Ring Murmansk Circus! Turn right 1 mile ahead at Iguana Boulevard, follow to red and white striped Big Top.

"We won't even have to ask directions," I said.

"Not unless you can't see the Big Top," Molly agreed.

But we could see the tent the minute we turned. The Big Top squatted like giant, round peppermint candy on the barren landscape. I pulled in and parked near a cluster of trailers off to one side. Two huge black dogs raced up to the car. They barked viciously, as though they ate only human flesh and hadn't seen a human in weeks.

I sounded a few short beeps on the horn and put my window down a crack. "Hello!" I called.

The dogs jumped up to try and squeeze their fangs through the window opening. A glob of dog slobber slid down the glass. I looked over at Molly. Her hands were clasped around her throat for protection, just in case they got in.

"Ha!" I laughed. "They can't rip out your throat from out there!"

She pointed a finger at me, and I looked down. My hands were around my neck, too.

A sharp knock at the car window right beside my head made me jump. A man in a sequined catsuit and a two-day beard stood by the car door. He was holding a machine gun, pointed at the ground. The man held up one finger in wait-a-minute mode.

I nodded to him and smiled. The smile frozen on my face, I said, "Molly, that guy's holding a Dragunov."

She pasted a smile onto her face as well. "What's a Drag-u-nov?" she asked.

We both kept our eyes on catsuit man.

"It's like a Kalashnikov, only better."

"Oh. What's a Kalash-hoo-ha?" she asked.

"A Russian AK-47. You can't even get them here; they're banned."

"Oh, I see," Molly said. "So what worries you about the gigantic gun is that it's illegal. Now I'm clear."

The man in the catsuit held one hand up in the air like a school crossing guard, and both dogs immediately sat down and looked up at him with eager faces, their panting tongues lolling. Then he gestured to Molly and me with his gun, and we emerged cautiously from the car.

"Thank you," I said, smiling. "We're looking for Irena?"

The man said nothing, but waved his gun toward the Big Top. He was still holding up his other hand and the dogs were still staring at it. We later found out that he was Irena's cousin and the Murmansk Circus tiger tamer, The Amazing Sergei.

"Thank you," we both said in unison and tiptoed off into the tent. As we entered, two men at either side of the entrance, also with two-day beards, sequined outfits, and Dragunovs in hand, pivoted toward us and aimed their guns at our heads.

"Uh...we're looking for Irena," I said again. I was getting the idea there was more to Irena's family circus than the Stones realized.

The men put down their weapons and stood aside. One of them uttered a single word. "Boris," he said, nodding his head toward the ringmaster, who thankfully held only a microphone in his armpit, no machine gun.

Inside, the tent was a whirl of activity. In one ring, a white horse cantered around the circle, while a sparkling girl hung off one side of it, swung up onto its back again, and then swooped down to hang from the other side. In another ring, Ivan the World Famous Dancing Bear's trainer had Ivan twirling in the center, while clowns plied their antics around the perimeter. In the ring nearest to us, acrobats made a human pyramid beneath a net, while two trapeze artists practiced hand-offs above. Ringmaster Boris, a man built like a tank, stood nearby in fancy dress with a tall hat. He watched the performers practice with a grim expression on his sharp face, stroking his bushy walrus-style moustache with two fingers.

"Excuse me," I called to the ringmaster, and we walked over to his side.

"May I help you ladies?" he asked, in a heavy Russian accent.

"We're looking for Irena," I said.

He turned to face the performers, put microphone to mouth and called, "Irena!"

At least six different women instantly stopped what they were doing and stared at Boris.

He shrugged. "Is very common name. Vhich vun?"

"I believe she's a trapeze artist," I said.

Indeed, one of the women who had frozen in place was hanging upside-down from a bar suspended by two cables reaching from a catwalk high above. The ringmaster waved her down, and the other Irenas returned to their previous activities. The woman swung a couple of times and then swooped up to a standing position on the bar. She then stepped off the bar-swing as though she were entering a swimming pool and dropped into the net below, rolled to an upright position, came to the edge of the net and flipped off, to land on the dirt floor of the tent with a dramatic flourish in front of us.

"Habit," she said, also in a Russian accent, and laughed.

Irena still looked like a supermodel. She stood six feet tall, with almond eyes set in a heart-shaped face. Rich red curls flounced around her head. Her willowy figure was dressed from head to toe in a glittering red-and-gold skintight outfit. No machine gun.

"Irena, thank you for coming down. Is there somewhere we can talk privately?" I asked.

"Sure, sure," she said. She turned to the ringmaster and said, "Uncle Boris, I go talk vith them for a minute."

"*Da,*" Uncle Boris said.

"Come," she said to us. "Ve go to my trailer." She retrieved a full-length fur coat from the bleachers and put it on, though it was about eighty degrees outside. Then she led us to a trailer with pictures of horses and dogs pasted on the door. Inside, books took up every available space, about half Russian and half English. She cleared seats for us at a dinette. We introduced ourselves, and I gave her my business card. She shut the door, plucked a large emerald ring from the table and put it on her index finger, and brewed a strong pot of tea.

"I doubt you remember me," I said, "but we met a couple years ago, back when you were married to Jack Stone."

"Vell, Jack and I vere happy together for long time," Irena said. "Almost four years. But no, sorry, I don't remember you." She poured the tea and brought forth a clear bottle with a Russian label. "Vodka?" she asked.

We both declined the vodka, but she poured some in her own tea. Then she stirred in a large spoonful of raspberry jam. Her fur coat flounced open, revealing the dazzle of glitter beneath it. She noticed us both looking at the coat and wrapped it around her again.

"I know is not cold. I just like vearing fur. Is like vearing a great big hug!"

"Sure, I could see that," Molly said, stirring her tea.

"So, you and Jack stayed friends after you divorced?" I asked.

"Yes, yes, very good friends alvays," she said.

"And I understand you were also friends with his other ex-wives," I said.

Irena took a big gulp of tea. "Yes, is true. Ve vere all good friends, alvays. But now"—she choked up—"is all my fault he is dead!" she wailed, and tears spilled into the depths of her plush brown mink.

CHAPTER 18

"You don't mean you killed him!" Molly cried.

"Is not vhat I meant," Irena said. "But, if not for me, maybe things vould be different, and Jack vould not be so sad to kill himself."

Irena grabbed a kitchen towel from the handle of her fridge and rubbed the tears off her cheeks, then honked her nose on it a few times. When she came up for air, her face was all red, especially her nose, but thick layers of obviously waterproof mascara remained intact and rigid, like black duct tape holding her swollen eyes open.

"Okay, feel better now." Irena raised her cup. "Cheers!" she said, her moment of sadness past. We all clanged our cups together and Irena downed most of her "tea."

"Irena," I said, "we came here today to talk to you about Linda Gross, Jack's second wife. I understand the two of you like to go to dog races?"

"Oh, yes. I love the pretty doggies," she said. "I love to vatch them run!"

"Where do you go? I didn't think there was a dog track anywhere in southern California," Molly said.

"No, is not. Ve go to Tijuana for doggie races. Place vhere movie stars used to go in old days. I get this calendar there, see?" She turned halfway and pointed to a Spanish language calendar with a photo of dogs racing and notes scribbled all over its squares.

"Uh-huh. Do you bet on the races?" I was trying to take it slow; I didn't know if she'd heard the bad news about Linda.

"Vell, I just like to vatch the doggies run, but Linda, she makes the bets."

"Has Linda won a lot?" I asked.

She clucked her tongue and shook her head. "Linda should not bet. She does not vin. Is vhy I say is my fault. I take Linda to races. Is all my fault she gambles."

"Has she lost a lot of money, do you think?"

"Oh, yes. Much money. She borrow money, then gamble that avay, too. She borrow money to pay back money. Linda owe everybody money. I vorry for her because racetrack men alvays vere buggink her to pay them the money."

"Who are they? Do you know their names?"

"The guy Linda deal vith is called Santiago. He is part owner and also manages track. He alvays have gang of big guys vith him." Irena hulked her shoulders up with a shrug, lowered her voice and grunted. "Linda say he have silent partner, but I don't know who."

"And has Linda paid Santiago the money?" I asked.

She looked at the floor. "Vell, I vorry for her, so I tell her to talk to Uncle Boris." She poured another vodka, this time skipping the tea and jam. "He lend her money to pay racetrack. Uncle Boris is very generous man. Cheers!" She gulped half her drink and laughed. "I do feel much better now."

"Do you know if Linda ever paid your uncle back?" I asked. I had a sinking feeling in my stomach. Irena seemed blind to the implications of someone borrowing money from a man with a compound out in the boonies, guarded by lots of other men with machine guns.

"Actually, I know for fact she have *not* paid him back. *Skoll!*" Irena downed the other half of her drink, then made another.

"Any idea how much she owes your uncle?" I asked.

"Give or take few dollars, around hundred thousand."

"A hundred thousand dollars!" Molly and I said together.

"*Da.* She vill have to sell a few condos," Irena said.

Molly and I looked at each other and winced.

"Irena, I've noticed all the men around here seem to wear glittering outfits, have beard stubble, and carry machine guns. Any idea why?" I asked.

"Vell, ve alvays have shiny clothes...is circus tradition," she said.

"Oh, sure."

"And is Monday, so men don't have to shave. Nobody go to

circus on Monday," she said.

"Okay."

She was silent.

"And the machine guns?" I asked.

"I ask Uncle Boris about that once. He says ve have lots of rabbits making holes in tent, and they have to be ready to shoot them."

"With machine guns?" Molly asked.

"Is all they have," Irena said.

"But you can't even get those guns in this country," I said. "They're banned. Illegal."

"They are Russian, like circus. Uncle Boris like Russian everything. He say he vill be less homesick that vay. He is very smart, Uncle Boris." She tapped her head with one finger. "Vhen there is audience, they put machine guns avay."

"Rabbits," I said.

"*Da,* rabbits." Irena seemed completely oblivious to how ridiculous that sounded.

I thrust my hands into my hair and shook my head, but only for a second. As an investigator, I see people in deep denial about their loved ones all the time. They're our bread and butter. Part of my job is to shatter that denial. But until I knew for sure if, or how far, Irena's family was involved in Linda's murder, all I planned to tell her was the bad news that Linda was dead.

"Well, never mind that," I said. "I have something to tell you, and it's not going to be easy for you to hear."

Irena, who had been standing all this time while we sat so the vodka bottle was within easy reach now grabbed the bottle by its neck and sank into a chair. "I have bad feelink," she said.

"There's no easy way to say this, so I'm just going to say it. Linda is dead. She was murdered three days ago. Gunshot wound."

Irena froze for a minute, like a gigantic mink in headlights.

"Irena?" Molly said. She reached out and put her hand over Irena's.

Irena pulled her hand back instantly. A single tear rolled down her red cheek. She poured a drink and raised her cup in the air. "To Linda," she said.

"To Linda," Molly and I said in unison, raising our cups high, and we all drank in big gulps.

CHAPTER 19

"Did you vork on Jessica's murder? Is that vhy ve met?" Irena asked me.

"Yes. Two years ago, I was asking you about Jessica. I don't remember much of it."

"I remember nothink. There vas lot going on then. Jack and I vere just getting divorce vhen his sister died," she said. She concentrated on pleating and unpleating the edge of her dishtowel.

"What was Jessica like?"

"She vas little bit older than Jack. She could get him to do anythink." Irena sneered. "He thought she vas God; to him, she could do no wrong!"

"I take it you didn't think much of her?" Molly asked.

"She could be cruel to Jack. The vay she vould laugh at him—it vas veird. It gave me the creeps," Irena said.

"When you and Linda went to Tijuana, who usually drove?" I asked.

"I drove, alvays. I not like Linda's driving," she said.

"Where did you pick her up?" I asked.

"Sometimes her office, sometimes her house before she sold house, sometimes at new house, sometimes even at places she have for sale," she said.

"Does the number four-five-three-five mean anything to you?" I asked.

She pressed her lips into a smooch. "I can't think of anything. Vhy? Is clue?"

"I don't really know. It could be nothing."

Irena suddenly brightened. "I just remember somethink! Last time I talk to Linda, she say she vant me to take care of something for her." Her face fell again. "She say she vill bring over something. I guess she vill never bring over now."

"She didn't say what it was?"

"No. Let me think, vhat she did say exactly?" Irena looked up at the ceiling. "I vant you to hold onto somethink for me. Sure, I say, no problem. She say somethink—Boris vas vaiting for me to get off phone, so I vasn't listening so vell—somethink about a *blue dragon.* And she vill bring over sometime in the next veek. Is all I remember."

"She told you she was bringing over a blue dragon?" Molly asked. I could read Molly's mind this time; she was thinking Irena might have drunk too much of her special tea.

"Was she into art?" I asked. "Could be a statue or painting worth a lot of money, maybe. Something she didn't want to lose to her gambling debts."

"Linda have blue tea jar vith dragon on it," Irena said. "Is that, maybe?"

"That's a very good possibility," I said. An especially good possibility because a tea jar is a container, and there could be something inside it that Linda wanted to keep safe and that could provide a clue to her killer's identity. I felt like screaming Eureka, but put on my poker face.

Molly didn't seem to have a poker face. "Maybe Linda hid something in the tea jar!" she cried. But Irena probably would have thought of it herself, anyway.

"Maybe if you get tea jar, you vill find out who killed her," Irena said.

"That would be great. Um, where did Linda live?" I asked her.

"She share leetle house vith creepy roommate in bad neighborhood." Irena grabbed a folder off her desk, flipped it open and located a piece of paper folded in half. It was a printout of an email from Linda with a phone number and a Google map beneath it. "She email me this map to her house so I pick her up. You can have." Tears welled in her eyes again, and she bolstered herself with a gulp of vodka. "I von't need anymore."

"That really is a bad part of town," Molly said.

I eyed the address on the map hopefully, but the house number was 15530, not even close to 4535. Still, the blue dragon tea jar might turn out to be supremely important. I had to get it.

"Vas terrible. Linda not like living there, but she have no money left. She hardly ever stay there. She even sleep in place for sale sometimes because of creepy roommate."

"Thanks, Irena. You've been a huge help. And don't you worry. I'm going to find out who killed Linda and bring them to justice," I said.

"I belief you vill try very hard, at least. Vatch out for creepy roommate, though. He is veird man; name is Villiam. That guy is crazy!"

"We'll be careful," I said.

We drove away from the Murmansk Circus amid vicious barking dogs and four or five glittering men with AK-47s smiling and waving goodbye to us alongside teary, sparkling Irena in her billowing fur. Just like any other rabbit-hunting family.

We went back into Sunspot City and hopped onto the 5 heading south.

"Aren't we going to Linda's?" Molly asked.

"Soon, but not right now. First I want to follow the money."

"You mean, Tijuana?"

I nodded. "The dog track. I need to find out what Linda was up to. How many people she was playing and for how much cash. She could've borrowed that money from Uncle Boris, but never paid this Santiago. Maybe she kept it and was planning to skip town, or worse, maybe she gambled that away, too. Obviously, she was out of control, a gambling addict."

"I never thought of that. You're right. She probably would gamble it."

"That's what addicts are like. Think of the most unthinkable thing someone could do, and they'll actually do it." The bitterness in my own voice surprised me. Molly must have noticed it, too, but she let it go without comment.

"So," she said, "if she never paid the dog race guys, they might've killed her to teach her a lesson."

"More likely to make an example of her. Or maybe they only wanted to talk to her, but caught her about to skip town, took the money she'd borrowed from Uncle Boris, and then killed her because she pissed them off. Or none of the above. We don't know anything about them yet. But I don't think they're any threat to us as long as I don't accuse them of anything. All they'd do, probably, is not answer my questions. But I can't be absolutely sure of that. If you don't want to come, Molly, I understand. I can drop you off, no problem."

"Are you kidding? I wouldn't miss it," she said. "I can do the unthinkable myself sometimes, addiction or no addiction."

I believed her. "Okay then, *vamonos!*"

CHAPTER 20

We drove down to the Mexican border and parked on the US side around two o'clock. The day was ripe and hot as a habanero. Yellow sun, blue sky. We had stopped quickly to change on the way down. Molly was now clothed in the red-orange-yellow part of the color spectrum. In the States her wardrobe made her stand out, but across the border she fit right in with Mexico's brilliant hues. My red hair fit in, too. I wore it big, along with a short khaki skirt, low-cut red top, chunky heels, and big dangling earrings that looked like wedges of oranges and lemons. I was walking sangria.

We walked through the claws of the border's tall metal turnstiles, then down the long, zigzagging walkways where people sold crafts from tables. Here and there, women and children begged for money. I stopped to give some coins to a tiny woman with a baby in her arms. As I raised my head, I caught a glimpse of a patch of black a few feet away from me, starkly out of place among the sun-baked colors. It gave me goose bumps, but when I looked around whatever it was had gone.

We soon came to the heart of Tijuana. The streets were full of pharmacies selling cheap drugs and bars selling cheap drinks. Music splashed down from bar balconies, mixing with laughter and chatter. Ribbons of people cruising the streets and vendors hawking their wares in Spanish made for a lively rhythm.

I had only a rough idea where the dog track was, but figured it couldn't be too tough to find. We stood at a crossroads trying to figure out which way to go. A man selling bobble-head dolls from a table next to us sat repeating, "*Pupitres. Pupitres aquí,*" in a low tone. His quiet words caught my attention.

"Excuse me, would you be kind enough to direct us to the dog races?" I asked him, in Spanish. My Spanish was merely okay. My parents, both first-generation Americans, hadn't taught us kids Spanish growing up, feeling it would be better for us to focus on English. I'd had to take Spanish in school, which I found slightly humiliating, and hadn't spoken it regularly since my school days.

The man's dark eyes twinkled. He answered my question with questions, in English. "You like to gamble, *sí?* You like card games?"

He figured I had money to burn.

"No, we're just looking for someone," I said.

"These dolls are very good luck. Especially the little frogs." He picked up a tiny, purple and green painted wooden bobble-head that looked like a small dinosaur. I strained to see its frogginess, but could not.

"I can always use more good luck," I said, my eyes meeting Molly's. I paid for the frogasaur and stuffed it into my bag, and we stepped away to find someone else to ask.

"Let's just get a taxi," Molly said.

"I don't want to do that without a pretty good idea where the track is first. Otherwise, it'll take way too long while they drive us all over the city to crank up the fare. You know, the tourist mark-up."

"*Señora!*" the doll seller called. He pointed to a bus pulling up across the street. "That bus goes to the racetrack." He bobbed his head up and down like one of his dolls. "You see, good luck already!"

"Thank you," I called to him, and Molly and I rushed across the street.

We climbed onto the bus, and I told the driver where we wanted to go. He nodded sagely without looking up at us. We paid and took seats near the front of the bus. I glanced out the window, and this time there was no mistaking the black thing. A man in a black trench coat stood across the street where we had just been, by the doll seller's table. He was staring straight into my eyes, a scowl on his face. A chill went through me.

I clutched Molly's arm. "Look," I whispered.

Molly looked out the window and gasped. She slid her hand over mine.

"You don't think those circus dogs can take human form, do you?"

When the bus pulled away from the curb, the man turned away and stalked off.

"I'd bet money that's the guy who attacked me in the parking lot the other night," I said.

"That guy gives me the creeps," Molly said. "If looks could kill, there'd be nothing left of you but a chalk outline."

"I don't mean to scare you," I said, "but anyone wearing a long black coat in this heat is probably packing a weapon."

"He could fit a lawn mower under that thing."

"Let's stick together every minute," I said, and she agreed.

As we bounced across town to the greyhound track, I wondered whether the trench-coated man was really tailing me, or if I was just being paranoid. But the look in his eye was pretty convincing. If he were to kill me and Molly on this side of the border and then retreat back to the States, he might just get away with it. We hadn't even told anyone where we were going. I was suddenly sorry I'd brought Molly along. She was in danger, and it was because of me.

The bus dropped us right in front of the dog track, and we headed for the manager's office. The door was open. Every inch of wall space was covered with posters of numbered dogs stretched out like rubber bands against blurred backgrounds. An air conditioner wheezed in the only window. Behind a desk, a man in a brown leather jacket sat talking on the phone, but I couldn't make out what he was saying. Another man in a chair thumbed through a biker magazine.

I knocked on the open door, and they both looked up at me. The man on the phone gave his dark mane a light toss and leaned forward. He looked Molly and me up and down with luscious brown eyes that made me catch my breath. He saw it, smiled, and waved us inside. He nodded to the man in the chair, a thick, tattooed guy with a goatee and shaved head who got up and left, but stood just outside the door.

The man behind the desk motioned us to take seats and wrapped up his conversation. Then he sat back comfortably and crossed his legs in a square. "Good afternoon, ladies. How can I help you?" he asked, in pleasantly accented English.

I wondered how he could be so sure we were American. No doubt he thought I was checking him out when my gaze lingered a beat too long on his fingers woven together in his lap. But what I was sizing up was his body language, and it suggested he was the type to give up absolutely nothing. I decided this man was not to be underestimated. All I could do was assure him we were not looking to cause trouble. And leaning over a lot might help. I decided to play it straight with him and make it clear that we were not police.

"*Señor*, are you the manager here?" I asked.

"Yes." He looked me square in the eye.

I waited.

"Santiago," he said, throwing me a bone.

Gee, thanks. "*Señor* Santiago, I'm Lola Vega, and this is my associate, Molly O'Reilly." I leaned forward and handed my business card across the desk to him, hoping to disable the frontal lobe of his brain with my cleavage. His eyes dived as expected, but only for an instant. "I'm a private investigator working on a case, not police. I'd like to ask you a few questions. Nothing about your operation here. It's about a…customer."

He looked my card over and set it on the desk, leaned back and folded his arms. "Who?"

"Linda Gross. I understand she ran up a sizeable debt."

He raised his eyebrows and nodded his head. "You could say that."

"Right. That part we know." I leaned forward in the chair. His gaze dipped ever so slightly longer this time. "What I'm wondering is, did she ever pay it?"

Santiago fixed his eyes on his desk. "Certainly, this is a private matter. It would be best for you to ask *Señora* Gross herself."

"I would love to do that, only she's dead."

He looked up, eyes wide. "Dead?" His poker face returned in an instant and he shifted in his seat. "I'm sorry to hear it. She was a pleasant woman. But it's nothing to do with us."

"No?"

In a split second, he calculated the odds and decided to talk. "Linda paid what she owed."

"All of it?"

"All of it."

"Do you know where she got the money?"

He brought a hand to his chin. "That is not my business. She didn't say, and I didn't ask." He hooked a finger over his top lip, looked off to one side and swiveled his chair a little. He was holding something back.

"But she gave you something else, didn't she?"

He set his eyes on me and folded his hands together on the desk. "Why would she?"

"Collateral, maybe? Or just because you have a safe? I don't know. But she gave you something, and you still have it." This was one of my "throw it out and see if it sticks" plays. They work in my favor about sixty percent of the time. But this time was different. I *knew* it was dead on, just as surely as I knew there was a safe in that room, although I saw no sign of it.

"You sure you're not cops?" He looked us both over again, this time probably sizing up whether our clothes would accommodate guns or maybe wires.

"We're not cops," I said.

Molly shook her head profusely. "We are not the police."

"There is something," he said. "But I'll have to pat you down before I open the safe." He stood up, but Molly and I didn't move. "I have to. Otherwise, I can't help you."

Molly jumped out of her seat. "How about if I just wait outside? Keep your boy out there company?" She bolted for the door.

"Take the bags with you!" Santiago called. Molly grabbed our handbags on her way out.

I wanted a peek inside the safe. "Fair enough," I said and stood.

Santiago's big brown eyes never moved from mine as he came toward me. Up close, he smelled of cigars, coconut, and leather. A tattoo on his neck registered as he touched me first on both arms and flashed a cheeky grin. I didn't think he'd be too thorough, me being a woman, but I was wrong. His hands explored my curves, lingering in places no gun could fit. Well, what had I expected, a gentleman? It was a racetrack. Had I been a smoker, I would have had a cigarette afterward. I really didn't mind. Sadly, this was the closest I'd come to a romantic liaison in some time.

Santiago took his hands off me reluctantly, flashed a grin, and motioned me to sit again. Then he walked over to a couple of battered grey filing cabinets and pushed them aside to expose a pocket door in the wall. The door slid open to reveal a safe. Santiago turned his back to me to hide the combination, and looked back over his shoulder after each number to make sure I hadn't seen it. Then he pulled the handle down, clunked the heavy door open and took a quick look back at me again, half smiling.

I stayed rooted to my chair, but the instant he turned his attention back to the safe, I strained to look past him to the contents. I caught a glimpse of several fat bundles of cash in the easily recognizable colors of both US and Mexican currencies. There was a third currency as well, but I couldn't make out what kind. He shuffled things around, then pushed the door shut and the handle up, and spun the lock dial. He hunched over a small bundle as he stood, then shifted it under an arm and brought it to the desk.

"This was Linda's," he said. "Maybe it will help you. You are right…she left it as collateral. But after she paid the debt, she didn't want it back. She said it was worthless to her now." With one arm, Santiago swept aside a small stack of magazines topped with a paperback novel, *Crime and Punishment*, and set the bundle down. It was about the size of a six-pack, wrapped in a crimson scarf with a black ribbon tied tightly around it. "It's probably only a matter of time before the police come sniffing around asking questions about Linda, anyway," he said.

"Possibly," I said. "I wouldn't really know."

"I'd rather you have it than them. Anyone but them."

"What is it?" I asked.

"I don't know; she made me promise her I wouldn't look."

That wasn't racketeer talk. I wondered if he was for real. I couldn't have resisted a peek, promise or no promise. I was practically salivating with anticipation, and I'd only known about it for ten minutes. But a second later, the wait was over.

Santiago pulled off the black ribbon, and the red cloth fell away.

CHAPTER 21

"Oh!" I said, on seeing it.

"Not what you expected?" he asked.

"No, not really."

It wasn't a tea jar, and it had no blue dragon on it. It was a wooden box, a simple mahogany rectangle, lacquered shiny. Santiago rotated it so we could both see and opened the hinged lid. The first few notes of the song "Over the Rainbow" drifted up and stopped short. We stood staring at the box for a second. It was empty except for the music mechanism.

"Some collateral, Linda," Santiago said. He sounded a little hurt. It was clear he had kept his promise and not looked. He had trusted Linda. And Linda had trusted him not to look. All of these facts surprised me.

There was a drawer at the bottom of the box. I leaned forward and pulled it open. The drawer was empty. I stood and looked it over. Apparently, what we had here was a simple music box, harboring no contents and no secrets. I sighed. "It's disappointing. I would like to take it with me, though. Maybe I can get it to her next of kin."

"Sure." He wrapped the box in the scarf, tied it up again, and pushed it toward me. "Here, take a bag." He pulled a shopping bag out of a desk drawer and opened it for me.

"Thanks." I put the bundle in.

"You got a car here?" he asked. He walked over to the safe, slid the pocket door shut, and moved the filing cabinets back in front of it.

Why did he want to know if we had a car? I thought about lying, but couldn't figure out any reason he'd want to kill us, hide our bodies in the trunk of the car, and dump it in a junkyard on such short acquaintance. So I told him the truth. "We took a bus here," I said.

"Good." He walked over to me. "Let me buy you and your friend a drink."

"Oh, no thank you. We should be getting back."

"Please, I insist. For the sake of international relations." He flashed me a sly smile, reached for one of my earrings and diddled my wedges with one finger. "We don't do things wham-bam-thank-you-ma'am down here. We like to take our time."

It sounds bad, but I found him irresistible. This probably stemmed from our little pat-down encounter earlier, which was also likely why he felt so free to finger my fruit. "Okay," I said, "one drink."

Molly rejoined us, and Santiago brought his security grunt along. We skirted the stands, aiming for the clubhouse. A race had just ended. Everywhere I looked, people were screaming, jumping up and down, hugging, or weeping. I could see the appeal. People love to feel things. The clubhouse was huge and had a stage at one end where a band was playing salsa music. A few people were dancing. It was about three o'clock in the afternoon.

Santiago ordered margaritas for all of us.

"Oh, no thank you, really. We'll just have Cokes or something," I said.

"Speak for yourself, girl!" Molly said. "I could use a drink."

I couldn't blame her. She had spent the last twenty minutes standing outside with a giant ex-con covered in prison tattoos glowering at her.

"There, you see?" Santiago said. "And you don't have to drive; you came on the bus. There is nothing to worry about."

I looked at Molly sideways.

"One drink," she said, shrugging her shoulders.

Three hours later, we were still drinking. And dancing. Molly was good. She knew all the Latin dances, and every guy in the place wanted to dance with her. And did. The music had grown loud, and the place was now packed with people. I shook booty with Santiago. He had a very hands-on style. At first, I kept peeling him off me, but a couple of hours and margaritas later, I didn't mind at all. I felt a hard lump in his jacket and wondered if it was legal. It was definitely a gun, and no doubt the reason he never took his jacket off, despite the heat.

We took a break from dancing and stood at one end of the bar sipping drinks. Santiago moved my hair aside and kissed my neck. I felt like melting butter just before it sizzles. He slid his hands smoothly over my curves like an Aston Martin cruising the Baja coast. Between his jacket hanging open and the way we were standing, no one could see, but it still felt way too public for me. I voiced a weak protest. He bit my neck and my whole body lit up. It was pure bliss. I could have let myself get lost in the moment, but my former relationships had started exactly this way, and it obviously wasn't working for me. I pulled away from Santiago.

"Um, I'm going to the ladies' room," I said. "Back in a sec." I started toward Molly to take her along. I didn't think we should be separated even for a few minutes, so I had been dragging her in there with me all evening and following her when she tried to go without me. She considered me as welcome as head lice at this point.

The crowd was packed in like the San Ysidro border at rush hour. I was standing five feet from Molly when I saw him about ten feet away from her over her left shoulder: the man in the black trench coat. Our eyes locked. Then everything happened fast. I leaped at Molly, grabbed her and made for the doors.

Trench Coat charged after me, mowing down the forest of dancers between him and me like a paper company exec rampaging through virgin trees. Santiago saw what was happening and went after Trench Coat. A bunch of his security grunts, all of them beefy, shaven-headed men with prison ink came out of nowhere and followed Santiago's lead. Molly and I were running blind; we could see nothing through the throng. We were slipping through the crowd of dancers by going with the flow of the dancing. We weren't as fast as Trench Coat, but we were more efficient because nobody slowed us down by stumbling or falling over in front of us. We reached the edge of the crowd, spotted a door, and went through it.

Molly and I found ourselves at the bottom of the stands, which were calm at the moment because the current race was mid-run. People stared like dogs at a dinner table, leaning forward, ready to spring. Their jaws were either set or mouthing prayers. The only thing we could do was lose ourselves in the crowd while making our way to another exit. We wound through the crowd, staying in the thick of it. Another exit came into sight, and we swerved for it. Just then, most of the crowd jumped up from their seats, waving their hands and shouting. Popcorn flew through the air like snowfall. The milling crowd bunched up to watch, clearing our path. Exposed, we ran for it.

But within fifteen feet of the exit, we stopped short. Santiago popped up in front of us, a grave look on his face. He took each of us by one arm and pulled us away from the exit. "This way," he said and led us through a heavy door beneath the stands.

The instant the door closed, the world outside muffled almost to silence. The air was cool. We went down some stairs and found ourselves in a large, curving concrete tunnel. It was lit every hundred feet or so and smelled faintly of urine.

"This tunnel runs under the whole place. We can cut across under the stands and come out on other side."

We kept moving, Molly's purple clogs and my chunky sandals echoing loudly in the tunnel. Santiago's sneakers barely made a sound.

At one point, we slowed down to catch our breath, but not for long. From behind us came the sound of the door opening and thudding shut once more. It echoed thunderously, and my stomach lurched. Molly looked about to say something, but I put a finger to my mouth and she stopped. I pulled my shoes off, she did the same, and we all took off running.

Footsteps echoed behind us, making no attempt to be quiet. It sounded like one person. I was impressed. How Trench Coat could've tracked us there, I couldn't imagine. We'd had a good lead on him. I wondered if he had managed to plant a tracking device on me somehow. The footsteps came louder and faster. They were gaining on us. All Trench Coat had to do was get within firing range.

We got to the other side of the tunnel. The footsteps were close, but still around a bend. Then the tunnel straightened out and we saw the stairs ahead of us. We'd just reached the bottom of the stairs when the footsteps stopped short. We froze. On the stairs we'd be easy targets, so that way was suicide. We were done. We turned in unison to face our captor.

It was one of Santiago's security men. He was bent over, hands on knees, catching his breath. Santiago laughed loudly and flashed an all-clear sign. I almost fainted.

"Who's the 007-wannabe?" Santiago asked me.

"I wish I knew!"

"But you're sure he's after you, right? I'm just trying to figure out if he's after you or came to bust up my place."

"He's been tailing me for a while now. He definitely has it in for me." But even as I said it, I wondered…assuming Trench Coat was the guy who'd grabbed me in the parking lot, why hadn't he hurt me when he'd had the chance, and what would he do if he did catch me? What did he want with me? Santiago snaked an arm around my waist.

"You sure he's not your boyfriend?"

I snorted. "No!"

"It's okay; you can tell me. I've had a few angry husbands and boyfriends after me."

"He's not my boyfriend!"

"Well then, I guess we can relax, eh, *mamacita?*" He pressed himself against me.

"Relaxing always leads to trouble," I said, hesitantly. I knew it was just flirting on his part, but this was not the right time. Even so, I wanted to have him right there on the stairs. I managed to tear myself away and climb the steps. Molly flashed me a raised eyebrow.

Santiago rushed ahead of us to get the door. We emerged into hot dry air again and walked out to the street. We looked around. There was no sign of Trench Coat.

"Can you point us to the right bus to get back to the border?" I asked Santiago.

"I'll drive you to the border," he said. "I insist. With that guy after you, I want to be sure you'll be safe."

I didn't protest. Trench Coat was lurking out there in the shadows somewhere, and anyway, I wasn't ready to say goodbye to Santiago. He was good looking, kind of macho, but not over the top, and he could dance. And he had great hands. And I liked him.

We picked up the shopping bag from the office and piled into Santiago's SUV, a black Cadillac Escalade with deeply tinted windows. It looked bulletproof. Santiago drove and two of his security grunts manned the back seat, probably in case of a shootout. Nobody seemed to be following us as we headed for the border.

After a few minutes, I relaxed. I pulled the music box out of the bag and unwrapped it to have a closer look. I turned the box all around and flipped it upside down. And there it was, the secret compartment I'd been looking for. A false bottom. It slid out lengthwise. Inside, a small, flat bundle of tissue paper was taped to the real bottom.

Santiago was excited. He kept looking at the box in my lap. "Come on…the suspense is killing me!" he said.

We swerved, and a car horn Dopplered past us.

"Watch the road," I said. I nicked the tissue off the box with a thumbnail and unfolded it. I could feel something in there, but not much. It was flat and lightweight. I held it up by the edges between my thumb and forefinger. It was a silver charm for a bracelet or necklace, a round disk engraved with a simple design and the message, "Good Luck! G.A."

I wondered who Linda knew with the initials G.A.

CHAPTER 22

Santiago drove us to the border, but not across it. We said goodbye; he said he would call me. Molly and I walked across the border and back to my car, and I figured that was the last I'd see of Santiago.

I stashed the bag with the music box in my trunk, and we headed back to up LA to find Linda's real place, the one where she paid rent and kept her things, the one with the creepy roommate. Traffic was bad, but once we got through San Diego, we got lucky again and found it mostly going the other direction.

A few freeways later, we found Linda's treeless neighborhood amid grafitti'd shops with bars on the windows. Cruising through rows of boxy houses with bare dirt yards, an urgency overtook me. I could think of nothing other than the fact that my twenty-four hours were slipping by. What was I thinking, staying in Tijuana so long?

"What is it about the bad boys that can make a perfectly sensible woman lose her mind with only hours left before she might be tossed into jail?" I asked Molly.

She said, "What I want to know is, what is it that can make a perfectly sensible woman drive around this hood so close to dark?"

We found Linda's house. It was a tiny pea-green bungalow with barred windows and a gravel front yard. It was one house off the corner of a main street, squeezed between a liquor store and another bungalow, identical but for the color, which was blue. I parked across the street, and we walked over to the house. Molly covered her ears, her face contorted in a grimace. I was about to ask her why, but by then we were at the door, so I let it go.

I rang the bell. No answer. After half a minute I rang again.

The door jerked open immediately, and a man in a brown terry bathrobe stood behind the barred outer door. The infamous William. His hair stood up in greasy clumps and spikes. He let loose a barrage of obscenities, the gist of which was, what did we want? He made sure we saw the butt of a shotgun he held at his side, the rest of it out of sight behind his bathrobe.

"We're looking for Linda," I said. I figured he might not have heard she was dead.

"She's dead," he said.

So much for Plan A, where we wait for her in her room, supposedly knowing she's on her way home. "Oh, no," I said. "You're kidding!"

"Would I kid?" William asked, and I felt sure he meant, not about her being dead, but at all, ever.

"No, likely not," I said. Molly was frozen, still holding her hands over her ears. On to Plan B: blurting out the first thing that came to mind. "Well, my friend here left her medication in Linda's room last time we were here. Could we just run and get it?"

"What do I look like, an idiot?" he said.

I felt sure he didn't want me to answer that. He slammed the door on us.

We sat in my car across the street, thinking up a Plan C.

"Maybe it's not the tea jar," Molly said. "Maybe it has to do with something else, like…a Chinese restaurant."

"Could be," I said. I pulled out my cell and called *Mami*. "Are you busy or could you do me a big favor?" She wasn't busy. "Would you look in Google maps for me and see if you can find a listing for any place called The Blue Dragon and call me right back? Thanks, *Mami*. Love you."

We waited. I noticed that at the house next to Linda's, a lot of people came, stayed for a short time, and then left. Several of them noticed us sitting in the car and shot us the evil eye.

"We've got to get out of here," Molly said, "or somebody's going to shoot us."

A minute later, *Mami* called back and said there was no Blue Dragon in the entire LA area. She had called information, which was a lot quicker than her dinosaur computer. I could have done that myself, but she liked to help, and it gave me time to think.

"Well, looks like it's probably the tea jar," I said to Molly, after I got off the phone. "At least, that's all we have to go on. How about this? I have the phone number, and we know his name is William. What if I call him up and lure him out of the house somehow, and you sneak inside and have a look around."

"Or how about *I* call the guy and *you* sneak inside and look around," Molly said, flashing me her "Are you crazy?" look that had become so familiar. "Anyway, does he look to you like the kind of guy who's going to leave his door unlocked?"

But luck was with us again. I gripped Molly's arm. "Look!"

William stalked out the front door, still in his bathrobe, but without the shotgun, and crunched across the gravel to the liquor store on the corner.

"You coming?" I asked.

"No way," Molly said, removing my claw from her arm.

"Okay, then keep an eye out. The second you see him coming back, call my cell."

Molly already had the number in her cell phone, which she pulled out to have ready. I ran across the street and up to the door. I figured if anyone was watching me they wouldn't have time to do anything about it, and they didn't look like the types to call the cops anyway. And besides, I had no Plan D.

I tried the doorknob. It turned; I was in. The house was dark inside and smelled like garbage. All the blinds were shut and the TV was on. William had left his shotgun behind, standing upright against the arm of a tattered couch. Plates of old food, trash, and plastic garbage bags full of who-knew-what were everywhere. There didn't seem to be anyone else inside.

"This guy should move to Sunspot City," I said aloud, picking my way through garbage bags. I looked into the kitchen at one side, noting the back door, then went on to the bedrooms. The first one looked just like the living room in its decor. Definitely William's.

There were only two bedrooms, so the next one had to be Linda's. The door was closed. I opened it and flipped up the wall switch for light. This room was neat and a stuffed badger sat on the bed, just like the badgers at the condo.

A dresser and bookshelf filled one corner of the room. I walked over and visually scanned the top of the dresser. Nothing. My cell rang.

"He's coming back!" Molly cried, so loudly I had to pull the phone away from my ear. "Get out of there!"

"Right," I said, ending the call. But I'd made it in there; I wasn't going to cut and run with nothing. I tracked my eyes along the bookshelves. Nothing on them looked even remotely like a blue dragon. Nor did anything have a blue dragon or the words "blue dragon" on it, so I gave up and made for the back door.

I switched the light off and pulled the door shut as I left. I hit the kitchen running and made it to the back door when I heard William open the front door. I hadn't locked the front door as I usually did when breaking and entering because I figured since he left on foot in his bathrobe and left the front door unlocked, he probably didn't have a key with him. I didn't want to leave the guy stranded outside. His footsteps thudded into the house.

The back door was locked. I turned the bolt and eased the back door open just as he shut the front door. The timing was perfect, but a grime-encrusted mini-blind on the back door window rattled.

"Hey!" he shouted. "Who's there?"

It was his dream come true, someone breaking into his house. Now he could shoot somebody legally. I heard the rustle of a heavy paper bag being thumped down hard on a table, then heavy footsteps coming my way. He was so close I could hear his robe swishing.

I whipped through the door, let it slam behind me, and I ran like crazy. The closed door would slow him down a little. The gravel backyard not only made a racket like a lawn mower chewing concrete, it was a tough surface to run over in my high wedges. I saw him come out the door just as I rounded the corner of the little house. A stunted date palm gasped for life around the corner, and my right shoulder smacked into it hard. Pain shot through me.

I darted around the palm and flew to the car, expecting to hear a gunshot at any second. Molly had hopped into the driver's seat and had the car running. I jumped in the car and we took off, wheels squealing. I could feel the eyes from the drug dealer house next door as its inhabitants crouched at the bottoms of windows to watch the shootout they thought was coming.

William chased after the car like a dog, but no gunshots came. He must have neglected to grab his shotgun when he came after me. Eventually, he stopped running and shook his fist after us like a cranky old man. I turned from the rear window, collapsed back in the seat and pulled my seat belt on.

"That was fun," I said, rubbing my aching shoulder.

Molly glanced at my empty hands. "Where's the jar?"

"It wasn't there," I said. "I looked all over. There was nothing remotely like a tea jar."

"Maybe William took it."

"Yeah, he looks like a tea man."

"Oh-oh, I feel somebody coming," Molly said and jerked the car over to the curb.

"Are you okay?" I asked.

Her eyes went glassy. "You must be Linda," Molly said with a big smile. After a few uh-huhs, she said, "Linda says she has something, and she wants you to have it now, Lola. She says it's at her condo, inside the blue dragon."

"What is it?" I practically screamed, but controlled myself.

"What's what?" Molly blinked and turned to me blankly. "Wha'd I say?"

I sighed and brought Molly up to speed on what she'd said in her brief trance. "Maybe you were experiencing static interference because that condo isn't Linda's."

"There wasn't any static interference," Molly said. "What other condo could she possibly mean? Seems clear to me."

I thought about the badger on the bed, Linda's territorial mark. "Yeah, maybe the condo at The Tides was Linda's after all, or she might've thought *I* thought of it as hers because we had our meeting there. Anyway, the important thing is, they both have badgers."

"Honey," Molly said, "I think you may have a little static problem yourself, because I have no idea what you're talking about."

"Molly, I think it's time we return to the scene of the crime."

CHAPTER 23

We cruised by The Tides just after nine P.M. I stayed out of the parking lot in case the police were watching the place. I'd gotten pretty good at spotting a stakeout when there was one around, but there wasn't much chance of it anyway. It was unlikely they could spare the warm bodies. LAPD didn't have that great a budget to begin with, and they'd had a number of lawsuits to pay out on in the last few years due to corruption problems.

Molly and I ditched my car two blocks away and walked over to the condo. I didn't spot any likely stakeout cars on the way. Police cars had a way of looking like police cars even when they were unmarked. They were always in decent shape and often had cigarette smoke trickling from a window or two. We stood at the bottom of a dark stairwell and looked up at number three-eleven. Nobody was posted outside the door, but a light was on inside.

"Somebody's in there," Molly said.

"Not necessarily," I said. "Places for sale usually have a light on a timer to help keep away bad guys, like us."

"Now, don't talk like that! I should go up there alone; they're not looking for me."

"No, *I* should go up there alone," I said. "There's no point in both of us getting into trouble. Besides, you don't know anything about breaking and entering." Then I realized maybe she did, for all I knew. "Do you?"

"No! But I'm going." She sprinted up the stairs before I could get out another word to protest. I followed right behind her.

I'd expected to find crime scene tape across the door, but there was none. The lockbox hung on the doorknob as before. There was no sign a murder had happened there. The blinds were tightly closed, so we couldn't see inside. I tried the door. It was locked.

"Now what do we do?" Molly whispered. "Oh-oh! Someone's coming!" She grabbed my arm.

A man jogged up the stairs below, whistling, his keys jingling loudly. We both froze, listening. The sounds grew louder, then receded. The man went on up the stairs to the floor above. We both exhaled, and Molly let go of me. She had dug her nails into my arm so hard it looked like the backside of a cheese grater.

"Ow!" I loud-whispered.

"Sorry," she mouthed.

I turned back to the lockbox. The last time I'd been here it had been closed incorrectly. What were the chances of that happening again, especially after a crime had taken place here? But it fell open in my hand just like before, and the key was inside. I took it out.

"I don't like this," I said, hesitating. This whole thing felt wrong to me, like maybe I was playing somebody else's game. But what choice did I have? All the fingers were already pointing at me.

I slid the key in the lock.

"What if there's somebody in there?" Molly said, grabbing my arm again.

"Ow!" I cried. I couldn't help it; she had grabbed the same spot again.

She sprang away from me. "Sorry!" So much for whispering.

"Well, if there is someone in there," I said, "they're probably calling the police right now because we're making so much noise they have to know we're here!"

I turned the key, opened the door and looked around. We went inside, and I shut the door softly behind us. A floor lamp was lit. I followed the cord with my eyes to the outlet where it was plugged in. There was a timer box on it. I pointed it out to Molly. We walked over to the bookshelf, the one Linda had taken Jack's headshot from that first day we'd met, in fact, the only time we'd met.

"And there it is," I said.

The tea jar sat dead center on a shelf, dark blue porcelain with a gold Chinese dragon painted on it. I took the jar from the shelf and opened it. There was loose tea inside.

"This has to be it." I tipped the jar, thrust my fingers in and felt around, showering the white carpet with a gush of tea leaves. Something was in there, smooth, flexible plastic. I pulled it out carefully, shaking off the tea.

It was a rolled-up plastic baggie. I stashed the baggie in my jacket pocket, set the jar back down, and put the top on.

"What is it?" Molly asked.

"I don't know, but we'd better get out of here and look at it later," I said, turning away from the bookshelf. "We have to hurry things up because I only had twenty-four hours, and my time is already half up."

"No, your time is *up.*"

Molly and I both jumped. We turned in the direction of the voice. A few feet away at the mouth of the hallway stood the man in the black trench coat, and he was holding a gun aimed straight at my chest.

CHAPTER 24

"Put your hands where I can see them," he ordered.

Molly and I both put our hands in the air. I felt annoyed with this guy; all I wanted to do was leave. This interruption was the last thing I needed at the moment. I felt myself sneering involuntarily, which usually meant I was about to say something I probably shouldn't.

"What's with the black trench coat?" I asked. "Isn't that a little clichéd?"

In spite of his five o'clock shadow, which was more of a ten o'clock shadow, I could see his face flush deeply. He was a pale blond guy, the type who go crimson at the slightest frustration. I had him off balance.

I went on, to buy time. "What are you, some kind of henchman, or just a common burglar? There's not much here, unless you know a stuffed badger collector. Look, we don't want to compete with you, Mr. Trench Coat. We'll just go." I dropped my arms and started for the door. I figured if nothing else it would draw his attention—and gun—away from Molly.

"Don't you move!" he yelled at me. He sounded as annoyed with me as I was with him.

I froze. All except my mouth. "Do you want the neighbors to hear? They'll call the cops." I was hoping he was from out of town and wouldn't know how silly a notion that was.

"Shut up," he said, but quietly.

And then I recognized the voice. No question...he was the guy who had grabbed me in the parking lot after I'd met with Linda. So he was definitely somebody's boy. I wondered who he worked for.

He may have been holding the gun, but I had him playing my game. "Somebody's called the cops by now, for sure. We should get out of here," I said, in a monotone.

Molly, who'd stood petrified throughout this exchange, seemed to catch on at that point. Our eyes met for a second and hers made a subtle shift.

"Let's go," he said, motioning toward the door with his gun. Molly and I walked ahead of him. He jammed the gun into his pocket, but kept it leveled at us. I'd thought I might go for his gun when he stopped to lock the door, but I never got the chance. He pulled the door shut behind us and left it unlocked. He never took his hand off the gun or his eyes off us.

As we jogged down the stairs together, Molly whispered to me, "Oprah says never to let the bad guy take you to a second location because he's probably taking you there to kill you."

"Oprah is a very wise woman," I said. "So we don't get in the car, right? When we get downstairs, hang back as much as you can. I'll need some room. If things go bad, we split up."

"Right," she said.

At the bottom of the stairs Trench Coat said, "Where's your car?"

"A couple blocks from here. We thought there might be cops around," I said. "The cops are after us. Because we're dangerous."

He laughed. He seemed to think that was very funny, which annoyed me even more. I had the impression he didn't think we could be dangerous at all, even though he had just caught us in more than one criminal activity.

"This way," he said and gestured around the back of the building. In back was another parking lot, about half full of cars. "I tried to tell you to stay out of this. You should've just taken the warning." He sounded irritated and a little tired. Maybe we were in the way of an early evening and a good night's sleep. Molly dawdled along like a six-year-old.

He steered us past all the other cars to a lonely sedan off in a corner away from the lights. I couldn't see the license plate. He switched the gun to his left hand and plunged his right into his trouser pocket for the keys. His eyes shifted to the car door for an instant. That was my chance.

I kicked my foot sideways toward the hand holding the gun,

giving it everything I had. It connected. The gun went flying out of his hand and scudded across the asphalt. Trench Coat let out a short cry. He grabbed his limp, empty hand and gawked at it for a beat in total disbelief.

Then we got lucky. A bunch of teenagers came around the corner into the parking lot, laughing and jostling each other. Molly ran toward them screaming for help. They stopped walking and watched us. Trench Coat hopped in his car and took off fast. I had to jump out of the way or he'd have run me over. Molly jogged back over to me, and the teens continued on their way like nothing had happened. The car flew out of the parking lot, lights off, silent as the swoop of a nighthawk, and was gone.

"Hybrid car," I said.

"Girl, where did you learn moves like that?" Molly asked.

"*Crouching Tiger, Hidden Dragon* is one of my favorite films," I said. "I've seen it a million times. Did you see it?"

"I saw it, but I didn't get as much out of it as you did," she said. "Let's get out of here."

"Wait! The gun." I ran over to look for the gun. It had slid into the shadows at the edge of the parking lot. "Here it is!" I picked it up. I could barely see it, but I could feel it. I put the safety on and stuck the gun in my other jacket pocket, the one without the baggie.

We walked back to my car, got in, and drove away from there to my mama's house, which seemed a million miles away.

At *Mami's* house, Molly and I went straight up to my room to look at the items we had acquired that evening through our illegal activities. I held the baggie up to the light, and we looked at the contents without opening it. It was a gold necklace. Stars of various sizes, all but three of them with a diamond at the center, hung from a delicate chain. The chain was broken. The backs of the three plain stars were each engraved with a word. Together they spelled out the sentence, For Ever 1979.

"What does it mean?" Molly asked.

"I don't know yet," I said. "But I'm guessing Jessica Stone was wearing this necklace when she was killed, and whoever killed her probably left fingerprints on it."

Molly gasped.

"Look at the break in the chain," I said. "It's uneven, not clean. My guess is the killer yanked it off her neck."

Molly put her hand softly around her neck and made a face.

Next, I pulled out the gun. We'd left in such a hurry that I didn't get a good look at it before, and it was too dark to see anyway. The serial number had been filed off.

"Oh, wow! This is a Varjag," I said.

"What's that?" Molly asked.

"It's the next generation Baghira."

"And what does that mean?"

"Both are newer, better replacements for the Makarov."

"Okay, never mind," she said, rolling her eyes.

"Sorry. It's a very accurate handgun, Molly. A Russian handgun."

CHAPTER 25

The next morning I wanted to ask Jennifer, extreme personal assistant, a few questions. After that, I would go and have the dreaded talk with LAPD. People like Jennifer get up early. Not only do they get up early, they're wide awake and functional, too. So I had no hesitation in calling her cell phone at 7:30 A.M., as soon as I managed to get my yawning under control and had sucked down some coffee. She agreed to meet me at the Bean at Third Street Promenade in half an hour. Molly was still sleeping when I left.

Jennifer got there first. I'm lucky if I don't find my clothes are on backwards at eight o'clock in the morning. She was the picture of order in a nobbly grey sweater with her hair pulled back in a bun. There were no message pins on her sweater, but she wore a green rubber bracelet that read: Choose Reality—The Climate Reality Project. She was sipping a pomegranate blueberry tea latte and playing with her iPhone when my coffee walked up with me in tow. She quickly stowed the iPhone in her cloth handbag and greeted me politely.

"Thanks so much for meeting me, Jennifer. I won't take much of your time. So, Morningstar, huh?" Her voicemail, which I'd gotten when I tried her the night before, said her first and last names.

She laughed, a high, nasal snicker. "Yeah, my parents are hippies. They live up in Bolinas, where I grew up."

"Mm. That's also the name of the big mutual funds rating group. And it was Lucifer's name before the infamous fall."

"How interesting," she said flatly.

"But enough chit-chat. We're busy women. I'm wondering if there's anything more you can tell me; maybe something you wouldn't feel free to mention around Leilani? I offer my discretion, of course."

"There's nothing I wouldn't say around Leilani."

"Not even that you were having an affair with her husband?"

"Not even that." She smiled, a little smugly and flicked the top of her straw back and forth.

"So, she knew? It didn't bother her?"

"No." She looked me straight in the eye. "Leilani couldn't keep up with him. Nobody could. He had very strong appetites. And anything or anyone Jack wanted, he got. Nobody got worked up about it. It was part of his charm." She smiled again, wistfully this time.

"And now you're involved with Leilani. I hope you'll understand when I say it looks a little…opportunistic."

Her smug smile returned. "You may be somewhat conventional in your orientation to personal relationships. I'm not. It's natural to become close with people one interacts with on a daily basis. I see no reason to fight it. When I was Jack's assistant, I saw him every day, and after he died, I became Leilani's assistant. Now I see her every day. Our lives are intertwined."

"So, man or woman, you have no preference?"

She snickered again. "I see people as more than their body parts."

"And nobody was jealous of anybody?"

"Not that I know of." She raised her eyebrows like the idea was preposterous.

"Okay, then. What do you think happened to Jack's will? As his assistant, you must've handled it?"

"No, I never did. He showed it to me once, though, right after he finished writing it."

"Where was that?"

"On the boat one day. That's where he wrote it. He would go out there to get away from it all. Jack used to say he was a better person out on the water."

"Why did he show it to you?"

"A couple of reasons. For one, he wanted me to witness it. He said it wasn't required, but it couldn't hurt. He didn't want anything to go wrong."

"That's sensible."

"Also because he added a few big fat donations to some animal rights and environmental organizations. They were to be ongoing, out of a foundation he wanted to set up. It was my influence that led him to do it, and he felt really good about it, so he was sort of thanking me. I was ecstatic, of course."

"Wow! Good for you; you really made a difference." I hoped the red flags that popped up behind my eyes with the word "motive" on them weren't too obvious.

"Yes. Jack and Leilani both became vegetarians because of me, too." She put one finger on a square napkin and pushed it around the tabletop in little patterns.

"Any idea where that will might be?"

She sighed. "I thought it must still be stashed away in the boat somewhere, but I've looked all over. I can't find it. It's a shame, but maybe when the money's freed up, Leilani will decide to honor Jack's wishes."

"Did Leilani ever see the will to know what's in it?"

"I don't think so. I don't know. As far as I know, he never took it off the boat, and Leilani never went down there."

"So she only has your word that it had those donations in it?"

Jennifer threw me a sneer. "True. But it's the truth, and she believes me. I don't lie. Everybody knows that about me."

"What about Linda? Was she in the new will?"

Another sneer. "Unfortunately, yes."

"I take it you didn't think much of her?"

"Linda was an idiot. Same goes for Irena with her fur coats and her enslaved bear. Same goes for anybody into dog racing. Do you know anything about dog racing?"

"No, not really."

"It's banned in most states because it's so disgusting how the dogs are treated. All day long they're kept muzzled in tiny cages too small for them, then forced to race in the scorching heat, and if they get injured or don't win, they're killed, or sold to research labs where they're further mistreated and then killed. The greed-driven slime who run these racetracks are too cheap to even kill them humanely. In Tijuana, where Irena goes, they abuse and kill unwanted dogs for so-called 'entertainment'! I won't even go into that; you'd get sick. Anyway, only about thirty percent of the dogs born into that industry ever make it to the track; they just kill the rest, tens of thousands every year. Only about five percent get adopted."

"I had no idea." I felt slightly nauseous and thoroughly disgusted.

"I told Linda all of that, but all she cared about was gambling. I'm not surprised she's dead, owing money to sleazebag abusers; she should get a Darwin Award. No, I didn't like her, I didn't have a high opinion of her, and I'm not sorry she's dead. But I didn't kill her, either, if that's your next question. I wouldn't kill a person any more than I'd kill an animal." Jennifer's face was flushed red, twisted with anger. She took a deep breath and exhaled. "I'm sorry; I get so bent about this stuff." She sucked down the last of her drink.

"I think it's great to be passionate about things," I said, "especially living ones. I'm glad you're trying to change the world. It needs a lot of work."

She shrugged. "Thank you. I probably should get going. Was there anything else?"

"No more questions, but there's something you might want to know. Jack's boat blew up a couple days ago."

"The *Alouette*! Oh, no." Her eyes grew wet. "Jack loved that boat. What happened?"

"I don't know, but I'll let you know when I hear something. Do you happen to know when Jack was last on the boat?"

"I know exactly when. It was the weekend before the weekend he died. He went down there for most of them, but he didn't go the weekend he died because *Rosebud* went missing. He could have gotten out to the *Alouette* some other way, but he just stayed up here. He was really down about it. I guess it doesn't have to make sense. Obviously, he was more depressed than any of us knew, and that was just one more thing wrong in his world. Poor Jack."

Poor Jack. I couldn't seem to feel that way. All I could think was, How could the man go from taking risks, from getting whatever and whoever he wants, to poor Jack?

We both got up to leave.

I shook her hand. "Thanks for your time, Jennifer. I hope the donations work out."

"Me, too. Um, by the way"—she lowered her sunglasses—"your top is on backwards."

CHAPTER 26

Jennifer went off to Malibu, and I headed for LAPD, armed with what I thought were some good strong leads and the baggie with the necklace in it from Linda's place. I called Michael and told him I was on my way. He sounded relieved. When I got there, Molly was standing in the waiting area with Detectives Whittaker and Parish.

"Molly, what are you doing here?" I asked.

She opened her mouth to speak, but Michael came around the corner with a coffee in his hand, which he gave to her.

"Well, the elusive Ms. Vega," he said. "I asked Mrs. O'Reilly to come down and answer a few questions, and she was kind enough to allow us to bring her down here without delay."

Molly, standing a little way behind Michael, wiggled her eyebrows at me twice, pointed to Michael with her thumb, then fanned herself with both hands. She looked so funny I busted up laughing. Michael seemed to think I was laughing at him and shot me an annoyed look. I averted my eyes from Molly, but still saw her in my mind.

A female detective walked up and stood unnaturally close to Michael. She was blonde, pretty, and in all obvious ways appeared perfect. I stopped laughing.

Michael turned to her. "Okay, Johnsen, we'll take Vega; Whittaker and Parish will talk with Mrs. O'Reilly."

Johnsen looked me over as though I were an insect, then turned on her heel, saying, "Let's go, Vega. I hear you're a *lawyer,* but I'm

113

still going to read you your rights."

I sneered behind her back and followed. Michael snickered. I wondered what else he had told her about me.

Detectives Whittaker and Parish took Molly into a room, and I managed to flash her a smile just before the door shut. Michael, Johnsen, and I went to a room a little farther down the hall. Michael and Johnsen sat across from me at a table. Michael turned on the recorder and stated the date and names of those present for the record.

I pulled the baggie with the necklace out of my purse and tossed it on the table. "I think Linda was using that to blackmail Jack Stone," I said.

Michael took a pen from his pocket and used it to pull the baggie closer to give it a once-over. He then pushed it toward Johnsen, who plucked a glove from her pocket. "Johnsen, take this to the lab, please. Tell them I want to hear the minute they have anything."

Johnsen nodded and left.

The instant she shut the door behind her, Michael shut off the recorder. Leaning in close, he said, "It appears you'll stop at nothing to be alone with me."

"Or to get rid of Officer Malibu Barbie. Listen, Michael—"

"That's my new partner, Detective Sally Johnsen. She just made detective. How do you like her?" He grinned.

"She's a real Miss Congeniality. What's she doing here? Shouldn't she be off marrying some ninety-year-old millionaire? Look…never mind her—"

"She does anything I tell her. She has to; I outrank her." His grin widened.

"Congratulations. Now you won't need that dog you've been thinking about getting." A bolt of pain in my temples made me hiss and cradle my head in my hands.

"You okay?"

"I'm fine, just a little headache," I said. "They pass quickly."

"You mean another one, besides Johnsen?"

"Hey!" I whipped my head up. "Aren't you going to offer me any coffee? You gave Molly coffee."

"Molly was nice to me," he said. "I'm just messing with you. You want some coffee?"

"No, I just wanted you to offer." I was glad Michael was making light of things while Johnsen was out of the room. I knew he was doing it to put me at ease, not because he didn't take my situation seriously. My papa used to do the same kind of thing with me.

"Sorry I can't offer you a margarita," he said.

"Michael, there's more." I hesitated because some people frown on a person making the same mistake twice, and I felt sure Michael was probably one of them. Eventually, I pulled Trench Coat's gun from my pocket and put it on the table between us.

Taking up the pen again, Michael used it to slide the gun toward himself. He sighed, his face grave. "What happened this time?" He grabbed a tissue, picked up the gun with it, and stuck it in the pocket of his tan trench coat that hung on the back of his chair.

I told him the whole story about going back to Linda's and running into Trench Coat, minimizing the breaking and entering aspects of the tale. He said nothing, just listened with an expression of utter disbelief on his face. At the end, I told him I hoped we could keep this to ourselves for a little while. He said he would try, but couldn't promise anything. He kept the gun in his pocket and didn't mention it again.

When Johnsen came back, Michael turned the recorder on and we went on the record again. It was a long, long day. They mixed things up a little, though. Occasionally, they did the good cop-bad cop routine in which Johnsen, in an instance of perfect casting, played the bad cop. At one point, the two teams switched, and I talked to Parish and Whittaker, while Molly talked to Johnsen and Michael. The whole time I didn't know if I'd be allowed to leave, or if they were going to arrest me. They had enough to hold me, but they might prefer to let me go and see what I would do.

They finally did cut us loose around ten P.M. I drove Molly back to *Mami's* with me. Neither of us said a word the whole way. When we got there, Molly went straight to bed, while I stayed up to give *Mami* the scoop.

"They think you killed that woman?" she asked me.

"They do, yeah," I said.

Mami held a hand on her mouth as I laid out their story for her.

"Their theory is: Linda killed Jessica Stone, and back when I was investigating Jessica's murder, I found out Linda killed her and had been blackmailing Linda ever since."

"That's ridiculous! You're not a blackmailer!" *Mami* said. "And even if you were, why would you kill her when she was paying you?"

"They figure she got tired of paying and threatened to go to the police, so I killed her."

"But they can't have evidence for any of it because it isn't true!"

"No, but they know she was paying somebody a lot of cash. I'm the last person they know of who saw her alive, and my fingerprints were all over the place." I left out the part about me having picked up the murder weapon and leaving my fingerprints on it. "They think I called the police just to throw suspicion off myself."

She asked no more questions after that, maybe so she wouldn't cry. She was being brave for me, which meant she was very worried. *Mami* tucked me into bed that night like when I was a child. She was afraid she was losing me. I slept a hard, exhausted sleep, like a coma.

CHAPTER 27

It was around noon when I finally got up the next day, feeling just as drained as before. *Mami* made me a big plate of *huevos rancheros*, which I picked at. Molly was still asleep.

"Don't worry; everything will be all right," *Mami* said. "I can feel it." Her instincts were usually right.

"Well, I told them everything I know, which is all I could do. I found out a lot in those twenty-four hours, though. It was a good day," I said.

Molly came into the kitchen. "I'll drink to that," she said, took a seat, and yawned.

Mami poured her some coffee.

"How did you tell them we got the tip on the baggie in the tea jar?" I asked Molly.

"I told them exactly what happened, what else?" she said.

"I told them Santiago told us about it. I said she'd left it with him as collateral, but he gave it back to her when she paid her debt."

"Why'd you tell them that? It's not true."

"It seemed…sort of true. They wouldn't have believed the truth." I pushed my *huevos* around with my fork.

"Oh, I see," Molly said. "You lied to cover up the truth so they wouldn't think you were lying. That makes sense."

"You lied to the police?" *Mami* said, upset again. "You're not supposed to lie to the police! What really happened?"

"What really happened," I said, "was that Linda's ghost appeared to Molly and told her to tell me to look for the tea jar, where we found the necklace. Oh, and did I mention we broke and entered another place where Linda used to live before we broke into the condo?"

"You can't tell them that!" *Mami* said.

"Exactly," I said. "It doesn't matter. They don't believe either story. All the trouble we went to getting the necklace, and the police probably just think I had it all along. And if Linda's prints turn up on it, it'll play right into their theory that she killed Jessica and I was blackmailing her with it."

"But that won't happen. You don't think Linda killed Jessica, do you?" Molly asked.

"No, but whether she did or not, she may have touched the necklace putting it in the baggie and left her prints on it then. Assuming it was Linda who put it in there, that is."

"We did go to some trouble, didn't we?" Molly said.

"Yes, *we* certainly did. And by the way, Molly, did you tell them about William, too?"

"Of course I did. I'm not going to lie to the police!"

I buried my face in my hands and shook my head, something I seemed to do an awful lot lately. "And the gun? Did you tell them about Trench Coat's gun?"

"They didn't ask me about any of that."

"Thank God there's *something* you didn't tell them!" I turned my attention back to the pursuit of caffeine.

"Hey, how 'bout that Detective Johnsen?" Molly said.

"What about her?" I asked, taking my fork into my fist and stabbing it into what was left of my *huevos.*

"What about her? Girl, she's a hottie. How long has she been partners with your friend?"

"She's new," I said. "Never saw her before yesterday." I pulverized the eggs repeatedly with my fork, imagining they were Detective Johnsen's breast implants. "But I don't think she's so hot. Her attitude is pretty ugly, for one thing."

"For the only thing," Molly said. "Anyway, she's on your case now. In more ways than one, I think." She stared at my plunging fork.

I returned to eating. "It doesn't matter. Michael's a player." I went on with my mouth full of eggs. "He just flirts with me out of habit. It's completely impersonal; it's like a language he speaks." I washed the eggs down with milk.

"You'll be single forever with that attitude," *Mami* said.

"He just likes to mess with you," Molly said.

"In his dreams," I said. "We're just friends, and that is all. In fact, barely that. Michael's a big fat pain!" I stabbed the last bite of *huevos,* shoved it into my mouth, and demolished it like a wood chipper. "I couldn't care less about his *America's Next Top Model* partner. All I care about is that they solve this case so I can get out of the hot seat."

The phone rang. *Mami* went to answer it. She came back and held the phone out to me.

"It's the pain," she said.

"*Mami!*" I could have died. "Hello? Who is it?" I asked, just in case he'd heard that.

"It's Michael," he said. "How's the world's most luscious spy this morning?"

"If you mean me, I've been better," I said.

"Well, listen...this may brighten your day. That necklace is actually a pretty big deal. The stars perfectly match the marks and lesions on Jessica Stone's neck."

I jumped out of my seat. "I knew it! Jessica was wearing that necklace when she was killed! And whoever killed her must've left their prints on it."

"Bingo. They're running it for prints right now."

"Did you seriously just say 'bingo'?" I was suddenly feeling much better.

"Very funny. Lola, listen, I'm coming over there right away. I've got something here you need to see."

CHAPTER 28

"Parish! Whittaker! Over here," Michael yelled. He stood outside one of the Murmansk Circus's red-and-white striped tents with Detective Johnsen. Parish and Whittaker got out of their car and walked over to join them.

"I look pretty good on camera, don't I?" Michael said.

"You should've been a movie star," I said. We were sitting in my mama's living room watching video footage from the camera mounted on Michael's car, taken that morning. He had come over so fast I was still wearing my fluffy black bedroom slippers.

The four police detectives were standing in the same area where Molly and I had parked when we were there. But everything was different. There were no barking dogs. Two glittering men came out to greet the detectives, but they carried no guns. They had even shaved. The detectives followed the circus men inside the tent.

I felt a sinking feeling in my gut. It looked like I had made it all up. "But...it was all different," I said.

Michael fast-forwarded the video. The four detectives emerged from the tent, followed by Boris and four men in glitter.

"Wait! Stop it a sec," I said. The picture froze, and I pointed at one man. "That guy looks like Trench Coat." I wavered. "Only, he's shaved."

Michael looked at the man's face for a while. "Is that him or not?"

"Yeah, that's him. I'm sure."

He pushed play again, and we watched the detectives get in their car and drive off.

Michael hit stop, walked over and took the disc out of the machine. "There were no guns inside, either," he said. "Just the usual circus stuff. But to really look around thoroughly, we'd need a warrant. Whittaker's on that right now, but I don't think we've got enough to get a judge to sign off on it. Boris, the ringmaster, says Irena Kuchikovna, formerly Stone, went back to Russia. Says she suddenly got homesick and took off."

"Oh, God! What is going on?" I plunged my forehead into my hands and grabbed handfuls of hair.

"Wait, there's more—this is the good part. After we left, Johnsen and I went to grab a bite." Michael tossed the disc onto the coffee table.

"Wow, that is good." I looked up. "I'll call the tabloids."

"Hey, at least she'll go to lunch with me. When we got back to our car, there was a paperback novel on the seat. And when we got back to the station we found out the same thing had happened to Whittaker and Parish, only they got a different book."

"Why, Detective, you should've locked your car."

"Yeah, I'll remember that. Whittaker and Parish got *Crime and Punishment*. Here's what we got." He pulled a thin paperback out of his jacket pocket and tossed it to me. I caught it and turned it right side up. It was *Notes from Underground*.

"Both Dostoyevsky," I said.

"Bingo." He pointed at me. "The name Dostoyevsky ring any bells?"

"Standard college reading," I said. "Come to think of it, *déjà vu!* I just saw a paperback of *Crime and Punishment* somewhere."

"Where?" He sat down next to me. "At the circus?"

"No, I don't think so. I can't think where it was, but it'll come to me. The novel Linda was reading when she was killed was a Dostoyevsky, remember? It was *The Gambler*. Read it in eleventh grade."

He popped up again like toast. "Lola, this is big. Dostoyevsky happens to be the code name of a top Russian mafia boss out of New York. No one knows who it is, but he's in charge of their push into LA."

"Linda probably wasn't even reading that book, huh?" I said.

Michael paced a lap across the living room and back. "They're into arms dealing, gambling, money laundering, drugs, human trafficking, you name it. With the Russian guns and now the Dostoyevsky novels, I think there's a connection."

"A circus would be a good cover for any of those activities," I said.

"That circus could be nothing but a cover for them, or maybe it's an ordinary circus and they're muscling in on it. Either way, the *Bratva* will crush anyone who gets in their way. Those books were a warning, probably the only one we'll get. The *Bratva* don't play with their food, they just eat it."

"Oh, I wonder if something has happened to Irena! That's a pretty sudden case of homesickness. They might've done something to her because she talked to me."

"We're looking for her," Michael said. "She wasn't on any flights to Russia today or yesterday, but there's still more checking to do. You sure you didn't get any of the plate on that hybrid car?"

"No. Maybe Molly did." I slumped deep into the sofa. "But I don't think so. She would've mentioned it."

"Maybe she can ask her ghosts what it was."

"Ha-ha," I said. "What about the gun that killed Linda?"

"You mean the *first* gun with your prints on it?"

"Yeah, that one. What kind of gun was it?"

"Nine millimeter, Russian made."

I perked up and put my feet up on the coffee table, fluffy slippers be damned. "So that's it. It's the Russian freaking mafia setting me up! They put the gun right in front of the door. In a narrow, dimly lit space. They knew I'd pick it up when I went in the bathroom. It's small—the kind of weapon a woman would use. Of course, it's not registered. They want it to look like it was my gun."

"Right, it's not registered. It could've been Linda's own gun, already there."

"Whatever. It's Russian. And the numbered bank account! That's something the Russian mafia would have, isn't it?"

"Them and lot of other people. We need proof."

"It all makes sense, though. If Linda owed the Russian mafia money, she'd have to do whatever they said. They planned to kill her, so they got her to set up the cover for her own murder! Unknowingly, of course. I was wondering why Linda put *me* on this case, why she led me to that condo in the first place. Who does the condo belong to, anyway?" I asked.

"It belongs to somebody out of state. Chinese name…Ang Lee or something."

"The film director?"

"No, that's not the right name, but it's something like that. I'll have to look."

"The necklace was in the condo," I said. "So, I guess Mr. Trench Coat is taking orders from the Russian mafia, too. The only thing that doesn't fit is, why did he try to warn me off at first? Anyway, it's clear from the bank accounts that Linda was blackmailing Jack. Maybe the necklace was the evidence she was blackmailing him with."

"Are you saying Jack Stone killed his sister?" Michael asked.

"No, that's not what I meant. I don't know what she had on him. A guy with Jack's life, it could've been anything. Maybe he was protecting somebody. No, I don't think he'd have killed his own sister. Not...the way it happened."

"What do you mean? I was working East Division at the time of the Jessica Stone case."

"Pretty grim stuff," I said. "It had all the indicators of a sexually motivated crime. She was garroted from behind in her bedroom. One of her own nylons was used; it was found next to her on the bed. No semen was found at the scene, but she was wearing some very sexy lingerie. The police chalked it up to a one-night-stand gone bad. I'm not saying it's impossible, but ew—it sure didn't look like a brother-sister spat."

"I see what you mean. Not the sentimental Jack Stone's style, anyway."

Michael's cell phone rang and he took the call. It was short, but not sweet.

"Just when you think nothing can surprise you anymore," he said, as he ended the call.

"Who was that?"

"The print lab. There are two sets of prints on the necklace, and neither of them are Linda's." He was still staring at the phone.

That was good news for me; it shredded their theory about me using it to blackmail Linda. I breathed a sigh of relief. "Whose are they?"

He tossed the phone on the couch, as if to get it as far away from himself as possible. "Well, for one," he said, "Jack Stone's."

CHAPTER 29

"I can't believe it," I said. "Though as far as Linda blackmailing Jack, it would be a *really* good reason for him to pay up." I tried to sort out whether I didn't believe it, or just didn't want to believe it. I flashed on my dream, the one where Jack had two faces. "Who were you, Jack Stone?" I mused aloud.

"Ang Gen!" Michael said.

"Huh?"

"The guy who owns the condo. His name is Ang Gen."

"Oh, right. But what about the other prints?"

"The only person who's been ruled out is Linda. The other prints are presumed to be Jessica Stone's. We're still waiting for DMV records, but they're most likely hers."

"No!"

"Whose do you think they are?"

"No, I mean I simply *do not* believe Jack Stone would've killed his own sister. Nope, there's more to that story, and I'm going to find out what it is. But first I think I'll check out Mr. Gen."

"It's Mr. Ang."

"Huh?"

"Chinese names have the family name first, so it's Mr. Ang," Michael said. "Unless... Some people do switch them around to Americanize them."

"So, how can I tell whether it's been Americanized or not?"

"I don't know. Good question," he said.

Then a thought hit me like lightning. If the name Ang Gen were switched around, it would be Gen Ang, with the initials GA. I uttered a small, guttural *oof,* like I'd been hit in the stomach with a basketball.

"What?" Michael asked.

"Oh, excuse me," I said, and held a fist in front of my mouth like I'd burped. I didn't want to share my lightning bolt with Michael, not until I knew whether it meant anything. I hadn't said a word to him about the silver charm or the music box. I had told him what I considered to be a harmless white lie in which I substituted the necklace for the music box and left out almost everything about Santiago, especially the parts with dancing and margaritas.

He looked at me funny. I wondered if he could see a little cartoon light bulb shining over my head. Thankfully, Molly walked into the room.

"What'd I miss?" she asked.

"I have to go," Michael said.

"I'll fill you in, Molly," I said, and practically shoved Michael out the front door so I could tell Molly everything.

*   *   *

I hadn't recognized the name, but when Ang Gen opened one side of the tall double-doors, I knew his face right away. He was a well-known character actor in the late eighties and early nineties, mostly in comedies, many of them buddy films. As it turned out, he hadn't moved out of the state for good, but had been working in an off-off-Broadway show in New York for eight months. The show had closed, and he'd been back for a month. Ang's hair had thinned, but he still had the same cherubic smile the public fell in love with.

He had Molly and me meet him at Beth Hillel Temple in North Hollywood. It was that purple velvet time of early evening. The faint scent of jasmine drifted on a lazy breeze. The temple was empty apart from the three of us. We sat in a meeting room full of folding chairs, and Ang gave us coffee in Styrofoam cups from a huge metal coffeemaker. I knew from our earlier phone conversation that the realty company had already told him Linda was dead.

"Mr. Ang, were you and Linda close friends?" I asked him.

"I don't know that I'd say close, but we go way back."

So, Ang was his family name. The name fit the initials on the charm. I raised my eyebrows. "Did you know Linda was using your condo for...activities other than selling it?"

"Uh-huh, I knew. She had my permission." Arms crossed, he then rubbed a spot under his lower lip with his fingers. "Look, I'm sorry. I don't know how much you know about Linda, and I don't want to invade her privacy."

"It's understandable you'd be sensitive to that. Linda was murdered, though, and I'm trying to find out who killed her. And to do that, I need information."

"Right. Sure," he said, but nothing more.

"I want to show you something," I said, then fished around in my purse for Linda's tissue-wrapped charm for a while. I did this for two reasons. One, to see if it would make him sweat. If so, then he might chatter nervously and give something away. And two, I couldn't find it. I unloaded my sunglasses, hand lotion, wallet, checkbook, and aspirin bottle onto the chair next to me so I could really get in there.

Ang wasn't sweating. He looked at his watch. "I only have about ten more minutes."

"What happens in ten minutes?" I asked, not even looking up. Molly sat quietly, looking around the room. She nudged me, but I ignored her.

"I'll be too busy to talk to you. I have a bunch of people coming," Ang said.

I found it. "Aha!" I dropped my purse on the floor, unwrapped the silver charm from Linda's music box, and held it out to him on the tissue paper. "Did you give this to Linda? It has your initials on it."

He plucked the charm from my open palm with two fingers, looked at it, and smiled wistfully. "Yeah, I gave it to her. A long time ago."

"Why did you give it to her?"

"To mark an anniversary. One year."

"I thought you said you weren't close?"

He looked confused for a second and then laughed out loud.

Molly laughed, too. She nudged me again and pointed at a flyer on a bulletin board by the door. It was a notice for Gamblers Anonymous meetings at Beth Hillel every Tuesday and Thursday evening. This was a Tuesday evening.

"G-A!" I said.

"Yep, you got it," Ang said. "Linda and I met at a GA meeting. We were both new then. That was back when she was married to Jack Stone."

"She'd been gambling again recently," I said. "She got into dog racing and ran up a pretty big debt."

"Yeah, I know about that," he said. "She called me a few times. I tried to get her to come to a meeting, but she said things had gone too far for that. Said she owed big money."

"Right. She sold her house because of it and was living in a nasty place with a nut job named William."

"Yeah, she told me that, too. Things were bad for a while, but then later she said her ex, Jack, was helping her. Said she'd quit gambling again. It seemed like everything was going to be all right."

"So, why did you let Linda use your place?"

"I met her for lunch one day over at Barney's Beanery. She told me Jack was dead and that they were saying he killed himself, only she didn't believe it. I agreed with her. I gave her some money to hire someone to look into it. And I let her use the place, no questions asked, just to help her get back some self respect."

"*You* gave her the money?"

"Yeah. I gave her access to an offshore account I have in Singapore to fund it. I can spare it; I haven't gambled in thirteen years. She used it once and then shredded the PIN."

"That's awfully...brave...of you, isn't it?" I was thinking, stupid. "Giving a gambling addict that kind of access?"

"I know what you're thinking," he said. "I must be an idiot. Look, she'd already paid off the big debt and quit. She was picking up the pieces, but her self-esteem took a huge hit. And she was really low over Jack's death. I thought she needed me to show some faith in her."

"I don't think you're an idiot," I said. *I think Linda was.*

He shrugged. "I figured if it turned out she was in Jack's will, she'd be able to pay me back. And if not, at least I'd have done what I could to help."

"How do you know she really quit gambling?"

"I don't. I took her word for it. She said she would hire someone, and I believed her."

"Mr. Ang, I'm that someone. Linda hired *me* to look into Jack's death. I'm only telling you because you paid me and she's now dead. But for a while now, it's looked to me like she was setting me up to take the fall for her blackmailing activities."

"Blackmailing activities?"

I nodded. "Jack."

Ang covered his eyes and shook his head. "Oh, Linda!" He looked at me sadly. "This addiction will drive people to do things they'd never do otherwise. I know that better than anyone. I'm surprised she'd turn to blackmail. She definitely wouldn't let someone else take the blame for her actions, though…no way. She had problems, but she wasn't that type of person."

"Maybe on someone else's orders she would."

"Nope. No way. Not Linda. I knew her as an addict, remember; I knew her worst behavior, her deepest fears. I'm sure. If somebody else got into trouble because of something she did, she'd have gone to the police at that point."

"Sounds to me like you knew her well," I said. "How on Earth do you define close?"

"Okay, I guess we were close in some ways, but we didn't hang out together. We sometimes went years without seeing each other. And we were never romantically involved."

"So, the condo and the bank account are yours. Those are the things that made me suspect her. You're not Russian mafia, are you?"

He laughed. "Nope."

And then it hit me. I knew the answer before asking the question, which I practically whispered. "Does the number four-five-three-five mean anything to you?"

He turned his head slowly and met my eyes with an expression that was part Kabuki samurai, part Howler monkey.

"It's the PIN to the numbered account, isn't it?"

The silent scream dissolved, and his face grew placid and a little sad. He sighed. "Maybe I didn't know Linda as well as I thought."

I leaned over in my chair and put my hand on his. "Look, I don't want to get your hopes up, but I don't think Linda emptied out your bank account. I found that number scribbled on a pad at the condo the day I found Linda's body."

"*You* found?"

"Yes, I found her." I winced at the memory. "I'm actually a suspect. But I didn't kill her! You'll just have to take my word for that, until I can find out who did."

He nodded. I think he believed me. "Okay, so you're saying the killer left the PIN behind. But they'd probably remember the number anyway, it's only four digits."

"But they'd need the account number, too, right? And a phone number? I didn't see those anywhere. I don't know, but if you hurry, maybe there's still time to change your PIN."

Three people came in the door, talking and laughing, and Ang waved and smiled.

He nodded. "I'll make a call right after the meeting. I can't thank you enough." Most people would have shot straight out the door, but apparently, his priorities were firm.

More people arrived, calling out boisterous greetings.

"I guess gamblers must be a pretty fun bunch, huh?" Molly said, standing to go.

"Yeah," he said, "we're the fun ones, all right. The twelve step programs each have a little different feel. Narc-Anon gets most of the music people, of course. GA and AA both get a lot of the Hollywood brass and talent, but the best deals are still made at AA. You want connections, AA is your program."

"Good to know," I said, sweeping my purse contents off the chair and back into my purse.

"You sure you're not a gambler?" Ang asked me.

"No. To be a gambler, you need something to gamble. Why?"

"That's a pretty big bottle of aspirin," he said, nodding toward my purse.

"I get a lot of headaches," I said. "Most of them are walking around. May I just mention, by the way, that you did some of my favorite movies."

"Oh, thank you. Which ones?"

"*Jokers Wild*, for example. Hilarious!"

"I wasn't in that."

"Oh. How about *Dark Ducks Two*?"

"I was in that."

"Good. That was my very favorite. Oh, one more thing. Did you and Jack Stone ever work on a film together?"

"Only the one that made him! *Stayin' Alive*," Ang said. "I was the beer-swilling taxi driver. I had two lines! Great movie. To this day, that's my favorite film."

As I walked with Molly to my car, I thought about how she was always calling me paranoid. I wondered if she was right, since I now knew Linda had not been framing me for blackmail. Apparently, the only people out to get me were the Russian mafia and the police.

CHAPTER 30

Ang had mentioned Barney's, which sounded good, so Molly and I went there for a pizza. We were finishing off a large vegetarian when I remembered where I saw the Dostoyevsky paperback. Molly had just asked me about a couple of ex-boyfriends I was still friendly with, neither of whom were dead, unlike most of the ex-boyfriends and ex-husbands she knew.

"Jimmy was my first love," I told her. "He was an actor and musician who made enough money working as an extra and street busking to pay half the rent. I was in my second year of college at the time and had a part time job cocktailing at a drag queen bar that used to be over on Hollywood Boulevard. It's long gone now. Believe it or not, the place was called Lola's. Every single night somebody would say to me, 'I can't believe you're a man!' And they meant it!"

"That sounds awful," Molly said.

"Nah, not at all. Drag queens are great tippers and a lot of fun. Those were good days! Jimmy and I were in love; we were happy. Eventually, he got a good speaking part in a pirate film and then he did a sequel, too."

"Wow! So, what went wrong?" Molly asked.

"I guess you could say we grew apart. After two solid years of being a pirate, Jimmy kind of lost himself. He took to wearing swashbuckling gear and talking like a pirate twenty-four-seven. At first it was fun. Then the studio made it a trilogy, but they didn't want him for the third one because his character had been killed off in the second one."

"That never stops anybody I know," Molly said.

"Or Hollywood, either, usually. But suddenly it was all over, and Jimmy had a major identity crisis. He was a pirate without a ship."

"I know what you mean," Molly said. "I once knew a biker without a bike. He had one, a nice one, but it got stolen. It was uninsured and he couldn't afford to replace it. A year later, he was a mess. He finally got caught stealing a Harley and went to jail. The last time I heard from him, he said he was very popular in prison, so I guess there's a bright side."

I let that one go and took a bite of my pizza. It was one of the few times I haven't talked with my mouth full.

"Anyway, so you left him?" she asked.

"Nope. He ran off with some wench he met working at a Renaissance Faire. She was a bastard child pretender to the throne-wannabe. I later heard they'd secretly been juggling together for months. They were made for each other—anyone could see that—but it still stung."

"Wow!" she said. "What about the second friendly ex?"

My cell phone rang. I held up one finger to Molly, swallowed my pizza, and picked up the phone to see who it was. I saw a string of numbers I didn't recognize, so I let it go to voicemail, then listened to the message right away.

"Hi, Lola. Santiago. Just seeing if you're still alive. Have you told anyone about Linda's box? Call me back and we can talk. About books, maybe. Just call me." He left his number. His voice sounded tense, restrained.

Santiago didn't strike me as a guy who spent his spare time reading; why would we talk about books? That's when I remembered. "Molly, that's it! I remember where I saw the Dostoyevsky novel. It was on Santiago's desk on a pile of papers."

"That's right! I noticed it, too," she said.

"Maybe Santiago is Dostoyevsky! Could he be Cuban? I don't think so. But he did mention books. He's hinting at something."

I put my phone on speaker and played the message for Molly. "That's the most words I've ever heard him say all at once." I hit End. "Do you think it's supposed to be some kind of threat?"

"Maybe. I guess it could be, but no, it doesn't really sound like that to me," Molly said. She stopped short of calling me paranoid, but I knew she was thinking it.

"Maybe he just doesn't want it to sound too obvious," I said. "It kind of sounds like he doesn't want me to tell anyone about the box. And the book thing sounds like a hint." He had also mentioned my life, as in whether I still had one, and I had seen him just a couple days ago. But having run through a tunnel with him in the belief we were being chased by a thug with a gun, a belief which wasn't a stretch for either of us, the "Are you still alive?" part didn't sound all that strange. I simply couldn't be sure whether the message was sincere or a veiled threat. I played it again.

"Why don't you just call him back and see what he says?" Molly said.

I thought about it. The only other option was not to call him back. I wanted to know what was going on, so I took a hefty gulp of wine in preparation for calling him. But I didn't have to because the next second, he called again.

"Santiago, hi," I said.

"I just left you a message, but I'm in a hurry," he said. "I'm in LA. Meet me somewhere."

"Where?"

"Anywhere. Where are you now?"

"I'm at Barney's Beanery on Santa Monica."

"I'll pick you up. We can talk in my car. Meet me out front in ten minutes." He hung up before I could object. I wasn't sure if I should go along with this, but Santiago had only helped me before. I felt I could trust him.

"Molly, you stay here. If I'm not back in half an hour, call the police."

She said, "No way! I'm coming with you as insurance."

"Molly, please. What good would it do for you to come? You've seen gangster movies. If there's trouble, they just bump off both people. The best protection you can give me is to get help if I don't come back." I checked out the window now and then for Santiago. "Just sit tight and relax. Order another drink. Everything will be fine."

She called the waitress over. "Another pizza, please. Make it a medium this time."

I couldn't believe it. "Molly! How can you order a medium pizza now? We just ate an entire large pizza."

"You know I eat when I'm stressed! But you do have a point."

She turned back to the waitress. "You'd better make that a large."

Santiago pulled up in front of Barney's in the same black SUV, with two security men in the back seat. One of the two jumped out and looked around, ready to open the car door for me.

"Thirty minutes," I said to Molly, and she checked the time. I went out to meet Santiago. He was driving; I got in the front seat.

"*Rica,*" Santiago said, as I got in the car. I ignored this.

"So, what are you doing in LA?" I asked him.

"I wanted to see you. I don't want to talk on the phone."

"*Nyet,*" I said. "You didn't come up here just to see me." I wanted to find out if he spoke Russian, but the only Russian words I knew were *da* and *nyet.*

"No," he said, a bewildered look on his face.

He had answered in English. From this and his blank expression, I figured he probably didn't speak Russian. I waited, as the lizard waits for the fly to come within range.

"I have a business partner up here," he said.

Oh, is that what you call the Russian mafia? And are you Dostoyevsky? I didn't ask those questions out loud, though. I remained silent. I was playing his game, but maybe I could beat him at it.

Santiago looked over at me. "There's something I didn't tell you before."

"You're kidding," I said. Even drinking, he'd been locked up tighter than an SUV at a carjackers convention. "What?"

"You're not the only one looking for that box."

Again, I said nothing, only looked at him. He met my gaze for a second, then looked out at the road and went on.

"A couple days before you showed up, a guy came to see me, and he brought some muscle with him. He wanted to know if Linda left something with me. I told him I didn't have anything of Linda's. I guess he didn't believe me because that night his muscle jumped my boys and searched the office. They found the safe, but they couldn't get it open." He laughed.

"So, why did you give me the music box after not letting him have it?"

"He didn't ask me nicely. Didn't look as pretty asking, either." He flashed me a smile. "Besides, they'll come back for it again, and I don't want it to be there when they do."

"What did this guy look like?" I asked.

"Big guy, had the biggest moustache I've ever seen. Thick accent. And he was kind of...overdressed."

"Boris!"

"You know him?"

"I'm getting to know him," I said.

"Oh—and they left me a little present."

He reached over in front of me, pulled a paperback novel from the glove box, and tossed it on the dash. It was the *Crime and Punishment* I'd seen on his desk.

"I found this on my desk," he said. "Does it mean anything to you?"

"I'm afraid so," I said, and told him about the Russian mafia and its phantom leader, Dostoyevsky.

"You think Boris is this Dostoyevsky?"

"Maybe. I don't know." I didn't mention that up until five minutes ago, I'd thought he might be Dostoyevsky. Boris had just moved up a notch on my list, but he could be someone else's pawn.

We drove around talking for a while. The whole time, Santiago insisted someone was following us. He looked in the rearview mirror more than where he was going. At one point, we got stuck near an accident. A motorcycle came up close on our right side, jamming up the road between the car lanes. The two guys in the back seat drew their guns. I could feel them itching for a shootout. But the biker kept both hands on his handlebars the whole time and rode on by. False alarm.

We finally got back to Barney's about forty-five minutes later. Santiago kept the engine running. His boys jumped out of the back seat like secret service agents on red alert.

"You're keeping that box someplace safe, right?" he asked.

"Yeah," I said. Not true. It was still in the trunk of my car.

"Good."

He leaned across to unlatch the door handle and one of his boys pulled it open for me. "Be careful, beautiful," Santiago said. As I was stepping out of the car, he helped himself to a generous handful of my bum, leaving me slightly stunned on the sidewalk as they sped off.

I turned to go into Barney's and found Michael standing ten feet away. Molly stood next to him, her hand over her eyes. The look on

Michael's face was somewhere between astonished and amused.

"Looks like everything here is *in hand,*" he said.

"Michael, hi," I said. "This is a surprise."

"When you didn't come back in half an hour, I called Michael instead of nine-one-one."

"Oh. Um, come have some pizza with us," I said.

Molly uncovered her eyes. "I ate it all. But we could get another one."

"No thanks," Michael said. "I have to get back." He walked Molly and me to my car in silence.

I could tell he wanted to say something, but was holding back. When we got to the car, he finally dug up some words. He opened the door for Molly, but he was looking at me.

"So, I guess you like more of a Lex Luthor than a Superman, huh?"

Molly ducked into the car.

"Of course not!" I said, thinking, of course Michael would compare himself to Superman.

"No, it's cool. I'm just surprised, that's all. I didn't know you went for the tats and steroids type."

"Don't be silly!" I said. "He's no Lex Luthor. Those beefy guys are just his henchmen."

Michael let my words drop into a deep and echoing silence. Then he walked around the front of the car to my side.

I jerked my car door open. "Well, thanks for turning up to save me, Superman," I said.

Michael came unnervingly close to me; the only thing between us was the car door, and he leaned into that. For a second, I thought he was going to kiss me.

"Baby, only the Lex Luthors have henchmen," he said, just in case I didn't get it.

Without another word, I got in the car, and Michael shut the door.

On the way home, despite very much wanting to, I decided against killing Molly. She had done the right thing in calling Michael rather than drawing more police attention to me. I quickly forgot all about it as we drove back to my place. I had a lot to think about. Mainly, if Santiago wasn't Dostoyevsky, then who was?

CHAPTER 31

The next morning I awoke to the telephone ringing, ringing, ringing. I tramped out to the kitchen to kill it. Right behind me, Molly stumbled in, wild-eyed, a rolled up magazine in her hand.

"Where is it?" she muttered.

I pulled the plug on the phone and held up the cord. "It's okay; I got it." I slouched into a chair and so did Molly. "I was having the coolest dream."

That seemed to perk Molly up. "Oh, tell me! You know how I love to hear dreams." She twisted around and turned on the burner under the kettle behind her.

"Okay," I said. "I was flying through the air on a car door, kind of body-surfing. And there was some guy with me. It was really fun! And then I mowed down some woman, only when we stopped to check her out, there was only a doll lying in the street. Its blonde hair was all squished up in the mud. Weird, huh?"

"Mmm. A shame the phone rang," she said.

Eventually, the kettle whistled, and we made coffee.

When I had some coffee in me and was finally awake, I plugged the phone in again. I picked up the phone to check the voicemail, but it rang in my hand, so I answered it. A nasal female voice assailed me.

"Ms. Vega, is it true you were the last person to see Linda Stone alive?"

I was stunned. "What? Who is this?"

"Kit Cooper, channel five *Star Sparks*. It's true, then?"

136

"No comment." I hit End, put the phone back in its cradle and sneered at it.

"Who was that?" Molly asked.

"It was a reporter from a television tabloid." The phone rang again. This time, it was *Mami.*

"I've been calling and calling you," she said. "Have you seen the celebrity news this morning?"

"I don't usually start my day with the celeb news, *Mami.* Let me look." I walked over to the coffee table and picked up the TV remote. Molly followed me into the living room and sat on the sofa. I sat on the arm. I turned on the TV, muted it, and flipped to channel five, Kit Cooper's channel. There were commercials on.

"Put on channel five," *Mami* said. "I saw a teaser for something; they'll probably show it after the commercials. Linda Gross's murder is all over the news, only they're calling her Linda Stone."

A picture of Linda with her name under it came up on the screen. "It's coming on," I said and turned up the volume. I listened to the TV with the phone to my ear.

Kit Cooper then appeared on the screen along with her name. I'd seen her in my living room many times before, all of them on TV. She said, "All we know at this point is that Linda Stone was found dead of a gunshot wound two days ago. No arrest has been made as yet. The former wife of Hollywood legend Jack Stone, they remained close friends over the years after an amicable divorce."

"Ha!" Molly said. "If you call blackmail friendly."

"Yeah, some friend," I said.

Linda's death was bound to get attention, coming so soon after Jack's suicide. That story still had legs, and now Linda was dead, too. But someone had told Kit Cooper that I was the last person to see Linda alive, maybe even that I was a suspect. I wondered who told her.

What I saw next made my heart stutter. The camera pulled back to a wider view. Kit Cooper was standing in a parking lot in front of condos I recognized instantly. "Oh my God," I cried. "They're right outside!"

Kit Cooper said, "I'm live in Burbank at the home of Lola Vega, the last known person to see Linda Stone alive. Police would not comment on whether Ms. Vega is a suspect at this time. I asked Ms. Vega for a comment by phone just moments ago, but she declined."

She arched one eyebrow as she said this, as though my lack of comment meant I must be Linda's murderer. Channel five cut to commercials.

A loud knock came at the door. I went to the window and peeked through one end of the closed blinds. The camera crew from the parking lot was outside. *Mami's* voice drifted up from far away; I'd forgotten I was on the phone.

"Oh God, they're here! They're outside my door. *Mami,* I'll call you back," I said, shrinking against the wall. I was still in my underwear.

"Lolita, I have to tell you something…"

"Mami, I have to go. Let me just call you back in a few minutes," I said and hit End. I super-tightened the blinds, and Molly checked that the door was bolted. "How did they get my name?" I felt dazed, like I was having dental surgery. "We haven't even had breakfast yet."

"The media all copy each other," Molly said. "It won't be long before it's everywhere."

I suddenly saw the bright side. "Molly, this is perfect! I wanted to go out of town for a couple days, but I didn't think LAPD would let me. You know, being a murder suspect and all."

The phone rang again. It was another reporter to whom I gave no comment. I unplugged the phone again, wondering if they could get my cell number, too. So far, the cell hadn't rung.

A thought struck me. "Molly, if those reporters see you, it won't take them long to identify you and figure out your connection to Jack Stone."

"It might be best if I go with you," she said. That was fine with me.

There was no chance of me eating breakfast now, but Molly was hungrier than ever. While she was eating, I took my cell into the bedroom and called Michael.

"Did you guys have to tell the whole world about me?" I asked him. "Reporters are camped outside my door now. With cameras. My phone hasn't stopped ringing."

"Lola, I'm sorry," he said. "I have no idea who talked to Kit Cooper. It was supposed to be kept quiet, of course. Do you know anyone who might've told her?"

I quickly made a mental list of who knew about me being the last person to see Linda alive. On the list were Molly, *Mami,* Michael, Detectives Johnsen, Parish, and Whittaker, their higher-ups at LAPD, and me. The only one on the list who seemed to have it in for me was Johnsen, Michael's partner. "Bet it was your new partner," I said.

"I don't know, but I'll get to the bottom of this. Just sit tight for a while."

"Sit tight? I've got a murder to solve, same as you. Only now I've got an audience, too. I need to get out of town, Michael, at least for a couple days. There's something I want to look into, anyway."

"Let me guess," he said, "Muscatawney, Pennsylvania."

"How did you—"

"Because we're working the same case, and great minds think alike. But do you have anything solid?"

"Nothing that'll make you scramble for a phone booth," I said.

"Are there still phone booths? And, um, why would I want one?"

"There probably are in Muscatawney. And I meant so you could rip your shirt off and fly right over."

"Did you just say, 'I want to rip your shirt off, so fly right over'?"

"Ugh! Seriously?" I found myself imagining Michael ripping his shirt open to reveal melted jack cheese sizzling on his pecs in the shape of an "S." I shook it away. "What were we talking about? Oh, yeah, I'm just following a hunch. I want to gather some lore about Jack from where it all began. I'm bringing Molly with me, and I'll call in regularly if you want."

"Oh, no. I'm not letting you out of my sight," Michael said. "I have a couple days off; I'm going with you."

"Are you crazy? Should you be kicking back with the prime suspect?"

"If we're out of town, how's anyone going to see us?"

"I guess. If we can get past the initial paparazzi mob at LAX. How do you plan to do that? Don't tell me—you're a master of disguise."

"Close," he said. "I'm a master of restricted access."

An hour later, Molly and I donned our shades, and with a couple of big tote bags, waded through the cameras to my car. By then, a second camera crew had shown up from another well-known entertainment tabloid. Neither of us made any comment, but Molly smiled nicely for the cameras as we drove off.

We went to a nearby Arco. I wanted to see if the reporters and cameras would follow us. If they did, I was prepared to do some very bad driving. They didn't, but there would be more at the airport, our next stop, where we'd meet up with Michael. I filled up the car and went inside to pay cash. Molly came in to pick up a magazine.

She grabbed my arm. "Look!"

Linda Stone's face smiled out from among the smaller photos on the covers of several magazines. A couple of them used the photo off her website, but most had old shots from the nineties of her with Jack. That was all fine with me, as long as my picture wasn't next to them. Molly bought six of the magazines with Linda on them, so we could look them over.

I remembered *Mami* wanted to talk, but when I called her back it went to voicemail. I left her a message that we were going out of town for a few days, and I would call her back when we returned. Hopefully, this would all blow over while we were gone.

CHAPTER 32

Muscatawney, Pennsylvania was Jack Stone's hometown. I wanted to do a little digging on Jack and see what turned up. I didn't know what I was looking for. I was going on a hunch, the same hunch Michael had, apparently. Molly understood that, and she would rather do something that might help than sit at home fending off reporters. Besides, her presence would keep Michael from getting any other ideas than work.

We got a flight to Harrisburg with only a quick stopover in Chicago on the way. Boarding the plane, I noticed Michael was fidgety. He'd barely said a word since we arrived at the airport.

"You're rather quiet," I said.

"I haven't been on an airplane since I was ten years old," he said.

"You're kidding! You should take the window seat." I tried to grab his ticket to switch with him, but he snatched his hand away and held it up out of my reach.

"No, you take it. I insist." He avoided my eyes. "I really don't care." No smile.

I shrugged. "Okay."

Molly ended up at the window, and I sat in the middle so we could chat. Michael took the aisle. As we prepared for takeoff, Michael went pale and sweat broke out along his hairline. He gripped the armrests like a man hanging from a ledge.

"Are you okay?" I asked him, keeping my voice low.

"I'll be fine," he said.

I looked at him sideways. "Don't forget to breathe."

"Right!" he said and gulped air because he'd been holding his breath without realizing it.

"Maybe you should put your head between your knees."

Molly said, "They only make you do that so you won't see the plane crash. It's true; an ex-flight attendant told me."

"Maybe that's why she was an *ex*-flight attendant." I flashed Molly a kill look.

Michael cleared his throat. "Could we not talk for a while?"

The plane started to gain speed down the runway and soon rose into the air. It climbed, and once we were on a steady course, Michael recovered. Molly soon dozed in her seat.

Michael spoke in a low tone. "Spygirl, can I ask you something?"

"Shoot."

"Are you seriously dating that Lex Luthor dude? Because, say the word and I'll chill."

"Oh my God!" I said, way too loud. I toned it down in response to critical looks from some nearby passengers. "I am not dating him! I basically told you that already."

"You owe that guy a slap then, because he took a super-sized scoop of you."

"I'll probably never see him again."

Michael grinned. "Great."

"Then again, that's what I thought before, too, so I guess you never know."

He ignored the remark. "Hey, let's try to have some fun on this trip."

"I couldn't even think of fun right now. We're here to work."

"Is there any law against having a little fun, too?"

In response, I put my headphones on and turned physically away from him. I could still hear his follow-up question, though, as we would have called it in the courtroom.

"Anyway," he asked, "if you couldn't even think of fun, why'd you bring a chaperone?"

During the stopover at O'Hare, we made our connection smoothly, though Michael did no better with the next takeoff. Just when I thought we might settle into a peaceful flight, Molly went wide-eyed.

"Oh-oh, somebody's trying to get through to me," she said, staring into the back of the seat two feet from her face.

"Are they coming through the headrest?" I asked.

"No, silly!"

142

"Oh, good. I was worried."

"The TV in the chair back." She stared intently at the little TV, her eyes glazed.

I looked at the screen. All I saw on it was a map showing our flight path and where we were on it.

Molly talked to the TV screen. "Hey! How you doing? Uh-huh. Oh, really? Why not?"

Molly was speaking too loudly, and people kept turning around in their seats to look at her. She didn't notice them. She never took her eyes off the TV screen.

"But...but..." she went on. "Well I can't do anything about it now! What am I going to do? Here?" This last question she squealed like a piglet, and several people looked over at us with scowls or suspicion in their eyes.

"What's the matter?" I asked, gripping her arm gently.

"It's Jack."

"What does Jack want?" I whispered to her, hoping she'd follow my lead and lower her voice. I was afraid the plane would make an emergency landing just to throw us off, or worse. Good thing the flight attendants were nowhere nearby.

It worked; she whispered, "He wants us to go back."

"Go back? Why?"

"He's getting mad now; he's turning red."

"Why does he want us to go back?"

She turned to me. "He's gone." The focus came back into her eyes. No point in asking again why Jack wanted us to go back.

A flight attendant, alerted by passengers complaining about Molly, came over to speak with us. "Is anything wrong?" she asked.

"Nope," Molly said, "not that I know of."

Molly had no more disembodied visitors after that, and the rest of the flight was blissfully uneventful.

Michael had reserved a car at the airport and a hotel in Muscatawney. A crisp, sunny autumn morning rolling through landscape lush with towering orange and yellow trees was just what I needed to de-stress. I was instantly glad we'd come. It was a world away from LA, where I seemed to be always getting into trouble, and what trouble could we possibly get into in a quiet little town like Muscatawney, Pennsylvania?

CHAPTER 33

By the time we checked into the hotel, the Muscatawney Inn, we were starving. Having lost our appetites on the plane, we'd recovered them even heftier at the baggage claim. We left the car at the hotel and walked over to Main Street to stretch our legs and grab a bite to eat.

Muscatawney was a small town with small town charm, the kind that would drive you crazy if you were sixteen years old or stayed up past ten P.M. The locals still got their kicks and withdrew their cash on Main Street. Bleary-eyed mothers with children in strollers wandered everywhere. The tidy storefronts we ambled past were decorated with Halloween masks, broomsticks, spiders, and orange and purple lights twinkling like dream stars.

We went into a diner called Up All Night. Molly and Michael ordered chocolate milkshakes; I aimed for a café latté, but settled for coffee. Our waitress, Terri, wore a pink uniform beneath curly brown hair and a perpetual smile, which she directed mainly at Michael.

My plan was to have a look at Jack's high school yearbook. I wanted to find out if Jack Stone was the man I thought he was, or if I'd had him all wrong. The school library would have the old yearbooks.

"Michael, you talk to her," I said. "She'll give you more information just to keep your attention. Maybe tone down the smile, though, or she might not be able to think straight."

"Very funny," he said.

I wasn't kidding, though.

When Terri brought the shakes, Michael asked her, "By the way, is there just the one high school in Muscatawney?"

"Yes-sir-ee," she said, holding her serving tray up high, next to her shoulder. "Just the one, Muscatawney High, home of the Badgers."

"Badgers!" I said aloud. Bells clanged in my head.

"Yep. State football champions two years in a row now." She hadn't taken her eyes off Michael.

He was smiling. I nudged him under the table with my foot, and when he turned to me, the spell he had on Terri broke.

"Wow, that's great to know, Terri, thanks," I said and waited until she was out of earshot to spill the rest. "Badgers! I knew it!" My gut told me we were on to something.

"What's so special about badgers?" Molly asked.

"I was sure those badgers all over the bedroom at the condo were Linda's, and there was one on her bed at William's place, too. Either there's a connection, or it's one of those synchronicities that let you know you're on the right track. Maybe Linda came from Muscatawney, too, like Jack and Jessica. Maybe she and Jack go back further than I realized."

"Way, way back," Molly said.

"But what about Jack's first wife?" Michael asked. "Didn't he go out to Hollywood when he was, like, eighteen? His first had to be a Muscatawnean."

"Maybe his first marriage was really short?" I said.

"Really, really short," Molly said.

"Or maybe she followed him out there?"

"Let's see if she shows up in a yearbook," Michael said.

We looked at the menus and ordered breakfast. When Terri brought the food, Michael asked her where the high school was located. She told him and then pointed out a man a couple booths away who sat drinking coffee and reading a newspaper.

"That's Coach Martin right over there," Terri said. "He was the football coach over at Muscatawney High for more than thirty years until he retired two years ago. Anything you want to know about the high school, he can tell you."

"What luck, running into him," Michael said. "Thanks!"

"Sure," Terri said, "only…a word of advice: Don't mention the championships." She looked around at all three of us.

We all nodded and thanked her.

"Synchronicity," Molly said.

We finished our food, which was excellent, and walked over to Coach Martin's table.

"Mr. Martin?" I said.

The man lowered his newspaper and looked over it at us, revealing bristly grey hair, a large nose, small eyes, a clean-shaven face, and a thick stump of neck holding it all up. He wore an orange T-shirt. The arms holding the paper showed exceptional muscle definition for a man his age. "Yes?" he said.

"Excuse me for interrupting your reading. I'm Lola, and these are my friends, Molly and Michael. We're visiting from out of town, and Terri mentioned you used to coach over at the high school. I wonder if we might ask you a few questions. We won't take too much of your time."

"Sure, sure. Have a seat." He folded his paper and stowed it on the seat next to him. We sat across from him, with Michael on the end. "I'm always up for talking to a couple of pretty girls such as yourselves. And your friend can come, too. What do you want to know?"

"Thanks. We wanted to ask about Jack Stone. Did you ever have him for a student?"

"Oh, sure. He was on the football team for three years. Fullback. Good player. Not afraid of anything."

"Really? Do you think he could've played professionally?"

"Maybe," Martin said. "He was offered scholarships out the wazoo to play at colleges. But he didn't take any of them."

"No? Why not?" I asked.

"Jack was in love. He followed his girlfriend out to Hollywood instead of college." Martin shook his head. "There was no stopping him. That's how he ended up in the movies."

"Do you remember his girlfriend's name?"

"Yep. Vanessa Rankin. She wanted to go to Hollywood and be a movie star, and she made him go with her. She could get that boy to do anything. Vanessa was a beautiful girl. Ironic, isn't it? That *he* became the big star. I never saw her in a single movie."

"So they left together for Hollywood," I said. "Pretty exciting stuff."

"Yep. Snuck out of town in the middle of the night," Martin said.

"That's so romantic," Molly said.

"Jack was like that. He was always like someone you read about, even before he became someone you read about."

"How did the families take it?" Michael asked.

"Vanessa's mother was heartbroken." Martin shook his head. "Vanessa was the only daughter. She had three brothers. Badgers, every one of 'em."

"No wonder she wanted to leave," Molly said.

I pinched her under the table. She grimaced, then tried to disguise it as a smile.

"Ha-ha, just kidding," she said, but Martin hadn't caught the remark anyway.

"It was the same with Jack's mom," Coach Martin said.

"No dad?" Michael asked.

"His dad was long gone." Martin lowered his voice. "Killed himself when the kids were little. Jessica might've been too young to remember it, but not Jack. He remembered."

"No!" Molly and I both were surprised to hear this. We'd thought of Jack Stone as someone who'd led an enchanted life with no heartaches, everything easy. Something else about this story bothered me, but I couldn't put my finger on what it was. Martin went on.

"Neither one of 'em ever came back. Jack's sister got the one letter from him about a month later and then, nothing."

"That's strange. He wrote to his sister, not his mom," I said, half to myself.

"He and Vanessa got married in Las Vegas on the way out to California, and that was it. Nobody here ever heard from either of 'em again. Folks here just wrote 'em off." Martin cleared his throat and crossed his arms. "Tell you the truth, some people took it personal. If Jack showed up on TV or something, we'd just turn it right off. Not his movies; I mean talk shows and such. Everybody loved his movies."

"Wait a second," I said. "You said Jessica was too young to remember, but not Jack. I thought Jack's sister was older than him. Did he have another sister?"

"Nope. Just the one, poor thing. Maybe you're thinking of Vanessa; she was a little older than Jack. He'd skipped a grade early on, but it wasn't so much age-wise anyhow. She was years ahead of him, the way some girls are at that age. If you know what I mean."

"I know what you mean," Michael said, nodding.

Something was tickling my brain and wouldn't stop. I went dead silent, sluiced into a muck of thought, half listening to Martin, but too preoccupied to respond. Trying to remember exactly what Irena had said about Jessica, I knocked a fist against my head.

"I know what you mean, too," Molly said, but the awkward silence stretched on.

"Do you have more questions, Lola?" Michael asked.

I said nothing.

Molly turned back to Martin. "Uh, so...how 'bout them Badgers?"

Coach Martin hesitated, then in an instant, his face turned bright scarlet, like he'd just chugged the hot sauce instead of his coffee.

"What, are you trying to be funny?" he said, loudly. All those years of yelling at players on the field had paid off in great projection. "Is that what you really came over here for, to make fun of an old man?"

Molly didn't get it. "No. No, we... No!"

Michael jumped up and tugged Molly by the sweater out of the booth. She headed straight for the door.

"Get out of here!" Martin's decibel level had gone from raised to yelling. "Go on, get!" He reopened his newspaper as violently as possible and barricaded himself behind it.

The yelling had brought me back to earth. I muttered an apology and slid across the booth. The second I was out, Michael grabbed my hand and pulled me to the front door, dropping some money on our table along the way. I caught Terri's eye as we skulked out and flashed her an apologetic look. We'd been in Muscatawney for an hour and a half, and already had disturbed the peace.

CHAPTER 34

We scurried back to the Muscatawney Inn to shower and change.

"What was Coach Martin so upset about?" Molly was clueless.

I stopped walking. "'How 'bout them Badgers?' Molly, remember what Terri said before? The Badgers have been state champions for two years in a row. And Coach Martin retired when?"

Molly had stopped, too. "Two years ago… Ouch, I get it! Missed that. I guess that's why you get the big bucks."

"Except, I don't get big bucks." I patted her back and we caught up with Michael.

We had barely checked in before, due to hunger. Molly and I were sharing a room, and Michael had a single across the hall. The rooms were surprisingly comfortable. I took a quick shower first. While Molly was still in the shower, my cell phone rang. It was Michael.

"Are you two ready to roll?" he asked. "I'm hoping to have time for a massage later."

I'll admit I rolled my eyes. Was he implying something? "And you're telling me this why?"

"Just trying to introduce an air of leisure. We should have time for some fun, too."

"I know these are your days off, but I'm only here to work."

"No fun allowed, huh?"

"How can I have fun while I'm a murder suspect?"

"Seems to me like all the more reason to squeeze some in."

"Well, to answer your question, we're not ready yet. Molly's still in the shower. Was that all you wanted?"

"Nope. I have news."

"Well, why didn't you say that first? Spill!"

"The other prints are Jessica's. DMV confirmed they match her driver's license."

"Really? Wow. That only leaves Jack to be her killer." I'd been sitting on the bed, but on hearing the news, I stood up and paced between the bed and desk. "I just don't believe it."

"Well, believe it. Fingerprints don't lie. Linda was blackmailing Jack with the necklace that could prove he killed his sister."

"Okay, okay. I guess that's that."

"Hey, give me a heads-up if Molly comes in, okay? I need to ask you something."

"What is it?"

"Molly told us a different story about how you two found the necklace. I'm not sure which was more entertaining, but which one is true?"

"Oh, right. Well, hers, but I didn't think you'd believe it. That's the reason I lied."

"Okay, so that happened. Apparently. But what if Molly didn't get a message from the great beyond about where to find that necklace? Then how did she know?"

"I...don't know. It was the next logical place to look, the next place we'd have gone anyway. And did." I glanced over at the bathroom door, behind which I could hear a steady sheet of water pouring down and Molly loudly singing, "I'm a Soul Man". She wasn't bad.

"Spygirl, how much do you know about Molly? Did you ever check her out?"

"No, I didn't. But I'm learning more about her all the time."

"Well, I told Johnsen to run her name through the system and see if anything comes up. Think about it; she's very well placed to be involved in setting you up."

"Molly? No way! It's the Russian mafia. What reason could Molly have?"

"I don't know, but she also knew about you being a suspect in Linda's murder. She could've been Kit Cooper's source, too."

Michael's points were reasonable, and that made me angry, even though he was only voicing doubts that had crossed my mind, too, but I'd shoved aside. "Look, I'm a pretty good judge of character," I said, "and I just don't think that's who she is."

"You didn't think Jack Stone killed his sister, either," he said, but gently. "Once in a while, anybody can be wrong. I'm just saying, watch yourself."

Though Michael's voice had soothed me, every single thing he'd said was depressing. The shower faucet squeaked off and the hiss of water spray ended abruptly. My intuition told me Molly wouldn't hurt a fly. But I didn't tell her about Michael's call or the fingerprints, for whatever reason.

✻　　✻　　✻

We drove over to Muscatawney High and went to the school office to register as visitors. A woman in her late sixties with a furrowed brow and a blonde wig in an upswept style dragged herself slowly to the counter, as though it took tremendous effort for her to make her way across the ten feet or so of linoleum floor. Once there, she leaned heavily on the counter for support to catch her breath. She could have spoken to us from her desk, but I'd been around long enough to know one thing: a lifelong actress never misses a performance, and whenever possible makes a strong entrance.

I started to speak, but she held up one index finger, her other hand splayed over her heart. At least one of her brand of office worker could be found in every public high school in the nation, a woman who has spent years finding excuses to say no to every request. She finally smiled sweetly, wheezed a little, and said, "How may I help you?"

"We'd like to visit the school library. There's someone we want to look up in an old yearbook," I said and smiled. Michael and Molly smiled, too.

"I'm sorry. The library is for students and staff of the school only," she said, still smiling.

"Oh, but Coach Martin sent us over. He said it was very important that we help him out with this."

Her smile turned into a concerned expression. "Well, I can help him with whatever it is. You have him call me."

I glanced at the nameplate on her desk. "Is Mrs. Hess in today?"

"I'm Mrs. Hess." She straightened her posture.

"Oh! Coach told us to speak with you in particular. He said, 'You need permission to use the library; talk to Mrs. Hess. She's the only person in the place who knows what's what over there.'"

She smiled again. "Well, *that's* certainly true! Okay, for Coach M, I'll get you visitor badges and you can go have a look-see around. Nobody will bother you with the badges on." She pulled a basket of blank nametags from under the counter, removed one, picked up a felt-tipped pen, and poised it over the tag.

"Okay, shoot," she said.

"Would you like us to write them down?" Michael asked, reaching for the basket.

"No, no. I'll do it." She nodded her head sagely.

We gave her our names, and within the hour, she had written them on the tags. She then peeled the backings off for us. She let us stick them on ourselves, but I could see it was a struggle for her not to help. She spent the next fifteen minutes giving us directions to the library, which was essentially next door.

"Now don't take those badges off until you leave," she said. "And keep quiet in the library, or Mrs. Waite will get on you. She's an officious one, she is!"

The library was empty of human life apart from the librarian, Mrs. Waite. She was also in her late sixties, with grey hair worn long and loose and wire-framed glasses. Immediately helpful, she walked us over to the yearbooks and left us to it.

"What year did Jack graduate?" Michael asked.

"I don't know," I said. "He was fifty; I'm going to guess 1982, maybe? Molly, try eighty-one, and Michael, try 1980." I had flipped open the eighty-two yearbook and was running a finger down the names of the seniors along the side of the page. "Let's look for Jessica, too. Coach Martin said she was younger than Jack. And Vanessa Rankin…she's in the same class as Jack."

"And we're keeping our eyes peeled for Linda Gross, too," Molly said.

"Right," I said.

"Martin said Jack skipped a grade, remember?" Michael said.

"That's right," I said and closed 1982 with a heavy thump. There were no Stones in 1982. I decided to look for Jessica and picked up 1984, thinking Jess was probably at least two years younger than Jack if she didn't remember their father's suicide, while Jack did.

"Jack Stone sounds like a stage name, doesn't it?" Michael said. "I'm surprised it's real."

"Gotcha!" Molly said. "Vanessa Rankin. And Jack…they're on

the same page. Oh, she is pretty. I'll bet she could get old Jack to do things."

"I've got Jessica on this list," I said. I had my finger tracking along the row of photos to find the fifth one to match it to the name. The photo was wrong. "That's not Jessica Stone," I said, way too loud for a library.

I gasped as the truth sank in.

"Molly, let me see that!" I came in close to get a look at 1981. I was right. In the spot where the list said Vanessa Rankin should be was a photograph of the woman I knew as Jessica Stone.

CHAPTER 35

"Jessica Stone was really Vanessa Rankin!" I cried. "I've never seen this other woman before." I pointed to the photo of the real Jessica Stone.

We heard the tick-tock of Mrs. Waite's shoes approaching. We were being too loud, and I was to blame.

"Is anything wrong?" Mrs. Waite asked, coming around the corner into view.

"Actually, something is right again," I said. "Do you have a copier we could use?"

We made copies of the yearbook photos, but didn't discuss the case any further until we could speak freely in the privacy of the hotel. We convened in the room Molly and I shared. I kicked off my shoes and threw myself and my purse down on a bed. Molly sprawled on the other bed, and Michael took a chair.

"So," I said, in my worst I-told-you-so tone, "the woman Jack killed *wasn't* his sister, but his first wife, Vanessa. I knew it! I knew Jack wouldn't have killed his own sister."

"No," Michael said, "just his own wife."

"Ex-wife," I said. "It's still awful, but at least it makes more sense." My moment of self-congratulatory triumph was cut short by a niggling thought. "Molly, how come you didn't notice the picture you found of Vanessa was the woman you knew as Jessica?"

"Huh?" Molly said, sounding unrehearsed, I noted.

"How come you didn't recognize Jessica in the photo? You've contacted her on the other side a bunch of times, right? So why didn't you recognize her?"

"Oh, that's not surprising." Molly flapped her hand dismissively.

"When I see spirits, most of the time I don't see them the way you see a living person."

"What do you mean?" Michael asked.

"At first there's just a presence, an energy. You get a feel for them, a sense of who they are, and then the superficial things from the way they were in life start to fill in, but they're different. I don't know how it works, whether they do it or we do it. But they've moved on, so they don't really have a form anymore at all."

"Right. That makes sense," I said, limply.

"Makes you think, doesn't it?" Molly said.

"Yeah," I said, "but they're so different. Vanessa had blonde hair, and Jessica was very dark, like Jack."

Molly shrugged and frogged her mouth. "I don't know what to tell you. Things just work differently on the other side."

Michael had succeeded in making me feel suspicious of Molly, and I didn't like it. I looked at him sideways, and he had to feel the fury coming off me.

"How come you're so sure Jack killed her all of a sudden?" Molly asked.

"Oh," Michael said, "the fingerprints came in. The other prints were Jessica's."

"Which Jessica's?" she asked.

"Whichever one has her picture on her driver's license," I said.

"Guess I'd better give Johnsen a call," Michael said, checking the time on his cell phone.

"So, Jack killed Jessica, who was really Vanessa," Molly said. "No wonder he got so mad on the plane about us coming to Muscatawney."

"You know what I still don't get?" I said. "Okay, so Jack killed Vanessa. Then, why was he so hot to get her ghost to say who killed her?"

"Jack spent *a lot* of time and lettuce on me talking to the other side," Molly said.

"But doesn't necessarily mean he wanted to identify her killer," I sprang upright. "He just wanted to know if she could!"

"And Vanessa kept him hanging on," Molly said, "just like when she was alive."

"In my experience," Michael said, "murderers often want to get caught. Maybe Jack wanted to get caught, too." He stood and shook off the gloom that had crept in. "I'll call Johnsen and get back to you on the driver's license photo." He showed himself out.

"Why does he have to go to his room to call Johnsen?" I asked.

Molly ignored my question. "When did you get word on the prints?"

"Oh, uh, you were in the shower. Sorry, I forgot to tell you." I didn't feel good about lying to her, and I wondered if she knew.

"Hard to believe you'd forget that," Molly said, a perplexed look on her face.

"I have to know what he's saying to her!"

I sneaked over to Michael's room and stood by the door. His voice sounded muffled. I pressed my ear tight against the door and the sound improved quite a bit. Michael's voice grew louder suddenly. Then the door opened and I was falling through it.

"Haven't you ever heard of knocking?" I cried from the floor.

"Usually the person outside the door knocks," Michael said.

"Oh! Yeah, I guess."

He helped me up. Since I'd avoided looking at Michael until then, only at that moment did I realize the naked pecs of my fantasy were before my eyes, in the flesh. No cheese, but I was definitely melting.

Michael was still holding me by the arm. "Are you okay?"

"I'm fine. You lost your shirt, though." A shadow crossed the ceiling, and I tried to get a look into the room behind him. "Or have you got a phone booth in there?"

"Did you want something, Lola?"

"Did *you* want something? Why did you come out?"

"I thought I heard someone out here."

"Always the detective," I said.

"And you?" he asked, unswayed from his original question.

"I, uh, just wanted to check on that license photo."

"I said I'd get back to you."

"I know. I just couldn't wait." I smiled. "What did Johnsen say?"

"I left her a detailed message and I'm waiting for a callback. And I have an appointment right now. So, if you'll excuse me, I really have to go."

A woman's voice chirped up from behind him. "Of course, it's fine if you need to reschedule!" I stood on my toes to see a hot blonde a few feet away. My mouth dropped open.

"Massage," Michael said, releasing my arm. "I told you." He

went back inside.

"Okay, then," I said to the closed door. There was no rational reason for this to upset me, but it did. As I pictured her hands stroking his back, they changed into mine.

Molly and I went shopping until we met up with Michael for dinner. We had finished eating and were about to head back to the hotel when the email from Johnsen finally came in. Michael set his cell phone on the table so Molly and I could look at the photo.

"She's a blonde," he said.

"Vanessa," Molly said.

"Could be bleached," I said, though I was thinking more about blondes in general.

"That's Vanessa," Michael said, flicking the photo to a much closer view.

I took the yearbook copy of Vanessa from my purse to compare. It was her.

"So the question now is, where's the real Jessica Stone?" Molly said.

"I need my computer. I have a hunch I know where she is," I said.

"Me, too," said Michael.

As soon as we got back to the hotel, Michael went to his room to make some calls, and Molly went to freshen up.

"Jack's here." Molly's eerie, singsong voice wafted in on the tinkling of running water. I walked over to the open bathroom door to find her standing by the sink, holding a tiny bar of hotel soap, staring into the mirror. "He says he's sorry. He didn't mean to kill her. Vanessa wanted him to do it, but she wasn't supposed to die. He says she just couldn't stop wanting someone to hurt her." Then Molly snapped out of it and finished washing her hands. "What'd I say?" she asked me.

I filled her in. Jack had confessed—apparently. If Molly was for real, that is.

"Poor Jack," Molly said.

Poor Jack again. All I could think was, nobody was what they seemed. And that none of this was helping my trust issues one bit.

I got on the Internet and looked for death certificates. I ran a search for Jessica and found out my hunch was right.

Jessica Stone had died over twenty years ago.

CHAPTER 36

"What's our next move?" Molly asked the next day.

"Let's try his mama," I said.

"Worth a shot," Michael said. "But she might not know anything if what Coach Martin said is true—that Jack never wrote home."

I looked at Molly. "Does that sound like any of the mothers and sons you know?"

Molly shook her head emphatically.

"I can think of a lot of things you might keep quiet about, though," I said, "in a town like Muscatawney, where everybody knows everybody."

"No kidding," Molly said. "It's as claustrophobic as an ant colony around here. I get the feeling this town has some big secret, like they eat strangers or something."

"Just in case," I said, "if we get invited to any cookouts, let's not go."

"I'll take my chances," said Michael.

We looked up Jack and Jessica's mother, Camille Stone, on the computer. We got an address, put it into the phone GPS, and off we went.

Pulling up to the address, we were surprised to find a huge wooden house with a wrap-around porch on several acres dotted with huge oak, maple, and willow trees. A sign on the lawn in front read: Explorer School. We walked up to the door and rang the bell. I paced little circles and twirled my keys. Jack had been dead only a month, and I was nervous about intruding on his mother's pain.

A teenage boy answered the door. He looked like he had just rolled out of bed, with his blond hair splayed about his face, a black tee shirt, over-long jeans with shredded hems, and bare feet. I told him we were looking for Camille Stone. He shyly waved us inside and showed us to a room to wait for her.

The boy shuffled off down the wood-floored hall, loudly calling, "Camille!"

Strains of melody, mismatched rhythms, and bursts of exuberant voices drifted up from other rooms like a bad band practice. The room was lovely, decorated in shades of white, light greens, and peach. Fresh air breezed in through two open windows, their gauzy white curtains waving. Wind chimes tinkled furiously out on the verandah, like fairies having a spat.

In three minutes, a slim woman in an African-style kaftan greeted us. Camille had a fast but easy walk, olive skin, intelligent eyes, dark hair streaked with grey. Her head made quick, small movements like a bird's as she listened to us speak. When we had told her the purpose of our visit, she smiled a gentle, closed-mouth smile.

"My dears, would you like something to drink or eat?" she asked, once we took the seats she offered. Her voice was soft and cool, like the room. "You seem so wound up. There's no hurry, is there? You could relax for a little while, couldn't you, while we talk?"

We could, of course. It wasn't as if we were expected somewhere else in Muscatawney, Pennsylvania. She brought us oatmeal raisin cookies fresh from the oven and a pot of mint tea, and closed one of the windows so the room was less blustery.

"You never know who you're going to outlive," Camille said, without bitterness. "Do any of you have children?"

"No," we said.

"A husband or wife who has passed on?"

"My husband died eight years ago," Molly said.

"Oh, Molly, I didn't know," I said. My hand went to my chest in Pledge of Allegiance fashion. This had been my most familiar gesture until recently. Lately face-planting and shaking my head in total disbelief had taken its place. I couldn't believe Molly had never mentioned this before. It drove home how truly little I knew about her.

"That's how I got into talking to the other side," Molly said. "My husband started talking to me. Then pretty soon he started bringing all his new buddies around, and they all wanted to talk to somebody. A lot of the time the other side is yacking away, only nobody's listening. I never asked for it. It just happened, not long after Dwight died. And now I'm like a one-woman Internet."

I reached over and gave Molly's arm a squeeze. "I'm so sorry."

"Thanks. I still miss him, even though we talk. It ain't the same!"

"No," Camille said, "it sure ain't! I lost my husband, and now both of my children. After Jess passed on, I began to look at all children as my children. I was drawn to them. I don't mean in a sad way. There's no sadness in it at all. I felt an urge to do for all children what I did—and would've done—for my own. That's why I started this school. I think it was my way of moving forward. And while Jess didn't exactly talk to me as your husband talks to you, Molly, I feel she communicated the vision of this school to me somehow. You see, in life she was an art teacher at Muscatawney High, very visual. She'd have loved this place."

"It's gorgeous," Molly said, and Michael and I agreed with ardent nodding.

"And it's a great school. We do all the academics, of course, but we also have yoga and meditation breaks, we cook meals together and have tea ceremonies. Everybody plays some kind of music and we all jam together. The central idea is self-expression within community."

"Nice...theory," I said, flashing on the cacophony I'd heard earlier. "I'm glad you've found a way to move forward. We wouldn't want to upset you with our questions."

"Thank you," Camille said. "And it's okay. You won't upset me. Ask away."

"Okay," I said. "First, would you mind telling us what happened to Jessica?"

"You mean, how did she die? She was crossing the street and a drunk driver hit her. She was on the way to her thirtieth birthday party at her favorite restaurant. We were all waiting there for her when we heard the sirens coming closer and closer. We went outside to see what was going on, and there was Jesse, lying in the street. She looked so small and broken. If she'd gotten three feet farther, the guy would've missed her."

"How horrible for you," Michael said.

"I'm so sorry," I said, thinking, Okay, the real Jessica Stone is definitely dead.

"I believe we'll be together again," Camille said, "and Jack, and their father, too."

"Is it true you never heard from Jack again after he went to California?" I asked.

"Oh no, we heard from him a lot off and on, Jess and I both, depending on how busy he was. Jack always traveled a lot, mostly incognito to evade the paparazzi. We would meet up somewhere, usually one of his houses. I went to LA several times, though, not since Leilani's been in the picture. She hates me. Won't let me near my own grandchildren."

Michael and I exchanged a look.

"We've never talked about Jack to folks here. People get to talking, and we didn't want him to be the subject of any more gossip and tabloid lies than he already was."

"Did you know Vanessa well?" I asked.

Her tone dropped. "Vanessa, yes. Jack and Vanessa dated all through high school. They were inseparable. She used to come over for dinner and hang out on weekends and so forth. I don't think her home was very happy. She preferred to hang around our place, which was fine."

"They went to California together?" I asked.

"Yes, she wanted Jackie to go with her. She was afraid to go alone. Vanessa was a weak person and she knew it, but Jackie was strong. I think she hoped he could save her from herself, and so did he. But he couldn't. Things didn't go well for her. Her career didn't take off as she'd hoped. She already drank and smoked a couple of packs of cigarettes a day, even in high school. Then Jackie wrote me that she'd gotten into drugs and was hooked on methamphetamine. He tried to get her straightened out, but he couldn't.

"Meanwhile Jackie was getting a lot of work, but half the time he would come home and find her hiding in the closet shaking, or sitting outside in her car talking to herself, smoking and crying. And she was bitter about his success. He finally had to let her go. They divorced, and eventually he lost touch with her. Later on, he heard from somebody that she was working in pornography. But that was all such a long time ago.

"More recently, Jack emailed me that Vanessa had gotten back in touch with him out of the blue. She'd gotten off drugs and wanted to get back on her feet, and had come to him for help. He said he would try and help her. And that was the last I heard about her."

"When was that?"

"Mmm...about two or three years ago."

I thought about telling her that Vanessa was dead, but decided against it. I couldn't see how it could do her any good at the moment. I figured one day she would hear it somehow, but it wouldn't be from me.

Camille stood. Her eyes looked glassy. She stretched and shook herself. "I feel tired now. Vanessa's energy can slime me even now, just talking about her. Funny how some people can do that. Anything else you want to ask me? I ought to get a few more things done today, and school will be letting out soon."

"We'll let you go," I said. "If I think of anything else, I'll call you. Thank you so much for your time and your candor."

Molly gave her a warm hug. I started to shake her hand, but then hugged her, too, and so did Michael, who had been a mostly quiet, but solid presence during the visit.

As we left, Camille walked over and opened the window she had closed earlier. "Does it smell like cigarette smoke in here?" she asked us.

*   *   *

We drove to the diner for a bite of food and milkshakes.

"I haven't had this many milkshakes since I was ten," Michael said.

Molly was quiet. She stared out the window at an empty park across the street.

"Molly, was Vanessa at Camille's? The cigarette smell—that was her, wasn't it?"

Molly nodded. "She was there, but not too close. She was pacing back and forth out on the porch, blowing smoke at those wind chimes."

Michael shot me a look, but I had no clue what it meant, whether he found Molly spooky or thought her an obvious charlatan. At some point, I realized I was staring at him, mainly because Molly waved her hand in front of my eyes to point out that I was staring.

"Why don't you just ask him the question you're dying to ask?" she said.

"What?" I asked, sincerely ignorant.

162

"Yeah, what?" Michael asked. "Go ahead; ask me anything."

"I don't know what she's talking about."

Molly did a cheesy fingers-on-temples gesture, like a stage psychic. "It starts with... Do you really... Do you really what? Complete the sentence."

"I have no idea what you're talking about," I said. And then the next words just blurted out of me through no volition of my own. "Do you really have a thing for blondes?" I clapped both hands over my mouth.

Michael laughed. "Why do I get the feeling you definitely were dying to ask that? No, I do not have a thing for blondes. I have a thing for women with brains between their ears, though, whatever color their hair is."

When Terri brought the shakes, Michael asked her, "Is this place really open all night?"

"'Til midnight!" Terri said, smiling as always.

He pointed with his thumb to the name in the window, Up All Night, in neon letters that were backwards from inside the place. "So what's up with the name?"

"The owner figures after midnight, it's really the next day. People try to tell him different, but he doesn't care." She giggled.

"So, what's there to do around here for fun?" he asked.

"Spotlighting deer, if you've got a car," she said. "You know, staring at deer staring at headlights, basically. I just think they're pretty to look at, but some people shoot 'em. You're not supposed to, though. You want something romantic, get yourself a bottle of something and go up to Miller's Hill."

"We're leaving tonight," I said. "Anything going on today?"

"The German place, *Der Speisewagen,* is having Oktoberfest all week. Nice place."

"We'll check it out," Michael said.

"By the way, we found another high school," I said.

"You mean Explorer? That's a private school," Terri said. "We call it 'Weirdo High.' They say strange things go on there."

"Like what?" I asked, wondering if she meant the yoga.

"I don't know. It's just what I hear. Oh, your food's up." She went to get our order.

All I could think was how very far from home Vanessa and Jack had traveled.

*　　*　　*

Oktoberfest at *Der Speisewagen*, which brewed its own craft beer from an old Munchen family recipe, was everything an Oktoberfest could be, short of importing the water and hops from Bavaria. Happy hour was all afternoon in the outdoor beer garden. Free food was abundant and our waitress, Kaylee, also informed us that the beer was two for one. Michael and Molly each ordered a beer, but the idea of a designated driver seemed lost on Kaylee. We discussed happy hour for a while until, eventually, I convinced her to bring me a cup of tea.

The look on Molly's face when Kaylee set two huge pints of beer in front of her was comically photogenic. Michael whipped out his cell phone and took her picture.

"I don't mind a drink once in a while, but I have a pretty low tolerance," Molly said, starting on her first one.

"I'll help you, since this one won't," Michael said, jerking a thumb toward me. He gulped down half of his first pint immediately.

"I know," said Molly, who had somehow managed to put away half of her first beer already. "The outlawer of fun."

"You don't have to drink to have fun," I said. If I'd worn glasses, I would have pushed them up my nose right then. Thank goodness I didn't say aloud what I was thinking, that "outlawer" is not a word, and thereby suggest the opposite might be true.

Kaylee came over with plates of free happy hour food, mostly things I couldn't identify. But we were in Pennsylvania Dutch country; I threw caution to the wind and ate exotic German foods. Molly forgot all about her low alcohol tolerance and drank her second beer as fast as the first one. Michael coaxed her up for a dance, and then me. We shared him. They drank more; we danced more. There was an all-male folk dance performance. We had a lot of fun. Having checked out of our hotel long before, we left hours after sundown to head for the airport in Harrisburg. We had plenty of time.

A little way outside Muscatawney, I was munching some fries from a to-go box, when I dripped a big blob of ketchup in my lap. I swerved, and the ketchup-laden fries went flying all over the car. Good thing it was a rental.

A flashing blue light appeared in my rear view mirror.

"Shoot!" I pulled over and buzzed my window down.

Michael leaned forward from the back seat, picked a fry from my hair, and ate it. He'd had a few beers, but wasn't drunk, just a little tipsy. He shot me a stern look and said, "License and registration."

The police officer walked over and said, "Can I see your license and registration?" He shined a flashlight into the car, while I fumbled around for my license. "Have you had a few drinks this evening, ma'am?"

"No, officer," I said, handing him my license. I turned to the glove box for the registration and handed it over.

"Where are you coming from?" He looked the license over.

"Oktoberfest at *Der* spice— *Der* speece— Uh, I can't remember, but *Der* something-*wagen*."

"So," the cop said, "you're coming from Oktoberfest at *Der Speisewagen,* but you didn't have a drink or two? Are you sure? Because you were all over the road back there, lady."

Molly piped up from the passenger seat, where I'd assumed she'd passed out ever since she stopped singing along to every single song on the radio. She said, "Oh, she doesn't need any help from drinkin'. She is one truly terrible driver, just naturally." Then she laughed a lot.

At that point, the officer asked me to get out of the car and was ready to give me a sobriety test, when Michael produced his badge. After that, we were soon on our way. Good thing, too, because at some point we noticed the cop's name was Martin, and after some further conversation realized he was Coach Martin's son.

Eventually, we made it to the airport and returned the rental car.

"Molly," I said, "could I just say that you suck as a chaperone?"

But once everybody sobered up and Oktoberfest was behind us, the fun lay behind us, too. My paranoia kicked in again.

CHAPTER 37

I had bought us return tickets home for that night on the redeye. The night flights were cheaper, and Linda's retainer money was running out. We would arrive at LAX at 3:50 A.M., which seemed all right to me. Michael was fine with it; not being able to see the distance to the ground made his fear of flying slightly easier to bear. This time I reached over and held his hand during takeoff, which also made the flight better for him. Molly was less than thrilled. Hopefully, she would be too tired to talk to her TV screen on the way back. As it turned out, we barely spoke to each other during the flight, but neither of us slept, either. Suspicion had silenced me, and Molly seemed preoccupied. Michael slept just fine.

We stumbled to my car in the long-term parking at LAX.

"I wonder how my place is doing," I said.

"I was just thinking the same thing about my place," Molly said.

"Want me to drive you home later?"

"You're going to be too tired. Let's just see how it goes."

"No, I won't," I said, but my words turned into a huge yawn.

Michael snatched my keys away. "I'll drive. I'm the only one who's had any sleep."

I was too tired to argue. It was still the wee hours of the morning when we pulled into my parking lot in Burbank. Michael turned the headlights off and approached my home sweet home warily. I had no idea if the tabloid vultures would still be circling at this point. I had traveled in a favorite little parrot green dress just in case I got my picture taken. This was the up side of being hounded by paparazzi:

both Molly and I had never looked better. To my great relief, no media presence was loitering in the parking lot. I felt like I could breathe again, even though in truth, it was probably just too early even for them. Michael walked us inside, checked the place out thoroughly, and then went home.

I had been gone so much lately there were cobwebs in the fridge. And the beginnings of a good-sized compost heap as well. The sun wouldn't be coming up for almost an hour, but neither Molly nor I felt sleepy, so instead of going to bed, I turned on the TV and we fell asleep in front of it. It would have been impossible not to with the brain-numbing crop of infomercials, televangelists, and fitness shows that comprise early morning television.

I woke suddenly. I couldn't tell if two minutes or two hours had passed, but it wasn't daylight yet, so it couldn't have been long. I thought I'd heard a loud bang somewhere. It could have been a knock. Whatever it was, it hadn't woken Molly.

I turned off the TV, got up, and went to the door. I saw no one through the peephole. I stood still as a deer listening for the slightest sound, staring at the dark shape of my pepper grinder on the dining table. A bird began to sing outside. The music relaxed me completely. I was tired to the point of zombie status from carrying around too much tension for too long and not having slept on the plane.

I twirled the rod on the front window miniblind and the slats flipped open. Resting my head against the wall, I stood listening to the melodic birdsong. Outside, the world was just blinking awake. Venus floated bright and low on the pink horizon, and the palm trees' fronds bobbed gently up and down in a light breeze. I thought about absolutely nothing for the first time in days.

A flash of light in the parking lot caught my eye. There were small movements there, too. Someone was hanging halfway out of a parked car, searching through it with a flashlight. When the person searching came up for air, I saw that it was a man wearing a very dark coat, possibly black. Only then did I realize it was my VW the man was searching. He turned off the flashlight, stepped out of the car, and shut the door. He looked straight up at my window. Definitely, the man was Trench Coat.

I went to Molly and shook her, hard. "Molly," I said, keeping it quiet, "wake up. We have to get out of here *now*."

She was really out. I pinched her arm. She didn't like it. She opened her eyes and glared at me with murderous intent.

"We have to get out of here! Trench Coat is out there."

Her eyes flared into suns and she sprang up.

Footsteps scuffed outside. Our heads jerked in unison toward the front window. I had forgotten to close the blind. I pulled Molly down in front of the sofa to hide, and we listened intently. I poked my head up. A shadow was hulking by the window, probably trying to see inside. With the lights and TV off, the room was dim. I put my head down, fast.

"He's at the window," I mouthed to Molly.

A bright light flashed. I thought Trench Coat must have shined his flashlight in through the window. The next second, I heard him run off.

We came out of hiding and went to the window. There was a police car outside, shining a search beam up at my window. Maybe the police would catch Trench Coat. It could happen. One miracle already had—one of my neighbors had called the police.

CHAPTER 38

The police didn't catch Trench Coat.

We sat around my living room drinking fresh coffee. It was six-fifty A.M. and we had the TV on, along with every light in the place. The black-and-whites had already taken off. Michael had barely gotten home when the police call came in. He'd been monitoring the police scanner and rushed back over.

Molly hunched bleary-eyed on the sofa bundled in a blanket, the spider-legs of her hair standing straight up. "I'll take a train home later," she said. "A train full of people will be quieter than hanging around here. I might even get some sleep."

"Molly, I don't think it's safe for you to be alone," I said from the floor, where I was sprawled by the coffee table in some old sweats I had thrown on. "That guy might come after you, too. If you don't have to get back, I think we should stick together a while longer." I went back to blowing on my coffee.

Michael shot me a look. I knew what he was thinking, but whether I should trust Molly or not, the closer she was to me, the better I could keep an eye on her. And if I had to, I figured I could take her in a fight. For one thing, I was better armed. I wore heels; she wore flats. For another, I probably outweighed her skinny frame in spite of her *sumo* appetite.

Molly shrugged. "Whatever. I just want some sleep, somewhere."

"I don't want my mama in any danger," I said. "I think we should go get our stuff from there and stay over here."

"Or somewhere else," Michael said.

"Any word on Irena?" I asked him, yawning.

"She wasn't on any flight we can find, and we've checked everything that went out," he said. "By the way, I've been reading the files on the Jessica Stone murder. Did you know it was Irena who found her body?"

"Mmm-hmm. I remember that," I said. "Irena must've found the necklace and kept it right then. Funny that her prints aren't on it. She must've picked it up with gloves on or something. I wonder why she kept it."

"Maybe she knew it was Jack who killed Jessica and wanted to protect him. Or blackmail him, herself," Michael said.

"But she didn't blackmail him."

"We don't know that. Or she could've kept it as insurance for later."

My cell phone rang. It was Jennifer Morningstar. I looked at the time—7:00 A.M.

"I hope I'm not calling too early," she said. "I remember you're an early riser like me." Boy, did I have her fooled.

"Oh, no, it's fine; of course I'm up." My dark-circled eyes crinkled with a fake smile.

"Good. Leilani wants to invite you to a Halloween masquerade party she's having at the end of the month, Saturday, the thirty-first. I just wanted to give you a heads-up and get your mailing address for the invitation. It's not on your business card."

"She wants to invite *me?* Really?" It was so early in the morning, I thought maybe I was dreaming.

"You and Molly both, actually. And guests, of course, if you wish."

"Great." I gave her my address and handed the phone off to Molly so she could tell Jennifer her address, too.

"Any word on who leaked my name to the media?" I asked Michael.

"Nothing," he said. "Not a clue."

"What about Leilani and Jennifer? Did you tell them I was a suspect?"

"Nope. I never mentioned it, just said I was looking for you. I was trying to *help* you with Leilani, remember?" he said.

When Molly was off the phone I said, "Either Jennifer didn't know our addresses or she's going to a lot of trouble to act like she doesn't know, right after Trench Coat was here. Maybe she just wanted to see if we're still alive."

"You still suspect Jennifer?" Molly asked.

"No, not really," I said. "Between Jennifer and the Russian mafia, I think it's more likely the Russian mafia. Plus we saw Trench Coat with the circus on the police DVD. It's just so hard to believe she honestly thinks I'm a morning person."

"Shouldn't Trenchy have a Russian accent if he's with the Russian mafia?" Molly asked.

"Not necessarily," Michael said. "And he did have a Russian gun. They're hard to come by, but not for *Bratva*."

"I'm sure Jennifer would be glad to know the Russian mafia uses hybrid cars," I said. "You don't expect organized crime to be green. The biggest thing I'm worried about—apart from global warming, of course—is whether Trench Coat came here looking for his gun, or he was having a look around for the gun since he was here to kill us anyway."

"It's a safe bet if that guy is *Bratva*, he plans to kill you. They don't spend a lot of time thinking about it. They'll kill people just for looking at them," Michael said.

"That's guys, Michael. They probably like women looking at them," Molly said.

Michael had that grave look on his face again. "Do you two understand how dangerous this is? Along with everything else, we still have no clue who tipped off that circus. It had to be somebody in the department. Until we know who that was, I feel like I can't trust *anyone*." His eyes slid away from me. The message was clear; he didn't completely, one hundred percent trust me, either. I couldn't blame him. I was still the number one suspect, after all.

"Michael, come with me to the kitchen for a second. I want to show you something," I said, standing.

He narrowed his eyes at me and stood.

I made for the kitchen. "Don't worry. No steak knives are involved."

Molly wiggled her eyebrows at me. I shot her a kill look and led Michael into the kitchen.

"You just want to be alone with me, don't you?" he said, standing in front of my dishwasher.

"True," I said. I stood with my back to the sink, hands propped up on the counter. "I have an idea."

He raised his eyebrows high. "Really?" He came across the room to me, which in my tiny kitchen, meant taking a single step forward.

He slipped his hands through the crooks of my arms and grasped the edge of the sink behind me. He wasn't actually touching any part of me. "What kind of idea?" This message was also clear: he didn't need to trust me completely to sleep with me.

Interesting.

"It's not what you think," I said, placing one finger on his chest to keep him at bay. But I wanted him close. I didn't want Molly to hear. My voice was almost a whisper. "Did you tell anybody about—the Varjag?"

He suddenly scooped me up. I grabbed his shoulders. He set me on the kitchen counter, knocking a cup over and scattering cutlery. A knife clanged to the floor. He nudged my knees open and pressed in between my thighs. I was stunned.

"Baby, we don't need Viagra," he said.

"Viagra!" I cried, but then lowered my voice again. "Michael, cut it out! Can you be serious for one minute?" I didn't believe for a second he'd misunderstood what I said. But since I wasn't drinking or anything, I couldn't find fault with him making a move.

"Oh, I'm serious." He still had his hands on my ass, but I didn't mind.

I wanted to be annoyed with him, but the whole thing had me pretty turned on. I wasn't going to tell him that, though. I was still holding him, too. One of my hands was on his neck. My usual impulse to shove him away simply wasn't kicking in.

Molly yelled from the other room. "Uh, I'm going back to bed for a while in the back bedroom. So, you know, don't worry about making any noise or anything. I won't hear a thing. I'll be asleep. Waaay down the hall." Her voice faded out.

A sharp pain bit me. "Ow!" I reached down and pulled a fork from beneath my butt and threw it in the sink. That brought me to my senses. I slid down from the counter and ducked away to the refrigerator, where I stood with my arms and legs crossed. "I said Varjag. The gun. Did you tell anyone about it?"

Michael sighed and leaned back against the kitchen counter. "Not yet. I couldn't see that it'd do anything but get you into more trouble at the moment, and you get into enough trouble on your own. Not to mention that some of the company you keep will probably lead you into even more."

I resisted rolling my eyes. When someone helps you out,

sometimes you have to keep a stray thought or expression of feeling to yourself. "Thank you. That was thoughtful of you."

"Don't thank me yet. I take that back—go ahead and show me your gratitude all you want." He came toward me. "But I might still have to give up the gun."

"Well, until that happens, here's my plan." He reached for a strand of my hair, and I lightly slapped his hand away. "Listen! As far as anyone knows, Trench Coat left the gun in the parking lot at the Tides. He probably came back for it later, but it was gone. Maybe Molly and I have the gun, maybe we don't, but it's not in that parking lot, so they probably think we took it. I'll bet that's why he was sniffing around here."

"Maybe. But I seriously think he might just want you dead."

"Work with me, Michael! He was searching my car. He must've been looking for the gun. What if we put the word out the gun is for sale? Maybe we can even get your mole to leak it. Bill it within the department as a sting aimed at street gangs. If we get a bite, then we set up the buy and see who shows up."

"That's not a bad idea," he said, rubbing his chin. "It would make me very happy to find out who the rat is."

"It's not rat, it's mole."

"Right. A rat is a stoolpigeon."

"A mole is a spy."

"Yeah. So how come you're leaving Molly out of this?" He cocked his head toward the living room.

"I don't want any more suspicion focused on her, especially by me, but also by you."

"Okay. Let's set it up. I'll put an ad in the *Times* and set up a reply box, and we'll see if anyone takes the bait. Meanwhile, I'll get a storage unit and put the word out in the department that it's locked up in there. Of course, we don't mention that in the ad. Then I make like I've got the info, the storage unit number, combo, and so forth in a certain place, a place that'll take fingerprints. Maybe...the bottom drawer of my desk. Then we stake out the storage unit and see who turns up. You just sit tight, spygirl. I'll arrange everything. This just might work."

"It'll work. It has to. Where is the gun, anyway?"

"Don't worry...it's in a safe place."

CHAPTER 39

"That's your idea of a safe place?" I asked Michael, as he tugged the Varjag out of his coat pocket, touching it only with the cloth lining. Back in my kitchen once again, twelve hours had passed since our visit from Trench Coat. Molly and I, both exhausted, had gone back to bed and ended up losing the entire day. Michael had posted surveillance outside my place to keep an eye on me and anyone else, then returned in the evening.

"To tell you the truth," he said, "I just kept forgetting to take it out of my pocket. It's been there since you gave it to me. But never mind that." He shoved the gun back into the depths of his coat. From another pocket, he pulled out his cell phone and tickled the screen. "Listen to the ad I put on Craigslist: Item found in back lot of Tides condos 3rd October. Describe plus reward and it's yours. Sound good?"

"Reward?"

"I want it to sound like some punk put the ad in."

"Perfect. How do they respond?" I asked.

"Same way as a personal ad."

"How's that?"

"You've never answered a personal ad?"

"No, I haven't." Why would he think I had?

"Seriously?"

I snorted. "No."

He looked dubious. "Guess that explains why I haven't heard from you. Well, the email address is randomized to protect the contact info. They can reply with an email or phone number, or just set up a meeting somewhere. The whole thing can be totally anonymous."

"And they say romance is dead."

"No kidding," he said. "I've got my bottom drawer set up and ready to go. Just need to put the word out. The mole will need the location, unit number, and gate code. They'll just cut the lock. I thought about setting up a computer file with the info, but it seems easier just to write it on a Post-it, stick it in a drawer, and get the prints on the drawer. Funny, isn't it? That in this age of computers, a case could hinge on a Post-it note."

"Just one more paradox of the post-modern world," I said, "like marriage."

"Marriage?"

"Yeah. We live in an age of serial monogamy, ex-spouses all over the place, and yet people keep getting married. Doesn't make a lot of sense, does it?" I said.

Michael smiled at me indulgently. "Why, spygirl, I didn't know you were so cynical! Are you saying you don't believe in marriage?"

I wished I hadn't said it, but I often spoke without thinking first. I kept meaning to do it the other way around. I just shrugged.

He went on, his brow furrowed. "I think marriage says something about the triumph of love and the human spirit. Just because something's old doesn't mean there's no place for it."

"Then I guess the same is true for Post-it notes." I flashed on the green Post-it pad at the condo where I had originally gotten Molly's address. I'd never figured out who wrote that note. It was still floating around somewhere in the bottomless pit that was my purse.

"You're a real optimist," Michael said.

But I was only half listening. I wanted to have another look at that note. I grabbed my purse and dug through it, looking for a flash of neon green.

"Anyway, I set up a camera, too, in case of gloves," Michael said.

"Mm. Good idea." I up-ended my bag on the counter, methodically shoved the large items aside, and then began going through the papers, tossing receipts, flyers, and candy wrappers into the trash bin under the sink. "Any idea who the mole is?" I asked.

"Johnsen," he said, without hesitation. "She came on right when all this started. And anyone who's just made detective is susceptible, untried."

I froze for a second in mild shock and looked him in the eye. "You're kidding. Detective Pamela Anderson? What if it is her? Are you going to call off the wedding?"

"Yeah, yeah."

"Guess we'll know soon enough, won't we?" I wiggled my eyebrows and returned my attention to my purse.

"What are you looking for?" He picked up my giant bottle of aspirin. I snatched it back.

"A Post-it I found by the telephone at the condo the day I found Linda dead. The handwriting on it wasn't Linda's, and the pad hadn't been there before. That means it might have belonged to her killer."

"What'd it say?"

"Molly's address was on it. That's how I found her." I spotted a flash of neon green.

"That's evidence. You should've told me about it."

"I know. I'm sorry. I forgot." Sort of. "Got it!" I pulled the neon green needle from my haystack of purse contents. It had been stuck to the register in my checkbook, the part where you balance it, which I hadn't seen a lot of lately. I looked the note over carefully. "Whoever wrote this dotted their 'i' with a circle, see?"

"Yep."

"I've seen that somewhere else recently," I said. "That's someone who wants a lot of attention. And look at that huge loop on the 'g' in 'San Diego.' That's very distinctive, too. Large lower loops indicate a strong sex drive."

"Really? Where'd you learn so much about handwriting?"

"Oh, I've been studying it for years. I just find it interesting," I said.

"You are full of surprises. Can you remember where else you saw it?"

"No. But it'll come to me."

"Okay." He stood to leave. "Well, the ad is in. Everything is set. Once I get a reply, we can stake out the unit. So now, we wait."

"Now we wait." I sighed. "I hate waiting."

"Yeah, me, too." Michael grabbed a brochure from my purse pile and shoved it toward me.

"Would you sign your name on here for me, please?"

"What for?"

"I want a look at your lower loops."

I growled, snatched the brochure and whacked him on the head with it.

My cell rang. It was *Mami.* Michael ducked out as I took the call.

"You know," *Mami* said, "I had something to tell you a long time ago, but I never got the chance. It just never seems to be the right time." Her voice shook a little.

"What is it?" I asked, worried by her tone.

She sighed. "I had a big Sweet Greets order a while back for gift baskets for a retirement party. They were really nice baskets; I found some great stuff. I really wanted to impress the customer who arranged the party because I thought I might get a lot of future business through her. She's very well known."

"Uh-huh. Sure."

"And we got to talking a lot." Long pause. "She's a TV reporter." She went quiet.

"Okay, so?"

"Lolita, I think…I messed up, I'm sorry. The customer was Kit Cooper."

I almost dropped the phone. "You, *Mami?* It was you?"

"I'm so sorry," she said. "I tried to tell you. I tried."

I was afraid she would cry. "*Mami,* it's okay. It's all over now, and it wasn't that bad."

"Really?"

"Really."

"You're not mad at me?"

"No! And even if I were, I could never stay mad at you. You know that."

She laughed. I could hear the relief in her voice. "You know, when you were away, they put your picture in some of the magazines and even on TV! I collected them. I'll show them to you sometime. And Molly, too. You both look beautiful!"

Great. For my fifteen minutes of fame, I was a murder suspect. I decided I could live with that, as long as the photos were good. There was one entirely good thing about *Mami's* revelation: I would now be able to prove to Michael that Molly had not been to blame for the tabloid stories.

CHAPTER 40

Michael got a flood of responses to the Craigslist ad. People sent emails describing all kinds of things they might have lost in the parking lot behind The Tides condominiums. An audio system, a bicycle, a pair of lovebirds in a cage, a suitcase full of money (yeah, right!), a set of dentures, and the obligatory wedding ring.

On the morning of the second day the ad ran, Michael got the email we were looking for: a guy who had lost a gun. He was a man of few words, apart from a phone number. I let Molly sleep and slipped out to meet Michael at the Golden Donut a block from my place. I wanted to be there when he called the guy. It was eight-thirty, and I was not feeling talkative. Michael looked ready for anything. I found him overly cheery and sneered.

"Dear God, you're a morning person, aren't you?" I said. "How did I not see it before?"

He shrugged. "I like morning, yeah. Not your thing, huh?" He laughed at me. Ha-ha.

I shaded my eyes, even though I was wearing sunglasses. "You going to make that call?"

"Yep."

Michael called the number. A man answered, probably Trench Coat, probably on a disposable cell phone. I could hear what the voice said, but not well enough to identify it because the call wasn't on speaker.

"You contacted me about a lost item," Michael said.

"Right," the man said. "You found my gun."

"Maybe. Can you describe it in detail?"

"Sure. Black plastic frame, fits in the hand nice. It's chambered for cartridges."

"Anything else?" Michael was trying to keep him on the phone as long as possible.

"What? What else?"

"Any numbers or letters?"

"Oh. There used to be numbers on the barrel, but they met with an unfortunate accident."

"Okay, I guess it's yours. Cool gun. What is it? I've never seen one like it before."

"What's your game, man? You going to give me my gun back or what?"

"I was just curious. It's a nice gun. Hey, I could've just kept it, you know."

"It's a Russian Varjag."

"Man, sounds hard to get. Probably worth a lot to you."

"How much do you want?" the man asked.

"Two hundred."

"I could buy another gun for that!"

"Not this gun. You want this one back, right? I might take one-fifty."

"Come on! Fifty bucks is about right."

"Okay, a hundred," Michael said. "I wouldn't mind keeping it. Or I could sell it. Definitely get more than that for it."

"Fine. A hundred."

"Deal."

"Where?" the man asked, quickly.

"I put it in storage for now."

"Where's that?"

"I'll go get it and we can meet up, someplace public."

"That's not a good idea."

"Listen, we can work it out later. I can't take care of this right now anyway. I'm going out of town for a few days." Michael said this just to make him antsy and push him to act.

There were a couple of possibilities. If the mole tipped him off it was a sting operation, whoever it was would forgo any meeting and just break into the storage unit once the mole supplied the information from Michael's desk. If the mole did nothing, we wouldn't catch the mole, but we could go through with the meeting in a few days and still catch whoever showed up for the gun.

"What? You're leaving town?"

"Hey, the ad's been in for a week," Michael lied.

"No, it hasn't. When are you leaving?"

"You just caught me on my way out the door."

"I'll meet you right now."

"I don't think the airport would be a good place for this particular transaction. I'll call you in a few days, I promise. Meanwhile, you can scrape together my hundred."

Click. The man ended the call.

"I think he was a little annoyed with me," Michael said.

"I keep meaning to ask you something, but now I can't remember what it is," I said. He wasn't listening. He was high on playing cops and robbers. Michael really loved his job.

"Time for stage two," he said. "So, I already showed the gun to some people in the department and talked up the sting before I went out to the storage unit. I made sure nobody saw me put the cameras in place at my desk and the storage. Now I have to get back to the station and make a little show of stashing the note in the drawer, mention it to a few key people, then make myself scarce for a few hours."

"Guess I should keep my head down," I said.

"Definitely. And we should try not to be seen together. If anyone gets the idea I have a conflict of interest concerning you, I'll be off this case. And you don't want that to happen, Lola."

"No, I certainly don't," I said. And I meant it. "But what about the stakeout? I get to go, right? It's not like anyone would see us there; only the bad guys will know the location."

"Which makes it more dangerous."

"Michael, please! You won't even know I'm there."

"We'll see." He didn't look at me when he said it.

So Michael took off alone to plant the seeds of stage two. As soon as he left, I remembered what I kept meaning to ask him: Where did he put the gun?

CHAPTER 41

When Michael came back, we took off for the Lock 'N' Load twenty-four hour self-storage facility just off the 10. I wore sensible shoes and brought a pulp private eye novel with me; I needed a good read in case we ended up on a long stakeout. This whole covert op thing was a big risk for both of us, and we knew it. Michael never would have done it if he'd known who he could and could not trust in the LAPD.

"When you don't know who to trust, you have to trust no one," he said. "At least you're not in the department."

"Well, it's obviously worth the risk for me, since I'm a suspect."

"The only suspect."

"Right. Thanks for reminding me. But I'm still surprised you're letting me come."

"I haven't got anybody else."

"Thanks a lot!" I said.

"Besides, it was your idea. I know how I'd feel about that. I'd damn well want to be there when it went down."

He was right; I did damn well want to be there. Michael punched in the code and the gate slid open. We drove past the unit first and continued on through all the rows of storage units and tarp-covered cars near ours. Nothing looked unusual. We found a good spot at the end of our unit's row, parked, closed the windows, and locked the doors. We threw a tarp with some strategic rips over Michael's car and positioned it so we could see out. His windows were also heavily tinted. It would be difficult, though not impossible, for someone to spot us. It could be a long night, or not. With luck, the mole would go to work quickly, but if not, our scheme might take a whole lot longer to play out.

We had brought cartons of Chinese food, but I was so wound up I couldn't eat. Michael could eat, no problem. Hours passed. Around midnight, we took turns trying to sleep, but I couldn't. Michael could sleep, no problem. Around four in the morning, he woke up after about three hours of sleep.

"Tell you what, spygirl," he said, "I didn't think when we finally spent the night together it would be like this."

Just then, an SUV turned into the row and crept along with its lights off. It was a black Cadillac Escalade with tinted windows.

"Looks like your boyfriend's car."

Eye roll. But it did look like Santiago's SUV. I wondered briefly if he had lied about finding the Dostoyevsky novel on his desk. It could've been in his glove box because he was the one delivering them to warn people off. But bottom line, I didn't feel that Santiago was Dostoyevsky. Mexican mafia, maybe, but Russian mafia, *nyet.*

"Half of southern California drives that car," I said.

The Escalade stopped midway down the row. The driver's window buzzed down and a flashlight beamed out at one of the storage units. The Escalade inched forward and the beam flashed on the next one, and the next. It stopped in front of our unit. The flashlight went off, then the rear window slid down.

"This is it," Michael whispered.

It suddenly hit me that what we were doing was insane. We had no backup. Worse, nobody knew we were there, not even Molly. If these people were Russian mafia, they would have AK-47s. They would gun us down without the least hesitation.

"Michael, we—"

"Sshhh. Later," he said. It was too late to back out.

The driver's door of the Escalade opened. Trench Coat emerged and walked up to the door of the storage unit. Another man got out on the passenger side and joined him. Trench Coat carried what looked like a gun, but it was a battery-op power saw. There was a brief, loud whine and yellow sparks flew and then the padlock fell off. Trench Coat put the saw in the back of the Escalade while his comrade pushed up the overhead door. The two men walked inside.

We sat straining to see them come back out. They were inside the storage unit for what seemed like twenty minutes, but was probably about thirty seconds. It couldn't have been long; the storage unit was empty. When they returned, Trench Coat shook his head at whoever sat in the back of the SUV. Then each man pulled a Dragunov from his coat and held it ready. They walked down the row of doors with their guns drawn. Trench Coat headed straight for our car. The other man set off in the opposite direction.

Michael drew his gun and we slid down as far as we could under the dash. Trench Coat walked right up to the car. He tried the driver's side handle through the tarp. I stifled a gasp. He tried the back door handle. He could have pointed his gun at the car and shot it, just in case, but he didn't. He could have thrown the tarp off the car and found us, but he didn't. We were lucky. He moved on, but made another pass on the way back, a large shadow sliding by soundlessly, like a barracuda. When he was gone, we came up for air.

Back at the Escalade, Trench Coat shook his head at the back seat, then approached the rear window and ducked down to confer for a minute. The second man pulled down the overhead door, then got back in the passenger side of the SUV. All the windows went up.

Trench Coat raised his Dragunov to his hip, his teeth clenched in a grimace, and shot up the door. The ear-splitting noise of bullets ripping metal stormed through my brain. I cried out, but it didn't matter. No one could have heard it through the din. Michael pulled me close and wrapped his arms around me, shielding my ears. Then the shooting stopped, and all I could hear was Michael's breath. I was holding mine. I was, however, keenly aware of Michael holding me, and it felt wonderful. Part of me didn't want the moment to end.

But it did end. A moment later, Trench Coat climbed into the driver's seat and the Escalade squealed away.

We stayed put for a while. There was a good chance they were hiding, waiting to see if anyone came out. I quickly fell asleep. When I woke, the smog outside had turned a lighter shade of brown, and I knew the sun would be fully up at any minute. Michael appeared wide awake. I looked out at the storage unit. An old man was standing in front of it, checking out the shot-up door. He bent stiffly, picked up the broken padlock and toddled off with it.

"Let's get out of here," Michael said.

We took off the tarp, threw it in the car, and drove down to the storage unit. The metal door, torn and warped with bullet hole graffiti, could have passed for contemporary art.

"So, where's the gun now?" I asked.

"I think you already know the answer to that." He patted his pocket. "With all that's happened and a mole in the department, it seemed the safest place for it."

Michael got out of the car. He walked over to the shot-up door and removed a small camera from a fire alarm box beside it, the top of which had been dented by a bullet.

"Still ticking?" Michael mumbled to the camera as he got back in the car.

"Good question." I felt for the pulse in my neck to be sure.

We took off. Michael had a faraway look in his eyes. At the exit, he silently tapped in the code and the gate slid forth.

"So, that's the guy you kicked the gun away from?" he asked, as we hit the road.

"That's the guy."

"You're very lucky to be alive."

"I know. He just didn't see me as a threat."

"Remind me not to make that mistake," Michael said.

CHAPTER 42

Michael dropped me off at my place and went back to the station. He wanted to lift the fingerprints off the drawer right away before anything could go wrong. He also wanted to analyze the film from the storage unit camera, though it could've been damaged in all the shooting.

I planned to collect Molly and go hang out at my mama's house for a little while. I wasn't worried anymore about Trench Coat coming after me, since he now thought someone else had the gun. But I was rattled from all the guns and shooting. I'd feel safer with my mama. I phoned her and said Molly and I would be over soon.

I went inside, kicked off my shoes, and called to Molly. She didn't answer. She wouldn't have gone anywhere; she was too frightened. The awful thought hit me that Trench Coat might have come straight over to my place after the storage unit. I went to check the back bedroom.

"Molly!" I called out. She wasn't in there, and I didn't hear water running in the shower.

I went down the hall to check out the shower off my room. "Molly?" The bedroom was dark, the blinds were drawn, but I hadn't left it like that. I flipped on the light.

Molly sat on my bed, her eyes glazed. She was muttering something.

"Are you all right?" I asked her and sat next to her.

"Lola?" She kept staring straight ahead.

"Yeah. Why are you sitting in the dark?"

"Your dad's here," she said. "He's very worried about you."

I caught a whiff of cigarette smoke. It put a chill right up my spine. "Me, too," I said.

"Well, look who else is here," Molly said. "Miss Jessica, or should I say, Vanessa?"

I went to the balcony and locked the door, which should've been locked already. No one was out there. No one I could see, at least. "Molly, come on. We have to go," I said.

"Vanessa says you should check out Jack's computer files. And Hector says you should go and stay with your mama for a while."

"That's what I'm trying to do," I said.

Molly came out of her trance.

"Come on...get your stuff," I said. "We're going to *Mami's*."

While we packed, I filled Molly in on what she'd said in her trance, and the cigarette smoke, too. Molly had been living out of a bag for so long, she was packed in minutes.

"I could get used to this," she said. "It's nice not having so much stuff." She sat on the bed waiting for me to finish. "So, how did the stakeout go?"

"Oh, it was great!" I talked fast, but Molly kept up. I gave her every detail.

"You know, this really is right for you," she said, "this private eye thing. Look at you. You're like a little kid, all lit up."

"You're right about that. Murder suspect or no, I love my job."

"And the fringe benefits aren't bad either, huh?"

"What fringe benefits? Being interrogated?" I stuffed in the last thing that could possibly be crammed into my bag, sat on it, and zipped it up.

"Too kinky for me." She snickered. "But hot detectives putting their arms around you on stakeouts doesn't sound bad."

I shrugged off her remark, but the truth was I had replayed those moments alone in the car with Michael again and again in my mind since then.

I'd been wearing sensible shoes for far too many hours. I grabbed a pair of Jimmy Choos out of the closet and put them on, my brown satins with two-and-a-half inches of heel. They'd always brought me good luck. We threw our stuff in the trunk of my car and took off for *Mami's* house.

We had just hopped onto the 405. Molly was digging through her purse looking for lip balm, when the worst possible thing happened.

"Ow! I broke my damn nail," Molly cried. "What the heck have I got in here?" Still digging in her purse, she twisted toward the back seat. The next thing I saw was her mouth moving like a goldfish, but no sounds coming out.

"Turn around," a voice said, a male voice with an accent.

A man filled my rearview mirror. He was so big I couldn't believe he could have hidden back there. The barrel of a pistol he held straight in front of Molly's face riveted my attention. My heart skipped. I swerved the car out of the lane, but pulled it back in. People honked and tires screeched. Molly and I tossed around, but the guy in the back kept his balance. The hand not holding the gun was gripping the road rage handle.

Molly was still staring at the gun.

"Turn around!" He said it louder this time.

Molly turned to face the front.

"You vill go different direction now, please. Take next exit," he said.

The accent was definitely Russian.

CHAPTER 43

I took the exit. "Where are we going?" I glanced in the rearview and tried to memorize his face. A flash of glitter beneath his coat caught my eye.

"You vill have good time." He let out a low, perforated laugh. "Ve go to circus."

It was a fairly long drive to the Murmansk Circus, and I was starving. It looked again like it had the first time, with dogs, guns, and glitter everywhere. The same guy as before showed up and called off the dogs.

The guy in the back seat said, "Sergei also tames the tigers. You vill see." Again, the staccato laugh. He got out of the car and clapped an arm around Sergei, who handed him a Dragunov.

Sergei motioned us out of the car with his Dragunov. We got out, both their guns pointed at us. Sergei said, "Viktor, you bring me new kittens to play vith!"

Viktor said, "You can play until Dostoyevsky is ready for them. Then ve have leetle goodbye party." They both laughed.

Goodbye party. That didn't sound good.

"Come," Sergei said, and he and Viktor marched us into the Big Top.

Inside, men stood guard with Russian AK-47s, and circus performers practiced their routines just as before. Ivan the dancing bear twirled in the first ring beneath the trapeze. I searched the high swings for Irena, but she was nowhere to be seen. I didn't see Boris, either.

In the second ring, where the bareback rider was running her horse, I saw someone else I knew. Trench Coat stood holding a gun, guarding one side of the tent. I didn't recognize him at first because instead of a black trench coat he was wearing a sparkly black skintight suit. I only recognized him because he saw me and shot me his distinctive glare. So that confirmed it—he was mafia. He obviously wanted to kill me, and it looked like he'd soon get his chance. I nudged Molly and pointed him out to her.

Sergei led us to the third ring, where a huge black cage was set up. Inside, round pedestals were positioned at one end of the cage. On two of these sat tigers. Big tigers.

Viktor doffed his coat in the bleachers, took a huge key ring from a pocket, unlocked the tiger cage, and stood outside by the door. Sergei waved us inside with his gun, walked in behind us and closed the cage door. Then he motioned us over to where the tigers sat watching us like we were live appetizers being served by waiters. One of them snarled loudly. They looked hungry. I couldn't tell if their ribs were showing or the striped pattern of their fur only made it look that way. A bunch of clowns came out of nowhere and started doing gymnastics around the perimeter of the cage.

When I looked at Sergei again, he had put down the gun and had a whip in his hand. He called to Viktor, "Vhere is Boris?"

Viktor said, "He is comink, vill be back any minute."

Sergei turned to the tigers. A crazed look in his eye, he cracked his whip on the ground and yelled something in Russian at them. They pounced effortlessly to the ground and stood on either side of him. They waited as he placed a hoop into brackets to suspend it a few feet above the ground. Then he stepped aside, raised one arm and called, "Bala!" The tigers leaped one at a time through the hoop and then circled back to their marks.

"Bala," Sergei commanded again, and the tigers jumped through once more. Then he cracked the whip again and pointed with his arm, and the tigers returned to their pedestals.

Sergei turned to us, his eyes sparkling to rival his cat suit. "Now you," he cried and cracked his whip. We exchanged nervous looks and went to his side, the side without the whip. "Go!" he shouted at Molly, a fierce look in his eye.

"Are you kidding me?" Molly turned her body to him like a wall and parked her hands on her hips. "I'm not jumping through no hoop!"

Sergei raised his whip.

"You leave her alone," I screamed at Sergei and charged at him, nails first. The tigers had inspired me. I aimed to knock him down and claw his face off.

He sidestepped my advance, and I went down, twisting my ankle. I yelped in pain. My left Jimmy Choo lay in the dirt a few feet away, its heel severed from its body. It was bad, but not beyond repair. I stretched toward it.

Sergei laughed at me. He leaped at the shoe and snatched it from my grasp. Then he did the unthinkable. He tossed my Jimmy Choo to one of the tigers. The tiger caught my shoe in its huge mouth full of tiger slobber, leaped down from its tuffet, and lay down to gnaw away at it.

"How could you do that?" I picked up the heel and tucked it in a pocket anyway.

Sergei only laughed. Then he turned his attention back to Molly. He cracked the whip by her feet, but she ran around the hoop to the other side of the cage and huddled near a pedestal.

"I'll take my chances with the tigers," she said. The tiger on the pedestal snarled and swiped at Molly with a paw the size of a truck tire. Thankfully, she was out of range.

Sergei laughed. "Good leetle kitten," he said. He walked across the cage, whip in hand.

I took off the other shoe and scrambled to my feet. If I couldn't wear it, maybe I could club him to death with it. I raised my weapon.

At that instant, Viktor yelled, "Boris is here!"

All around, people passed the word along. Some shouted, some spoke. "Boris is here. Look…here he is!" Sergei abruptly turned his attention to the first ring. I lowered my shoe and stuffed it in my jacket pocket. With Sergei distracted, I hopped over to Molly and leaned against the bars, rubbing my ankle. We gawked in the same direction as Sergei.

The ringmaster had just walked in. He was quickly surrounded by people. Clowns leap-frogged over one another to join the others at Boris's side. Throughout the Big Top, people dropped what they were doing and flocked to him. I considered a run for the cage door, but Viktor stood right next to it, gun in hand.

Molly spoke quietly. "I guess Boris must be Dostoyevsky."

I snorted. "The ringmaster is the ringmaster? Puh-lease! No one could be that tacky."

"Have you looked at the wardrobe around here?"

She had a point, but I hoped she was wrong. If Boris was Dostoyevsky, we were probably about to be killed. What was it the sparkle-boys had said? Dostoyevsky would have a goodbye party for us.

Sergei spotted us huddled against the bars and clucked his tongue. "Ve can't play no more now! Sorry, kittens." He put down the whip and picked up his gun. I looked around for a weapon, but all I had was the shoe in my pocket. But Sergei surprised me. He motioned to Viktor to unlock the door and stepped out of the cage to join him.

Viktor locked us inside, then tucked the keys in the waistband of his sparkling outfit. The two of them stood with their guns trained on us, rubbing their beard stubble and talking. Molly and I eyed the tigers nervously, but they showed no interest in us. If only the same could be said of my satin pump, which the one tiger was still nibbling.

The crowd around Boris began to spread out again, but I couldn't see what was going on.

Two clowns came skipping and leapfrogging back our way. They bounced and landed right in front of Sergei and Viktor with a flourish and bowed deeply.

"Greetings from the ringmaster," the clowns said, in unison. Together, they held something out toward Sergei.

CHAPTER 44

It was a brown paper bag. Sergei took the bag, and when the clowns skipped away, he and Viktor sat in the bleachers to open it. They pulled out submarine sandwiches and started eating. They waved and shouted, "Thanks, Boris!"

Boris waved. At that point, I noticed everyone was sitting in the bleachers eating. We weren't going to die yet. Boris had just brought lunch. He was only an errand boy.

"So, Boris isn't Dostoyevsky?" I asked Viktor and Sergei from behind the bars.

They cracked up laughing.

"Boris?" Sergei said. "Dostoyevsky is brilliant criminal mastermind. Boris is un-brilliant, criminal ringmaster. But don't vorry! You vill meet Dostoyevsky very soon."

I wondered if Trench Coat could be Dostoyevsky. I noticed he wasn't standing guard where I'd seen him before. In fact, he was nowhere in sight. I looked around for escape routes and tried to come up with a plan, but I wasn't getting anywhere. I decided to work on Viktor. I kept stealing looks at him while he was eating. Viktor was watching me, too. He blew me a kiss; I threw him a seductive glance. Then he blew me another kiss and accidentally spit out a chunk of his sandwich. That put a stop to our flirtation for a while.

Right about then, another commotion kicked up over at ring number one. Viktor and Sergei put their food aside. They made some hand signals back and forth with some clowns, then came over to the tiger cage and stood beside it with their guns ready. As I made my way over to where Viktor stood, I noticed my ankle had recovered.

I smiled at Viktor, reached through the bars to touch his firm, spangled leg and slid my hand upward, keeping away from the gun. He smiled back at me. My hand traveled over his hip. He closed his eyes, dreamily. He moaned when I played my fingers around his waistband, teasing my hand a little way into forbidden territory. It was enough. I got the keys and crushed them in my fist so they wouldn't make a sound. Smoothly substituting my other hand on Viktor's hip, I stashed the keys in my bra. They were cold. Bulky, too. I pushed them in securely.

"Your dream is comink true," Sergei called to Molly and me. "Dostoyevsky is comink!"

Viktor opened his eyes and moved away from the cage, a regretful look on his face.

A small crowd was approaching, an entourage surrounding the mysterious Dostoyevsky.

I huddled close to Molly and whispered, "Once we know who Dostoyevsky is, they'll have to kill us, even if they weren't planning to."

Molly took hold of my hand and gave it a squeeze. "You never know who you're going to outlive," she said, quoting Camille.

I pictured Camille, and images of all the people we had met during the case popped into my mind. I saw them all pinned against a slowly spinning roulette wheel. But the wheel was all different colors, some pastel and some neon, like Post-it pads. And then it hit me. Except for the yellow ones, colored Post-it pads always came in stacks of different colors, in either neon or pastel bundles. The roulette wheel in my head stopped spinning and landed on one person. And I knew it was right.

"I know who Dostoyevsky is," I cried.

"Who?" Molly asked.

"Who had a neon Post-it pad, the type that would have been bundled with other neon pads, like the neon green one I found at Linda's? Who had a supply of actual books on her shelf, some of which were paperbacks, some of which were very likely authored by Dostoyevsky?"

Molly looked lost. "I don't know. Who?"

"I've been so stupid!" I clapped my hands against my head.

"Who is it?" She was jumping up and down.

"Irena! Irena is Dostoyevsky."

"Oh-oh!" She stopped jumping and nodded at the circus people, no more than twenty feet away from us. "I don't know if figuring that out is going to do us any good at this point."

The small crowd had stopped and parted, as if for royalty. Striding down the center was the elusive, brilliant mastermind behind California's Russian mafia. Irena wore her big fur coat and led two wispy greyhounds on leashes, one in each hand. Her red hair bounced and shone like a shampoo commercial.

She pointed at Molly and me, crammed against the bars, threw her head back and laughed. "If you could see look on your faces!" She looked around. "Ve have camera? Vhere is camera?" She snapped her fingers. "Qvickly!" But her entourage threw their hands up; no one had a camera.

"Irena, I knew it was you," I said.

"Vhoopee! Good for you! You still look funny. Now, vhere is that music box?"

"The music box? Why?"

"I vill ask qvestions, please. Vhere is box?"

"It's in my car. The green shopping bag in the trunk."

"You have keys, please?"

"I left everything in the car."

"Boris!" She motioned with her chin for Boris to go and get it. Boris ran off.

I was still thinking, putting it all together. My mind went back to the day we were talking at her place. "And your calendar," I said. "That's where I saw the 'i' with the circle dot, and the big loops. Besides the pad, it was your handwriting on that Post-it note at Linda's place. You killed Linda!"

"Correct. She tell me Jack's psychic vas 'the real deal' and give me her address so I can talk to my darlink mama I miss so much. Then I kill her."

A chill went through me. Irena had seemed so torn up about Linda's death, but it was just an act. "How can you be so cold?" I asked.

Irena sneered. "Linda vas a pain in the ass! She owed lot of money. I help her again and again, and still she owes more money. I just like to vatch the leetle doggies run, but she have to gamble all the time. I never get back all that money. So I kill her, bang bang!"

"I'll bet it was you who blew up the yacht, too. But you weren't after me. I just happened to be there. You and Jack were still married when he bought that boat, weren't you? You were after the insurance money."

"*Da,* it vas me who blew up Jack's leetle boat. I am the benefoosh...the venifeesh...the one who gets the insurance money. So I blow it up, boom! Still it not cover Linda's debts. She say she give me offshore money, but she write down wrong account number. Too late now."

"You are full of surprises. But how do you know about the music box?"

"Boris told me about it."

"How did Boris find out about it? Santiago didn't talk."

"Everybody talk, eventually."

I felt sick. Santiago may be part of society's dark underbelly, but he was a smoking hot part who had both saved my ass and fondled it. I had mixed feelings about Santiago, but he didn't deserve to die, in any case. "You didn't...kill Santiago?" I asked.

"He vill recover. Eventually." She laughed wickedly. "Is perfect plan, yes? I let you get necklace for me, then I take."

"Necklace? What necklace?" I said, hoping she would think we never found it.

Boris rushed in with the green shopping bag in his hands.

"That's a good color for you, Boris," Molly said.

Boris frowned.

Irena grabbed the bag from Boris, took the music box out and let the bag fall. She tore the cloth off the box and threw it on the ground, too. "Necklace is in box?"

"I not look in box." Boris's left eye began to twitch. "You ask for vhat Linda give racetrack man. This is vhat she give him. Then racetrack man give to her." He nodded at me, looked back at Irena and shrugged.

Irena opened the box. Two notes of music rose from it like a question. "Vhere is necklace?" she asked. "Linda stole the necklace from me!"

"You yanked it off a dead woman's neck," I said.

"Eh, she not need it anymore." Irena turned the box upside down and shook it. Linda's tissue-wrapped packet fell out. She hurled the music box to the ground where it smashed to pieces. She snatched up the tissue and clawed it open to find the Gamblers Anonymous charm inside.

"Aaagh!" She threw the charm across the tent. "Vorthless junk!"

I said, "The necklace was in the tea jar, the tea jar *you* told us about."

"But henchman told me he find jar, but nothink vas in it. So I think Linda put necklace in music box and give to Santiago."

"Nope," I said. "I just got to the jar before your guy. The police have that necklace now."

"Aak! Vhat a vaste. I could've sold that necklace for big money on eBay. People pay big for celebrity stuff."

Molly was horrified by Irena's tantrum. She said, "We were worried about you! We were afraid someone had hurt you, but look at you. All you care about is money." Then she got that glassy look in her eyes. "Your mama says you ought to be ashamed of yourself. She says she didn't raise her daughter up to be no criminal mastermind. And she wants to know where are the grandchildren you promised her?"

"Mama," Irena said, clutching her fur-covered heart. "She is here?"

I sensed an opportunity. "Molly is the psychic Linda told you about. That's how I found her...from the Post-It note you wrote at Linda's. You left it there."

Irena stared at Molly wide-eyed. "*You* are real-deal psychic?" She dropped her dogs' leashes, threw herself at the tiger cage, and gripped the bars in front of Molly. "Are you sure is my mama? My mama, she look just like me, only vith leetle moustache."

The instant they were free, the greyhounds ran toward the bareback rider's cantering horse, barking all the way. A group of clowns ran after the dogs to catch them. The horse spooked and reared up at the dogs, then bucked the bareback rider off. She flew forward over the horse's head. One of the trapeze artists just missed catching her in midair. She fell instead into the safety net, bounced off, and landed on her feet unharmed, with a flourish. Ivan, the dancing bear, was running loose on all fours, with several people trying to catch him.

Sergei went running after Ivan. Viktor ran to the bareback rider's side. Irena stood clutching the bars in front of Molly, listening intently while Molly zoned out.

With Irena engrossed, I plucked the keys from my bra, reached around through the bars, and unlocked the cage door. For what I had to do next, I needed to access my angry thoughts and go dark side. Thoughts flashed through my head at lightning speed: how Irena had fooled Molly and me; how Sergei tried to make us jump through a hoop, like animals. None of that put me over the edge of fury. It was Sergei giving his slobbery tiger my Jimmy Choo to munch on that really got to me.

I sneaked up behind Irena, grabbed her gorgeous hair with both hands and yanked her head back. She screamed and clawed at the air, but I ducked her grasp. Channeling fifth grade, I slammed her head against the bars as hard as I could, and she slid down the side of the cage like a melting wicked witch. Nobody noticed. The circus people were all preoccupied in the other two rings, engulfed in chaos. I tried to pick Irena up, but she was too heavy.

"Molly, help me!" I looked over at her. She was just giving her head that telltale shake that signaled her return to planet Earth.

"How'd you get out there?" Molly cried.

"Never mind; come help me! We can use her as a human shield."

Molly ran out the door of the tiger cage. The tigers watched her, blinking, and then sprung lightly off their pedestals and followed her out the door. They slunk right past us toward freedom. One of them slid out through a side flap of the tent and the other went after it.

"Come on!" I nodded at the flap where the tigers had just escaped. Molly and I tried together to pick up Irena, but she was dead weight. Her fur coat slid off in our hands and she lay limp on the ground. We stood holding the fur for a second, then let it drop.

"Forget it," I said. "Let's just go, while nobody's looking." We made for the side of the tent. Molly got there, but I stopped short.

"Hang on a sec!" I ran back in and picked up what was left of my beloved shoe. I'd hoped it could be saved, but it was mangled beyond recognition.

"Leave it!" Molly grabbed her head with both hands. Just then, two rings over, I saw Viktor grab Boris and point at Molly. They ran toward us. Worse, Trench Coat had reappeared near the spot where we planned to slip out. He was ten feet from Molly. It looked like he was saying something to her, but he held his gun down.

I ran, barefoot. When I was in range, I threw my mangled shoe at Trench Coat's head and then hurled the good shoe after it. I fished the heel out of my pocket and tossed that, too. It wasn't much, but it was enough. He dropped his gun. I grabbed Molly's hand as I flew by, and we managed to escape through the tent flap together, not as stylishly as tigers, but alive.

We inhaled fresh, cool air on the other side, something we might easily not have felt or breathed ever again.

"It's a beautiful day," I said, running.

"It certainly is," she agreed, also running.

My car was right where I'd left it, with the keys still in the ignition. We jumped in just as Trench Coat, Boris, and Viktor came through the tent behind us. My hand was shaking as I turned the key and gunned it. We high-tailed it out of there and left them choking down our dust. I got on the freeway and drove even worse than usual in case they were following us. We flew down the freeway until we got near LA, where the traffic slowed us down. Molly called Michael from her cell phone and blathered to him that we'd been kidnapped by circus people.

"Molly, put it on speaker," I said. She did, but at first we heard only background noise.

A few seconds later Michael's voice came back. "Okay, I've got a SWAT team on the way. Just keep moving!" We were at a standstill.

"No chance of that," I said. "We're stuck in traffic. But don't worry about it…just listen. Irena is Dostoyevsky. She killed Linda, and she blew up Jack's yacht."

"She admitted that?"

"Yep."

"I don't suppose she confessed to killing Jack, too."

"Uh, no. But isn't that great? When last we saw her, she was out cold."

"I hope she's still chillin' when the SWAT team makes it to the Big Top. Got to go. We'll talk later. Good work, spygirl!"

I high-fived Molly. "What did Trench Coat say to you?"

"I didn't hear him say anything," she said.

"That guy just cannot hold onto a gun," I said and then I gasped so loudly, it made Molly jump. "*Mami!* We were supposed to be at her place hours ago. She'll be worried sick!" I called her to say we were all right, and I'd explain when we got there. She screamed when she heard my voice, and I could almost hear her crossing herself over the phone.

Two hours later, Michael called back. I turned the radio way down. Molly and I had the music cranked up and were dancing in our seats, having only made about ten miles of progress since our last talk with Michael.

"Things are wrapping up here," he said. "We've got Irena."

"Oh, thank God!" I said. "We're still sitting in traffic, by the way, but it's starting to open up now. We're on our way to my mama's."

"Good, because the one person who slipped the net is Trench Coat, so be careful. He's on the loose out there...somewhere."

CHAPTER 45

We didn't get to my mama's house for another hour and a half. When we finally arrived, *Mami* looked about ten years older. She'd been crying. No doubt that wouldn't have happened if I were practicing law. I didn't tell her most of what had happened because I didn't want to upset her any more, but I think she sensed that she'd almost lost me.

Molly and I slept for a while. When we got up it was dinnertime. *Mami* told me Michael had called and she'd invited him over for dinner. I didn't even know he had her number. I ran upstairs to change out of my sweatpants.

When I came back down, Michael was standing in the kitchen talking to *Mami.* He looked different. I'd always seen him wearing a suit. He was obviously off duty because he was in dark jeans and a black button-down shirt. He looked over at me and smiled, and I had the urge to run over and hug him. I didn't do it, but it threw me for a second, and I must have seemed nervous because he walked over to me with a questioning look on his face.

"You okay?" he asked, as he reached to tuck a sprig of my hair behind an ear.

"I'm fine. Why wouldn't I be?" I snapped.

"Sorry," he said and backed off. He held up a DVD. "I've got something to show you."

"Sure," I said and marched quickly down the hall to the den. I plopped down hard on the sofa and crossed my arms and legs. "There it is," I said, looking at the DVD player. I had no idea why I was acting this way.

"Did I do something?" Michael asked.

"What?" I squinted at him like he was crazy. I just kept making it worse. Each word I spoke moved me further away from what I was really feeling. I knew I was doing it, but I couldn't stop myself.

"Never mind," he said. "I thought you'd like to see the surveillance. Was I wrong?"

"Of course I want to see it."

"Okay." He popped the DVD into the player.

I grabbed the remote and turned on the TV. Michael came and sat down next to me on the sofa. My heart beat faster. I stared at the TV screen.

"First is the storage unit. Here, let me fast-forward it." He took the remote from me, putting his hand over mine.

His touch on my hand felt electric. It was unmistakable. I was falling for him.

"Okay, watch." He stopped fast-forwarding.

On the TV screen, the rear window of the black SUV slid down and the flashlight shone out from it. At first, all I could see was the blinding light of the beam. Then the flashlight clicked off. The person in the back seat leaned out of the darkness and became visible in the ambient light of the storage facility.

"There!" Michael hit the pause button and the picture froze. It was clearly Irena's face, surrounded by blackness, like her heart.

"Unmistakable," I said, shaking my head. Watching the DVD, my mind was right back in that car with Michael.

"At first, the only word she knew in English was 'lawyer.' Then I showed her the DVD, along with my irresistible smile, and pretty soon she confessed everything. Everything to do with Linda, anyway. That and the illegal guns we confiscated at the circus should put her away for a good long while." He flashed me his irresistible smile.

"Unmistakable," I said again.

"Yeah. And you won't believe this. At least I didn't." He fast-forwarded again.

There was Michael's desk and someone's back as they approached it. The mole. But it wasn't Johnsen; it was a man. He knelt by the bottom drawer and opened it with a paper napkin in his hand so he wouldn't leave prints. The word "Donuts" was imprinted in pink letters on the part of the napkin that was visible.

"Definitely a cop," I said.

"Good thing I put the camera there, huh?"

"But do we get to see who it is?"

"Yep. He's going to turn around…right…here." The man turned to go, and Michael froze the picture.

It was Detective Roger Parish.

"No," I said. "I can't believe it!"

"Twenty-three years on the force. You believe that? Internal Affairs popped him a couple hours ago."

"Wow."

"Yeah."

We sat in silence for a few long seconds.

"You don't seem yourself," Michael said. "You sure you're okay? Maybe you have post-traumatic stress disorder." He looked into my eyes.

I looked away. He only leaned in closer.

"I'm great, really." I quickly got up and went over to the DVD player, opened it, and took out the DVD. I held it out to Michael. "You don't want to forget this."

"Keep it. I made copies," he said. "IAD wanted a bunch." He leaned back and sprawled out with his hands behind his head. "Not a bad week's work, huh?"

I set the DVD on the table in front of him. "Yeah."

"We make a pretty good team, don't you think?" he said. "My brains, your brawn…"

I sat down in a chair across from the sofa. "I'm completely cleared now, right?"

He sat up straight. "Oh, yeah, absolutely. You're no longer a suspect."

I smiled. The sense of relief was huge.

"Is that what's been bothering you?" He smiled. "I'm sorry. I should've said it before."

I knew right then that Michael's irresistible smile would never get old.

Mami showed up in the doorway. "Dinner is ready. Go wash your hands, you two."

I already knew that mothers never stopped being mothers.

CHAPTER 46

The next morning, I called Leilani. I asked her for permission to look at the files in Jack's computer, to which she agreed. She told me his password and said to come by any time after one. Molly and I showed up at one-oh-one.

We went into Jack's study. It was a dream room filled with books and comfy furniture. The only side without bookshelves had floor-to-ceiling windows edged with framed maps. A slim white laptop computer lay on the desk. I sat in Jack's chair, opened the computer, and turned it on. I typed in the password Leilani had given me: leilani. It didn't work. I tried it with a capital L. That didn't work, either.

"Guess he changed it," I said. I tried all the kids' names. It was none of them.

Molly said, "Try his harem…I mean wives."

I did, but it wasn't any of them, either. I tried "jessica," "jennifer," "alouette," "rosebud," and "stayinalive," with and without capitals. I tried a bunch of his other film titles. Nothing.

"I don't really want to be the one to tell her he changed it from her name," I said. "He probably changed it because their marriage was on the rocks."

"I get it," Molly said, arms akimbo. "You want me to tell her. Fine, I'll tell her. She can pitch a dolphin at me." She walked away and opened the door, but stopped. "Wait a second—she won't know the right password anyway, because she thought it was Leilani. So why tell her?"

That gave me a hunch. "Molly, wait!" I typed it in with a question mark: "leilani?"

Molly closed the door and came back to the desk. I clicked Enter.

"It worked!" I couldn't believe it, but the computer started ticking away, putting Jack's settings in place. A minute later, Molly and I were staring at the desktop, trying to find the file called "away" or "a way," if it existed at all. It was just a hunch of mine. The one small error in Jack's suicide note had been bugging me all this time.

I looked through My Documents. It wasn't there, so I clicked the Start button and tried both "away" and "a way" in the search box to search the whole computer. The file didn't turn up. I opened his browser history to see if any websites in it contained that string of letters. Nothing.

"There's no place left to look," I said.

I closed the browser and went back to the desktop. I was about to shut it down, when Molly noticed the wallpaper. It was a photo of the *Alouette*.

"He sure did love that boat," she said.

"His boat-neighbor, Barnaby, told me he used to take her out almost every weekend, unless he was away on location shooting a film."

Then I noticed the trash bin icon and realized I hadn't looked there, so I clicked it. I was used to trash bins being empty, but Jack's was full of discarded photos. Then I saw it. The file called "Away" had been deleted, but the trash bin had not been emptied.

"There it is," I said and clicked it. "I wonder why he threw it away?"

"Maybe he knew he wasn't going to be using it ever again," Molly said.

The file contained charts of sea current and tidal information for the Pacific Ocean for a two-year period ending with the end of that very month. I couldn't make anything of it, nor could Molly, except that maybe he was planning a sailing trip somewhere. But we both knew what trip Jack apparently had been planning, and it wasn't on any charts.

I copied the file to a flash drive I'd brought with me and shut the computer down, feeling deeply disappointed. I knew this should be important, but I had no idea how I was going to figure out what it meant or could be used for. We thanked Leilani and left, promising to come up with good costumes for her upcoming party.

Now that I was no longer a murder suspect, I felt free to drop in on Michael at the police station. I asked Molly if she'd mind stopping there. I wanted to apologize to him for my weird behavior the previous evening.

We swung by the station. Michael worked on the sixth floor. As Molly and I walked up to the elevator, the doors were closing. I saw a face, just as the doors slipped together. The eyes met mine, and I froze. Time slowed down. No question about it; the man on the elevator was Trench Coat.

"Molly, did you see him?" I grabbed her arm.

"I saw him!"

The elevator had only one way to go—up.

"Come on!" I sprinted for the stairwell.

We raced up the stairs, but Molly fell behind around the fourth floor.

"Go ahead," she yelled. "I'll catch up. I'll just follow the smell of doughnuts."

"Sixth floor," I yelled down to her. I didn't know where Trench Coat was going or what he was doing. Maybe he found out Michael placed the gun ad and was bold enough to walk right into a police station to get it back, though that seemed highly unlikely. All I knew was that he always carried a gun. Maybe he was planning a showdown.

I got to the sixth floor, wrenched open the heavy stairwell door, and charged over to Michael's office. No Trench Coat. Detectives at tables were using phones and computers or talking.

"A guy with a gun is on his way up here," I said, gasping for breath. "He was on the elevator." I spotted Michael over by the coffeemaker. He saw me just as all the detectives looked up from what they were doing. At the same moment, Trench Coat appeared in the doorway.

I launched myself at Trench Coat before he could draw a gun, before he could think. I knocked him flat and heard the crack of his head hitting the floor. Then I straddled him, pinning his arms at his sides with my knees. But he came up fast and turned. He threw me over sideways like I was no more than a housecat. I went sprawling across the hallway until my back smacked into the wall. He was already up, standing over me, ready to repel another attack. I had to admire his moves. I was not even close to a match for him, but I'd bought some time. There were plenty of cops around to take him down.

"Freeze!" a cop yelled.

About six cops had guns on him. I kicked off from the wall and crawled away.

"Wait," Trench Coat said. "I'm FBI." His hands were in the air.

Nobody moved.

"Let me take out my badge." Trench Coat carefully flipped his jacket open and slowly reached a hand to his inside pocket. He picked a wallet out with thumb and finger and threw it to the floor. Michael pulled the wallet over and flipped it open with his foot. There was a badge, all right.

"Federal Agent Henry Becker," Michael read aloud.

The guns dropped instantly.

"Organized crime unit...I was working undercover," Becker said. He turned to me, reached down and gave me a hand up. "I'm starting to think you've got a crush on me."

I sneered at him and straightened my clothing.

"I want to thank you, Ms. Vega," Becker said, turning the hand-up into a handshake, "for your help in tying up the evidence on the Russian mafia operatives here in LA. We couldn't have bagged Dostoyevsky this quickly without you. Though it pains me to say it."

"Why didn't you just tell me you were FBI?" I said. God, I wanted to hit him.

"For one thing, you were the main suspect in Linda Gross's murder."

"Oh, that."

"Not that I thought you did it," he said.

"I thought *you* did it," I said.

"Most people would've dropped it right in the beginning, or very soon after. The client being dead and all," he said.

"Oh, that."

"I did try to warn you off."

"That's your idea of a warning? Assaulting me in a dark, empty parking lot?"

"I couldn't chance blowing my cover. And it's a good bet you wouldn't have backed off if I'd simply asked you to, so I tried to scare you off. You PIs cause us a lot of headaches."

"Oh. Well." I was ready to change the subject. I had seen only

Becker's face on the elevator. Now I noticed he was wearing jeans and a yellow polo shirt. "I see you finally lost the trench coat," I said, for small talk. "That glitter actually wasn't a bad look for you."

Molly staggered in, breathless from climbing the stairs. She leaned heavily on the doorframe, pointing at Becker.

"It's okay, Molly," I said. "He's an undercover fed. Can you believe that?"

Molly nodded, made an okay sign, and struggled to speak. She kept pointing, but not at Becker. I brought her a cup of water, which she gulped down.

When she finally could speak, all she said was, "Starving…doughnuts?"

CHAPTER 47

That evening, Molly, *Mami,* and I rented a DVD and planned a quiet evening at *Mami's.* We rented the Bollywood film, *Bride and Prejudice. Mami* had gone Bollywood crazy in the past year. She said the music and dance in them made her feel light and happy.

In the past three months, she also had been going to all sorts of places to sketch her surroundings. She was meditating regularly, as well. I had never known her to do any of these things before my papa died. But it was typical of her to sense exactly what she needed to do to regenerate herself after a fall or loss. I couldn't remember a time when anything had defeated her strong spirit. But the way she'd looked the day before tore at my heart.

"*Mami,* I'm thinking of going back to practicing law," I said, as we stood in the kitchen making popcorn for the movie.

"What?" She looked astounded. "Why would you do that?"

I shrugged. "I thought maybe I should do something less dangerous."

"That's not my Lolita talking! What's wrong?"

"Nothing!"

"She's right," Molly said. "That doesn't sound like you."

Mami tipped her head to one side, came to me and took my hands in hers. "*Mija,* if I thought you'd be happy as an attorney, I'd be all for it. But I think you figured out long ago that you would not. You've got to do what will make you happy and not look for anyone's approval but your own. All your papa and I ever really wanted for you in this world is for you to be happy. So, please, don't do something like that for anyone but you."

"Are you sure?"

"I'm sure."

We shared a big hug.

"Thanks, *Mami.*"

The microwave dinged. Molly poured the popcorn into a big bowl.

"I would still like grandchildren, though."

I tossed a popped kernel at her, and we all went into the den. I put in the DVD and sat between them on the sofa.

Mami said, "There's more to happiness than work, of course."

"Amen to that," said Molly.

"Why were you so cold to Michael the other night, after he's done so much to help you?" *Mami* asked.

"I was kind of awful to him, wasn't I?" I said, wishing the DVD's FBI warning would end; wishing my mama hadn't heard every word of my conversation with Michael. "But it's okay. I apologized for that. He probably just thinks I was having a hormone surge."

"Maybe you were. Only not that kind."

I sighed. "Okay, I was afraid something was happening with us. I guess I just got scared." I picked up the remote to fast-forward through the trailers.

"That's scary?" Molly said. "Girl, if you keep on like this, you're going to end up as one of those cat ladies."

"Right. Thanks."

"Nuking single-serving dinners at night and arguing with your TV set."

"Molly!" If only I could fast-forward her.

"The neighborhood children will call you a witch and dare each other to ring your doorbell."

"Okay, okay!" I said. She had broken my concentration. I'd forwarded past the last trailer. I saw credits and a woman's mouth moving, so I had to back it up again.

"I do know what I'm talking about," she said. "I ended up talking to ghosts instead of the TV, and I have newspapers instead of a cat, but believe me, honey, having somebody to love is a good thing."

"Molly, my track record with men is so bad, it's more of a prison record." I managed to hit the perfect spot at the end of the final trailer and pushed Play.

"Even prisoners get conjugal visits," Molly said.

"Sshh! The movie's starting."

On the TV screen, the credits faded in and out as a woman gazed out her window at smears of red and yellow lights on the rain-slick streets of Mumbai. "Time waits for no one," the woman said, turning away from the window to consider her empty, untouched bed before bursting into song. It seemed like a cosmic conspiracy was afoot. I'd not yet realized that all Bollywood films have the same plot.

"Why don't you ask Michael to Leilani's masquerade party?" *Mami* said. "It's not a big deal. He's your friend."

"Okay, okay," I said. "Whatever you say. Wow, I *love* this song!" I figured I could conveniently forget to invite him to the party.

"Have you got a costume figured out yet?" *Mami* whispered.

I put my finger to my lips and shook my head no, pretending to be engrossed in the movie. On the screen, the woman was now wearing a gold and crimson sari. She was dancing on a rooftop with a man, surrounded by about a hundred backup dancers. All I could think was, if I took Michael to the party, he would probably think it was a date.

*   *   *

I drove Molly down to San Diego the next day. She planned to come back up for Leilani's party, but until then, it was time for her to go home for a while. A long drive was a perfect plan because earlier that morning, I had dyed my hair back to brown and left the dye in a little too long. It looked chalky and too dark. It would be okay after a few shampoos, but for now, I didn't want to be seen in public. After everything we'd been through with Irena, I didn't want to be a redhead anymore. It reminded me of her, but it wasn't only that. I always looked at changing my hair color as beginning a new chapter of my life, and the time was ripe for it to happen. I felt restless.

"Did you ask Michael to the party yet?" Molly asked me.

"Um, no," I said.

"What are you waiting for? The day of the party, so he'll be busy?"

"No! I just…haven't gotten around to it yet."

"There's no time like the present!" She'd taken my phone out of its pocket in my purse and was scrolling through my contacts.

I grabbed at the phone. "Molly! What are you doing?"

She dodged my grasp and held the phone down low by the door. "I'm looking for Michael's number, of course. I know he's on your speed dial. Why don't you make it easy and tell me which number he is? I can just call him on my phone if you're going to be difficult."

In my most authoritative voice I said, "Molly, step away from the phone."

She didn't buy it. "There he is." She pushed a button and held the phone to her ear, then thrust it at my head.

I snatched the phone from her to kill the call, but heard Michael's voice.

"Hello? Lola?"

Freaking caller ID. I thought about driving into a tree, but that would kill me as well as Molly. "Michael, hi," I said. "Um, how are you?"

"Good," he said. "You?"

"Great," I said. "Yeah, never better. Now that I'm free and everything. You know."

"Good, good. So, what's up?" he asked.

"Um...I...well. I don't know."

Molly said loudly, "You want me to ask him?"

"Sshhh!"

"I didn't say anything," Michael said.

"Not you, sorry." I flashed Molly the evil eye. "Um, actually, I wondered if you'd maybe like to come to a party with me."

Silence.

"At Leilani's," I added.

All I heard was rustling and muffled talk.

Then he said, "Sorry, somebody had a question for me. What did you say?"

It was like some kind of torture. I wondered for a second if he and Molly had arranged this phone call.

"Lola?"

"Yep. I'm here."

"You know there's nobody I'd rather talk to, but I'm kind of busy right now. What's up?"

That was a nice thing for him to say. It bolstered my courage. "Do you want to come to a party at Leilani's with me?"

"A party? Sure."

I could hear him smile through the phone.

"It's not for a couple weeks," I said. "It's a costume party, so...you'd have to wear a costume. Is that okay?"

"Yeah, sure. I mean, I don't have to be the back end of a horse or anything, right?"

I laughed. "No! You can be whatever you want."

"Shouldn't we, you know, coordinate?"

"Um, okay. I hadn't thought about it, but I guess that's a good idea."

"Well, think about it and we'll talk. I have to get back to work, okay?"

"Okay." I hit End.

Molly said, "Now, that wasn't so bad, was it?"

"Yes, it was," I said. But I couldn't stop smiling.

CHAPTER 48

When we got to San Diego, I skirted the harbor where Jack used to keep the *Alouette*. The mooring ball had not yet taken on a new tenant, surprisingly. It bobbed alone on the water like a beach ball waiting for someone to come play with it.

"Want to walk down there?" I'd forgotten all about my hair.

"Sure," Molly said. We found a parking space and walked down to the dock.

"I can't help but feel I've let everyone down," I said.

"What are you talking about?" Molly said. "You busted the Russian mafia and solved two murders, including your client's!"

"But, Molly, I accomplished neither one of the things I was hired to do. I was supposed to find evidence Jack was murdered, which I didn't find, and the lost will, which I also didn't find." We got to the top of the metal ramp, opened the gate, and headed down.

"If Jack wasn't murdered, you can't prove he was."

"I know, but I wish I'd at least found the will. Not that it matters anymore, not to Linda, anyway. It's the principle of the thing."

At the bottom of the ramp, we stood on the concrete dock with the water rolling beneath it, bobbing up and down like a giant sleeping dog.

"Look!" I pointed. Tied up to the side of the dock like a faithful horse was Jack's little blue buddy. "*Rosebud*!"

I phoned Barnaby Watts. He was on his boat. He came out on the deck with the phone at his ear, and we waved at each other.

"Hey, *Rosebud* is back," I said.

"Yep, I know," Barnaby said. "Turns out some homeless guy was living on her. Coast Guard popped him." He laughed. "He tried to sell 'em a story that some lady gave it to him, but they didn't buy it."

"Some lady? Do you know the story?"

"Yep. He said a tall, drop-dead gorgeous redhead told him he could have it. Hey, wait a minute…that wasn't you, was it?"

I snorted. "Me? I'm certainly not…um…tall. Is this guy in jail now?"

"Been and gone. Only got three days. Good deal for him…at least he got three squares while he was in there."

"I guess. Listen, I know this'll sound awful, but I want to take *Rosebud's* seats off." This was no hunch, just a possibility. "Do you have any power tools I could borrow? A driver?"

"Yeah. But you could just pry 'em up with a crowbar."

"I know, but I want to put them back on right. Can you help me out?"

Minutes later, Barnaby came gliding over in his dinghy, leaving a long, S-shaped line on the water. He hoisted a toolbox up onto the dock and then himself, and threw open the toolbox.

"Hey, you changed your hair!" he said.

"Oh. Yeah."

"I liked it red." He handed me the driver.

"Thanks." At least he was honest. I climbed into *Rosebud*. Right away I knew this search would be fruitless. The seat boards and screws were old. Had he hidden his will under one of the seats, Jack would've taken them off and put them back on fairly recently. These screws didn't look like they had budged within the last decade, even given that the salt water of the bay weathered things rapidly. On top of that, I could see it would be a challenge to remove the boards without splitting them.

I took off the seat in *Rosebud's* stern, and the wood did split a little. There was nothing under the seat. Then I tried the triangular seat at the bow. Again, nothing. The center seat was a plank with no compartment under it. So that was that.

"I thought the will might be on *Rosebud*," I said, "just because she was missing."

"Maybe it was in here and somebody already got to it," Molly said.

"Yeah, sure." If that were true, the factors concerning the wood and screws still applied, and I saw no evidence of it. I didn't say that to Molly, though, just put everything back together without another word. I was out of ideas. Jack's will was last seen on the *Alouette*, and it had most likely blown up along with her.

I took Molly to her place. Her car was still orange, her sign was still broken; everything was in order. But her stacks of newspapers annoyed her. She kept telling them to get out of her way. When she started moving them outside the door, I helped her, and pretty soon we had cleared a big space around the table. Once she found the phone, we ordered pizza. After lunch, we said a slightly tearful goodbye, and I headed back up to LA.

All the way back, I kept thinking there must be something I missed. I went through events in my head, but came up with nothing. I flipped on the radio. It was choked with loud commercials, so I knew it was on AM. I was about to turn it to FM when I heard a familiar voice. It was Clay Parker. He was doing a spot for his upcoming show, which I'd forgotten all about.

That's when I remembered I'd never gone back to listen to the rest of the tapes.

CHAPTER 49

When I got back to the City of Angels, I shampooed my hair twice and super-conditioned it. Then I headed for KFX to listen to some more of the *Clay Parker Show* archives. I'd just settled in when my phone rang. It was Michael.

"Have you given any thought to this costume business?" he asked.

"Actually, I haven't. I'm still obsessing on finding Jack Stone's will."

"Baby, that will is gone."

"Yeah, I know it probably blew up with the boat. But *Rosebud* was gone, too, and she's turned up again."

"Yeah? Maybe the will's on *Rosebud*."

"Nope, I tried that."

"Well, if anyone can find it, you will," he said.

"Thanks," I said.

"Maybe we should just surprise each other."

"Huh?"

"The costumes."

"That could be tricky," I said. "What if I'm, say, a bunch of grapes and you're a fox?"

"Woof," he said. "I'm not touching that one. But, please, don't be a bunch of grapes. Wear something sexy. I mean, pretty."

Revelation. He definitely thought it was a date. Of course he did. It was, I had to admit, a date. There was no other way to look at it. I was heading straight into enemy territory.

"Um, I have to go," I said.

"So, are we going to just surprise each other?"

"Yeah, sure. Just...please, don't turn up as Superman. I had enough of men in tights back in my Ren Faire days."

I turned my attention back to the tapes and went through them in succession. Jack Stone was so popular they had keyworded his name for use in filing and cross-referencing, so it was easy to pick out the shows he was on. I listened to them in chronological order.

In his final call, about a month before his death, he sounded like he had been drinking. His words were slightly slurred and uneven.

———

"Caller, you have the *Clay Parker Show*."

"Jack Stone here. How ya doing, Clay?"

"Great, Jack. What've you been up to?"

"I've been looking at patterns. And currents. You know the oceans are rising?"

"O-oh, yes, they most certainly are. Heard from your sister lately?"

"My sister. I wish I could just let the whole thing go. I really do. I'm sick of thinking about her. Honestly, I think she's driving me a little crazy."

"Could be the bottle talking to you, not your sister."

"Nah, it's her. She never stops. I shouldn't have gone looking for her 'cause now she's haunting me. She never, ever shuts up."

"Oh, now that's very interesting. So you've contacted a ghost, and now you can't get rid of her."

"Right. A ghost that never shuts up. And everything I do is wrong."

"Sounds more like a wife."

"I don't know how much more I can take. If you don't hear from me, you'll know why."

"I will? Why?"

"Because she keeps trying to get me to kill myself, telling me ways to do it. If you don't hear from me, it'll mean she finally killed me from beyond the grave. By my own hand."

"Uh...well, I certainly hope not. Thank you, Mr. Jack Stone. I have to break for a commercial now. I wish you the very best of luck. Please hang in there, and keep us posted."

———

Jack sounded like he was losing it, as well as drinking heavily. He'd said "the whole thing." That must've been a reference to Linda blackmailing him, asking for more and more money, with no end in sight. That and the guilt of having killed Vanessa could drive a man to suicide. I'd seen firsthand how some people could have such a deep sense of guilt that they would agonize over their smallest dishonesties, while other, fortunately rarer, people had no conscience at all, and even their most extreme acts of betrayal left them unmoved.

I was convinced—Jack did kill himself. What I couldn't understand was why, when he planned to do it, he hadn't left the will someplace where it would be found. Okay, he probably didn't expect Irena to blow up the *Alouette*. Still, I couldn't accept it as over. Logic be damned; my gut told me the will was still out there somewhere.

*   *   *

The day of the Leilani's masquerade party came. I still hadn't found Jack's will, but I had managed to rent a costume. I was going as a flamenco dancer. The dress was red and black, with layers of ruffled skirts that were short in the front and long in back. It had a black lace *mantilla* with it and a little black mask. I fell in love with it the minute I saw it in the shop.

I picked Molly up at the train station around noon. She had her costume with her, but wouldn't tell me what it was.

"I want you to be surprised," she said.

"What about this date of yours? Where is he meeting us?"

"He's meeting us in Malibu. He says he lives in Brentwood, but he knows Malibu well."

"Brentwood!" I snorted. "Are you kidding me? What does he do?"

"He's an actor," she said.

"An actor? Where do you know this guy from?"

"I met him on the Internet."

"Molly! The Internet?"

"People get together online all the time."

"Sure. People *lie* online all the time, too. Brentwood? An actor? Come on!"

"Now, don't be silly. Are you going to be paranoid all night? Because I'd like to have a good time."

"Okay, okay! Never mind. But—"

"What is it?"

"You did tell him it's a costume party?"

"Oh, I told him. He said he'd bring something from some film wardrobe, so it should be a good one."

"Unless he comes as a wookie."

We went to *Mami's,* and she made us lunch. Then *Mami* and I went upstairs to her bedroom, and she helped me with my costume. Molly wanted to surprise us both and went in the den to change. I was dying of curiosity, both about her costume and her date.

When I was ready, we called downstairs to Molly.

"I'm ready! Come on down," she yelled.

Molly stood in the den decked out in a gorgeous black and silver vintage nineteen-thirties evening gown, with a wisp of silver scarf around her shoulders and her hair swept up.

"Molly, you look beautiful," I said.

"Breathtaking!" *Mami* said.

"Billie Holiday," she said. "Always wanted to be her for a day. You look gorgeous, Lola!"

Things got squeaky at that point. The party didn't start for hours, but I had a lot of running around to do. *Mami* took pictures of us, then we did some errands and by the time we wound up at my place, it was almost time to leave. Half an hour later, we were on our way to Leilani's. We would pick up the guys on the way.

Michael lived in Santa Monica. I stood outside his door at the precise moment I'd said I would pick him up, rang the bell, and called him on my cell. He answered the phone.

"You ready? I'm outside," I said.

"Are you grapes?" he asked.

The door opened and there stood Michael, looking hotter than ever, dressed as Zorro, the fox, entirely in black clothes and hat, with his cell phone in hand. Our costumes went together perfectly. He looked me over. A salad of surprise, delight, and lust tossed in his eyes.

"We were made for each other," he said. He pushed the End button on his phone with his thumb. "You look beautiful." He pecked my cheek in an intimate way that made me blush. "And I like your hair this color."

"Thanks. So, you're the fox after all!"

"Just in case. I thought it was a good idea."

"You look great."

"Thanks. I thought about going as Lex Luthor."

"You made the right choice. Are you ready to go?"

He held up one finger, ducked behind the door for a second, and came out with a sword and a black silk mask. The sword was big, and it looked real. He slid it into its scabbard, and we slipped into the night beneath a rising opalescent moon.

"Is that thing real?" I asked.

"Only the real thing for me, baby," he said. "But don't worry; it won't hurt you."

We headed up the PCH to Malibu.

CHAPTER 50

"We're meeting him at a *gas station?*" I said.

"What's wrong with that?" Molly asked. "If you needed gas you'd think it was okay."

"But why? Why are we meeting him at a gas station?"

"We're meeting him at a gas station because it's easy to find. It's right on the PCH. Maybe he thought it would make things easier for us. Maybe he's being considerate."

"Or maybe he's homeless," I said. "Libraries have computers, you know. What do you even know about this guy?"

"He's thirty-something, from New York, and his name is Donald. He's been married before and has four kids."

"Busy guy," Michael said.

"He's been in a lot of movies, too," she said.

"Really? What movies?" he asked.

"He was in *Bachelor Party Mardi Gras* and *Uptown Chicks.*"

"Those sound like porn movies," I said.

"I've seen the first one. It's not a porn movie," Michael said. "It's a comedy."

"He said he was in a movie called *Huge Fat Liar*, too," Molly said.

"I'll bet he starred in that one," I said.

"He's been on TV a lot, too," Molly said. "He's a fine-looking man. He sent me a picture."

"Do you really believe all that?" I asked. "The picture is probably fake, too."

"Why shouldn't I believe it?" Molly said. "You don't know that it *isn't* true. You don't believe anything!"

That shut me up. I didn't want to get into how cynical and paranoid I was again, so I quietly headed for the Chevron station a little before Malibu Canyon to meet Donald. I figured maybe the guy wouldn't even show up, but didn't want Molly to be disappointed.

When we got there, a man was standing by the doors. He was African-American, with close-cut hair, wearing a white dinner jacket and bowtie, and holding a trumpet.

"That's him," Molly said.

"Go, Molly!" I said. He looked good, very good. He also looked quite a bit younger than Molly. "Um…what did you tell him about yourself?" I asked.

"I know what you're getting at," she said. "And yes, I told him ahead of time that I was going to be Billie Holiday."

Molly slid out of the car and went over to greet her mystery date. They talked for a minute, then came over and crammed into the backseat of my car. Molly's date held the trumpet across his lap. It was then that I recognized him. He was one of the stars of my favorite TV show, a comedy about medical students and the hijinks they get up to in the hospital.

"Oh! You're really him," I said, brilliantly. I felt so relieved for Molly.

"Yes, I am really me," he said. "But tonight, you can call me Satchmo."

At Leilani's house, the gate was open and already a sea of parked cars had inundated the grounds. Anyone in a hurry to leave would be out of luck. A Philippino valet in a red vest and white shirt came to the car window.

He smiled. "Good evening, ma'am. May I take care of your car?"

I handed him the keys, and we all got out and followed a trail of lanterns up the driveway.

The house smelled like cinnamon and was lavishly decorated in black and gold, with ring-wraiths on rearing black horses from *The Lord of the Rings* positioned around the ballroom. They looked like film props, and probably were, contrasting strangely with the ever-present dolphins. A band that consisted entirely of vampires was playing a medley of Danny Elfman songs. I scanned the room for Leilani, but didn't see her.

222

Movie stars were abundant among the crowd. Their costumes were all gorgeous, but none of them wore masks, probably in case of photo-ops. I spotted every one of the hot couples of the moment: Mila and Ashton, Blake and Ryan, and Shakira and Gerard, to name a few.

Donald swept Molly onto the dance floor. The party was so full of people, I wondered if we'd ever see them again. Michael took me into his arms and grinned. "Want to dance?" he asked. I went stiff as a corpse.

"Um, let's have a drink first," I said.

"Okay."

Costumed people stood in clusters around a table laden with champagne and glasses. A tanned, college-age surfer girl behind the table kept the bottles and ice buckets replenished. We picked up filled glasses.

I clinked glasses with Michael. "Happy Halloween!" I may have been a little nervous. I downed the bubbly like a shot, then grabbed another glass.

"Have you eaten?" Michael asked.

"Uh-huh," I said.

"Good. There's some food over there, though, if you get hungry." He nodded at a food table a few feet away.

"Great." I looked over at it as I sucked down more champagne. Then I saw what he was getting at and sipped the rest. A pirate came over next to us to get a drink. He had dark eyes with tons of eyeliner and long, dark hair. He looked awfully familiar.

"The costumes here are amazing," I said, sipping the last of my champagne.

The pirate slurred, "Arrgh! They be plunder from films." He sounded sloshed already. I thought, Some people just don't know when they've had enough, and plucked another glass.

A woman walked up to the pirate and poured herself over him. She babbled to him in messy French and pulled him away from the table to dance. A zombie and a banshee walked over and took drinks.

The banshee living up to its reputation for being loud, yelling, "You know what Bogey's last words were? 'I should never have switched from Scotch to martinis.'"

Laughter erupted from everyone in earshot.

"Ever heard Ed Gwenn's?" asked the zombie. "'Dying is tough, but not as tough as comedy.'"

Everybody laughed and laughed. Comedy didn't look so tough to me.

"Come on. Let's dance," Michael said, and he wasn't taking no for an answer this time. He took the glass from my hand, set it on the table, and whirled me onto the dance floor. The band was good, and soon we were having a blast. After three numbers that really rocked, they played a slow one, and a lot of people left the dance floor. Michael wanted to dance the slow one. It was nice, floating around the floor…no murders, no death.

When that song ended, the band asked if anyone wanted to come up and sing a song with them. The drummer spotted Molly.

"Hey, Billie Holiday," he called to her, "can you sing?"

"A little," she said.

"Well, come on up here and sing us one!"

Everyone cheered her on, and within seconds, Molly was up on the stage. She sang "God Bless the Child." She must have channeled Billie Holiday's ghost because she was fantastic and got roaring applause.

After that, we danced some more until the band took a break.

"Let's go outside," I said. "I love the grounds here. Have you seen them?" We went through the doors to the gardens.

"A little," he said. "Mostly I've seen the garage."

And then I had a hunch. It was as clear as someone tapping me on the shoulder. It's hard facts that put a detective's dinner on the table, but so often it's the hunch that gets them in your sights so you can hunt them down. I had a hunch about the garage.

"Oh! I've always wanted to have a look at that garage," I said. How many people have always wanted to see a garage? Any garage. Especially on a date. But Michael was a cop. He would understand. "Come on!" I said, pulling him by the hand. He didn't protest.

The garage stood closed, with cars parked in front of it.

"There's a side door," Michael said and led me to it, around a corner. It was unlocked. We walked into darkness. There were windows, but not much light came through them. I felt for a wall switch by the door and flipped on the light. There sat Jack's bright red Ferrari Enzo.

"How big is the gas tank on that thing?" I asked.

"Twenty-eight point five-three gallons," Michael said.

"That's a lot."

"It has to have a good-size tank; it only gets about eight miles per gallon. It's a twelve cylinder. That car goes from zero to sixty in three-point-two seconds."

"Impressive. And I'm sure you guys did the math on the size of this garage and how long it would take to fill up with carbon monoxide."

"Sure," he said. "With his tank full, he just made it. A lot of suicides don't realize what it takes with a car with a catalytic converter. It takes a lot longer to build up enough carbon monoxide to kill you, especially in a garage this size."

I sighed. Jack killed himself, end of story. Sometimes, hunches could be wrong.

"Hey, can we talk about something else besides work?" Michael put his arm around me and turned me toward him. "Or better yet, let's not talk at all." He leaned toward me.

"Michael...here?" I squirmed away from him.

"What's the matter? Want me to turn off the light?"

"Oh, God, no; it's way too dark in here." I gasped. "Wait! Michael! It is. You can't see a thing in here with the light off. Look!" I snapped the switch off, and we stood in the dark.

And in that darkness, he saw what I was driving at. I could almost hear his brain ticking. He was thinking exactly what I was thinking.

I flipped the light back on and put it into words. "Leilani came home that night at two in the morning. The power to the garage was completely shut off. How could she possibly have read the note? How could she even have found it on the floor of the car?"

"She must've found him earlier, much earlier, when there was still light," Michael said. Then he made an abrupt, harsh grunt.

"Put your hands where I can see them," a voice behind us said.

Michael raised his hands in the air. I did the same. I looked sideways at him and saw the barrel of a gun against his ribs.

I knew that voice. It was Leilani's.

CHAPTER 51

"That's the last time I invite you to a party, Lola," Leilani said. "Couldn't you have just let it go?"

"I've never been any good at that," I said. I turned a little so I could see her. The sight of her was a mild shock; she was dressed as Marie Antoinette. Her hair and skirt were huge, an excellent choice for her full hips. "Love your costume, by the way," I said.

"Thanks," she said. "Look, if Jack—or anyone—wants to kill himself, who am I to stop him? It's obviously what he wanted. He shut the garage door, snuggled up in his favorite car, with his favorite Scotch, and wrote us a note to say goodbye. Then he turned on the ignition and fell asleep, expecting never to wake up again. That was his choice! The genius just forgot to make sure his tank was full first. Oz had sneaked the car out for a drive the night before, so the tank was half empty."

"So you helped him," I said.

"Yes," she confessed. "He tried and almost did it. He was passed out, but he still had a strong pulse. I went down and got more gas and put it in his tank. I had to make two trips! And with a truly hideous brown scarf over my face, I might add, or I might've gone bye-bye, too."

"Wow! That was so nice of you," I said. "I don't suppose it crossed your mind that he might just need some counseling?"

"Look; it's over and done with. I've forgiven myself."

"So, you're both an altruistic and forgiving person," Michael said. "You're practically a saint."

"And what did you do with the will? Burn it?" I asked.

"I don't know anything about the will," she said.

"Oh, come on!" I said. "It's driving me crazy trying to figure out where it is."

"I know nothing about it. Really, that's the truth. Now, come on. Let's go for a ride in your car."

She took a step back and waved us in front of her with the gun.

I flashed Michael a slow-motion blink and darted my eyes at the wall switch to signal what I was about to do. As we turned, our hands in the air, I flipped the light switch down with my elbow.

Darkness. Leilani screamed. I twisted and dived at where I thought Leilani's feet should be. My hands found fabric; I clenched it and pulled with all my might. Someone tugged on me, hard. I heard something rip amid the scuffling, grunts, and screams, but had no idea what was going on. I felt for the handrail, hooked an elbow over it, and kicked out blindly.

"Ow!" It was Michael.

"Sorry!" I cried and stopped kicking.

Leilani gave a shrill scream. I could hear Michael and Leilani struggling. The gun scudded along the floor. Both their heads slammed sharply into my stomach, and I doubled over. My face pushed into something like cotton candy, which I shoved up off my face so I could breathe.

Michael yelled, "I've got her!"

I pulled myself along the handrail, felt for the wall switch and snapped the light back on. We all blinked. My *mantilla* was on the ground, trampled, and Leilani's gigantic white wig sat on my head. Michael was holding onto Leilani by one wrist and one ankle, and his mask was bunched up around Leilani's foot. I looked down at my hand and realized I was holding a handful of red satin and black lace. I had ripped off a long swath of my own skirt.

"I guess Marie Antoinette lost her head," I said, then snatched the wig off my head and stuck it back on hers.

Michael pulled a pair of handcuffs from some unknown depth of his costume and clamped Leilani to the leg of a workbench. As a final touch, he stood back, unsheathed his sword and traced a "Z" in the air over her big skirt.

I tugged my phone from the ruffles of my skirt and called LAPD. The gun was several feet away on the garage floor. For once, I didn't touch it. The trip to Leilani's place took the police five minutes. Getting up her driveway took them twenty.

The party soon broke up and scattered as the better-known celebs escaped ahead of the arriving paparazzi and the less well-known ones positioned themselves in front of cameras.

Leilani held up her fist and yelled, "Right to die!" to the news cameras, glowing with moral indignation, as the police led her away.

Molly and Donald snaked their way toward us through cars and past police as they were hauling Leilani away.

"What happened?" Molly cried.

Michael said, "Marie Antoinette lost her head."

"Hey, that's my joke," I said.

He laughed, hooked an arm around my waist and looked me dead in the eye. It was one of those mongoose and cobra moments. I couldn't seem to unlock my eyes from his. He leaned in like he was going to kiss me, and my reflexes kicked in. Instinctively, I dodged it with what must have looked like a full-body spasm. As I jerked, what was left of my skirt caught on Michael's sword and the rest of it ripped away. I was wearing a scarlet satin Victoria's Secret thong I had splurged on that afternoon. What little fabric there was to it now matched the color of my face. I'd never regretted a lingerie decision so much in my life. I buried my face in my hands and backed away from Michael.

"This must be one of those accidents our mamas warned us about," Molly said, wrapping her silver scarf around me for cover. My violent reaction had surprised even me, but I figured, if my instinct to keep Michael away was that strong, we would certainly be better off just staying friends.

Michael insisted on driving home. We all crammed ourselves into my car and went to Donald's place. In Brentwood. It was still pretty early.

Molly held up a bottle of wine sporting an orange and black bow. "Let's open this!"

"Where'd you get that?" I asked.

"Some pirate gave it to me just as we were leaving," she said. "I'm surprised it isn't rum. He said he liked my song."

Donald took the bottle and looked at the label. He said, "This is a 1955 Tuscan Biondi-Santi. Not a bad haul." He opened it and poured us all glasses.

"To Jack Stone," Molly said.

"To Jack," everyone said, and we all clinked glasses. I gulped my wine. I'd been feeling I needed a drink since the whole Leilani thing, and that had been at least an hour ago.

"That's really good," I said, drinking some more.

"Oh, you don't want to gulp that," Donald said. That's a four-thousand-dollar bottle of wine."

I almost spit my wine. "You're kidding?"

"No, I'm not kidding." He turned to Molly and put an arm around her shoulder. "You know who that pirate was, don't you?"

"No, but he sure did look familiar," she said. "Lola, that wasn't your ex?"

"You're kidding, right? Although, he was in the same movies as my ex. But he had a much better part."

"That was Captain Jack Sparrow himself," Donald said.

"You mean that was…"

"Yep."

"Wow," Molly said, "a real pirate!"

We all groaned with disbelief. Molly had spent too much time with the dead and not enough with life. All I could think was, why would a guy with a vineyard in France give Molly an Italian wine?

CHAPTER 52

Molly hung around LA for a few days before I drove her down to San Diego. I had just pulled into her parking lot and shut off the engine. Below the stone and glass forest of office and condo towers, San Diego Bay shimmered in the sunlight and sailboats rocked gently in the harbor. I'd been mentally reviewing the case, pondering the bigger picture.

"Molly, you and I are not so different," I said. "I follow instincts I can't see, but they're as real as you are sitting next to me. I don't understand what you do, but I'd be the last person to call you a fake."

"Thanks," she said. "I wouldn't mind trying something different now, though. It might be time for me to move on from...all this." She swept her arm out to take in the urban parking lot, former gas station, and broken sign that comprised her small empire.

"Yeah? What are you thinking?"

"Donald knows a lot of musicians. He said he could get me some gigs up in LA."

"Singing? Wow! That would be great!" I leaned over and gave her a big hug. "I'd love it if you lived up there! But could you make a living at it?"

"Oh, I don't need the money. My husband left me pretty well off. I just haven't wanted to do much but talk to him for so long. I haven't wanted to move on, but now I think I might be ready. Think you could help me move when I find a place?"

"You bet I could. I'll help you look for a place, too."

"Let's get some LA papers and start looking," she said.

I started to pull out, but Molly pointed out a 7-11 right across the street, so we walked over. I picked up the *Sun* and Molly grabbed an *LA Times*.

Before she even unpacked her clothes, we made coffee, pulled the newspapers apart, and sprawled them all over the kitchen table. An item on the front of the *Times* weekend section caught my eye.

"Molly! Look at this," I said and showed her the picture.

It was a photo entitled Message in a Bottle and showed a little Asian girl on a beach, smiling and holding up a wine bottle. A caption appeared beside the photo.

———

Sienna Stone, adopted daughter of film legend Jack Stone, with the bottle she found washed up on Malibu Beach yesterday morning, on what happened to be her seventh birthday. The bottle has captured the imagination of local residents because of the as yet unopened message it contains. Sienna plans to open the bottle at sunset this Sunday, on the beach where she found it.

———

"Isn't that Jack's kid?" she asked.

"Sure is. What a cool thing to find. She's going to open it in three days. I'd like to go on Sunday and see what's in it."

"You're the person who busted her mama! I wouldn't go near the place," Molly said.

"That's not fair," I said. "Leilani got herself busted. She probably could've gotten away with what she did if she hadn't pulled a gun on Michael and me and tried to kill us! For crying out loud, she could've just lied and said she had a flashlight on her when she found him. Talk about a genius!"

"I know. I was just messing with you," Molly said.

I rolled up some newspaper and threw it at her head. Molly's squeak when the paper hit made me think. "I wonder what Leilani's dolphins think of her behavior," I said.

*   *   *

The next day, I had a call from Jack's alpha attorney, J.M. Klein.

"Ms. Vega, I heard about your crucial role in the Jack Stone investigation. Very impressive. Well done."

"Thank you very much, Mr. Klein. I didn't realize it had gotten around that much."

"Oh, we hear everything over here," Klein said. "Any chance you'd be interested in practicing law again?"

"Have you heard somewhere I was interested?"

"No, I didn't mean that." He chuckled. "Jack Stone was my client for many years. I've rarely heard of such persistence as you displayed in solving the puzzle of his death. Ms. Vega, what you did was extraordinary. I think we could use someone like you here at Bishop, Sigorsky, and Klein."

"That's very kind of you, sir."

"I'm prepared to make you an offer only a damned fool would refuse."

"Oh, Mr. Klein, thank you, but I haven't even been thinking about going back to practicing law."

"Now, hear me out. I'm prepared to offer you a full partnership and everything that comes with it."

"I don't know what to say."

"You don't have to decide right now. Just tell me you'll think about it. I'll call you back in, say…a week? Long enough?"

"Yes, all right, that would be fine."

"Great. Talk to you in a week. Partner."

Just when you think there are no more surprises.

CHAPTER 53

Sunday, late in the afternoon, I put on my blonde wig and a pair of sunglasses and went up to Malibu Beach incognito. Michael went with me, wearing a hat and sunglasses. We wanted to see little Sienna open the bottle. City of angels, city of dreams; like everybody else in this town, we were dying to know what was in that bottle.

Sienna stood on the beach with her brothers, their nanny, Jennifer, and an aunt and uncle. Dreamers and media people crowded the beach.

Sienna said, "On the day I found this bottle, I attained the age of reason. But I vow never to forget the wonders of childhood."

A little over the top. She was Jack Stone's kid, all right.

She went on, "It is with a sense of wonder that I open this bottle today. May it bring that wonder alive in all our hearts."

A hush fell as she worked at the cork, which looked only halfway in, rocking it back and forth. The cork had been thoroughly sealed with wax or something waterproof. Finally, the girl's uncle pulled a corkscrew from his pocket and used it on the bottle. He left the cork in just a little bit so the girl could be the one to pull it out.

Sienna pulled out the cork, but then couldn't get the paper out. Her uncle poked something into the bottle to grab hold of it, but couldn't get it. He ended up bashing the bottle against the inside of a trash bin until it broke, and then picking the paper out from the broken glass. He handed it to the girl to a hefty round of applause. Things don't always go as planned.

Sienna unrolled the paper. She looked at it intently for a moment, struggling to read it, but she couldn't make out the handwriting. So, she handed it to her uncle, who looked at it intently for a few more seconds. The uncle gasped. With a shocked expression, he turned the paper around and showed it to the world.

"It's the will," he cried. "It's Jack's will!"

The crowd went wild. People hugged each other and cried. A man let go a bunch of red balloons, and we watched them float away into the sunset. Jennifer had a huge, genuine smile on her face. A dance party broke out on the beach and continued until Sienna and her siblings were eventually whisked away, waving to the cheering crowd.

I thought about the "Away" file, with all its charts of currents and tides and dates and groaned loudly. Jack must have known Sienna would come to the beach on her birthday. "Where there's 'Away' there's a will," I said to Michael. "I should've known!"

"Nobody would've gotten that," Michael said, taking my hand in his. "Only a dreamer like Jack could've ever imagined it would work."

"And it did. How perfectly Jack Stone—brilliant and spectacular. Truly an amazing guy."

"Among other things: romantic, heroic, homicidal, suicidal. A walking contradiction."

As I gazed out at the great blue Pacific, trying to imagine what it would be like to be Jack, a thought popped into my head. Or maybe it was a phone call from the other side. "I think I know what Jack was counting when he died!" Unexpected tears filled my eyes. "I think he was counting the people who loved him."

After the dancing faded, the whole scene turned into a spontaneous wake for Jack, and made a nice final sendoff. Later, Michael and I walked down the beach away from the crowd to have a picnic dinner. All I could think was, were we still just friends, or was this our third date?

CHAPTER 54

We hung around the beach for hours, like I usually did only on vacation. The moon was a new, pointy crescent in the black, star-dotted sky, and a soft warm breeze blew in off the desert to fly to the ocean. We stood at the water's edge. I turned to Michael and found him looking at me. I had to squint to be sure, but yes, the glimmer two feet away from me was his eyes. They made me feel warm and a little giddy.

If it hadn't been so dark out, if gentle waves hadn't been whispering suggestive things to the sand, if I hadn't failed utterly to cure myself of speaking without thinking first, I never would have blurted out my next words. But I did. I said, "Do you think there's something going on with us? I mean, maybe there's some chemistry?"

"There's one way to know for sure," he said, moving toward me.

Before I had time to think, he pulled me close and kissed me. Sparks did fly, and they were trailing from skyrockets. His lips were soft on mine, and I wanted more and more. When we came up for air, I felt like the tide had rushed in, spun us in an eddy, then carried us back to where we stood. Oh yes, there was chemistry.

He scooped me up in the air and his hands discovered my thong and all that it revealed. Never had I been happier about a lingerie decision. I wrapped myself around him and we made love on the sand under the stars. When we were finally spent, the only sound in the world was the waves softly lapping the shore. They seemed to be sighing and asking for a light.

I said, "It's been a long time since I made love on the beach!"

"Really?" he said. That's all, just "really."

Instantly, the doubts jammed themselves into my brain. I propped myself on an elbow. "What do you mean, 'really'? I guess you do it all the time, huh?"

He laughed. "Molly's right about you. You are paranoid."

"Michael!"

"No, I did not mean that I do it all the time."

"What did you mean?"

"Nothing. Just 'really.'"

I rolled onto my back, not sure what to think. Then I jumped up and started putting my clothes on.

"Hey, come on," Michael said.

"Somebody could see us here."

"It's pitch black! And tomorrow's Monday. Everybody's home in bed."

I said nothing. It was true we hadn't seen anyone in about four hours, but I didn't want to feel naked right then.

Michael put his clothes on, too. Then he reached for me and kissed me again, and I wasn't going anywhere. Yet.

"Lola, why are you so suspicious of me?"

"This was a mistake, wasn't it?" I started pulling away.

"Why are you saying that?" Michael looked me in the eye.

"Because we have a professional relationship, and I don't want to screw that up. We probably should've kept it all business."

"Well, it's too late to change that now. We've already anted up. It'd be pretty lame to fold before we even play our hands."

"Of course, you'd use a game analogy," I said. "It's things like that that make you seem like such a player."

"There's the suspicion again. This isn't going to work if you can't trust me."

I looked away. "I guess I'm just afraid you're playing with my heart, and you'll toss me away when you're done with me."

"Wow!" He took me by the arms and made me look him in the eye. "Is that who you think I am?" His nostrils flared, but on him it looked hot.

Once again, I had let my mouth run ahead of my brain. But it was honest. "No. Oh, I don't know. That story about you and Valerie Farrell is like a legend now. I don't know what to think."

"Do you want to hear my side of it?" He was getting all worked up. He jammed his hands in his pockets and took a breath to hold onto his temper. "Valerie was having a thing with her partner off and on for years, including while we were together. And he was married. When I found out, I broke it off with her. I didn't talk about it because I didn't want it to get back to the guy's wife and maybe break up his family. Valerie went nuts. She started following me around, going through my trash, spreading lies about me." He kicked the sand.

"She stalked you?" This was even better than the gossip version, far more twisted. But—ugh!—I wouldn't be able to tell anyone for the same reason as Michael.

"That part you can check out. I had to get a restraining order on her. The department had to transfer her or she'd have ended up losing her job. Or doing something stupid."

"Wow!" I said, briefly wondering if I were unstable enough to end up, a year from now, following Michael around the city or going through his garbage at night with a flashlight, feeling I'd struck gold on finding a discarded photo or receipt. I decided, probably not.

"What do you think?" Michael asked.

"I can't believe Valerie Farrell's a bunny boiler!"

"She didn't go that far."

"She didn't have far to go." I went to him and slid my arms through his. "I'm sorry you went through all that. It sounds awful."

"Really?" He took his hands from his pockets and held me close.

"Really," I said. "See, I knew what that one meant." I nestled into his arms, feeling a surprising emotion called hope.

"So, are we going to give this thing a chance?" he asked me.

"I trust you with my heart. Let's give it a shot," I said. "But please, you must promise never to call me Lois Lane."

CHAPTER 55

The next day, Michael was off, and since I made my own hours, we slept off and on, among other things, through most of the day. Later, we ate dinner out, and after that, each of us went home. We had been together for almost twenty-four hours by then. The last couple of days had been almost unreal, in a wonderful way, but I wanted some time to myself.

The media ran headlines like,

LITTLE GIRL OPENS BOTTLE TO FIND FATHER'S WILL INSIDE

None of them mentioned her uncle and his head was cut off in every photo. Some said it was all a hoax; some said it was a miracle. The handwriting was quickly authenticated; it was Jack's.

I ended up the focus of another flurry of media attention from the events at Leilani's party, and this time, so did Michael. The harsh gaze of the public eye wasn't a very comfortable place to be. But our fifteen minutes of fame, in my case thirty, came to a quick and painless end. I got a lot of new work out of the whole thing, and if it kept up, I'd finally be able to make a good living at investigation. Maybe I'd even get that office I wanted.

J.M. Klein called me back one morning about a week later.

"I guess you heard about the message in the bottle," he said and chuckled.

"I sure did," I said. "Leave it to Jack to do something like that and have his own daughter find it."

"Do you actually believe she found that bottle on the beach?" Klein asked.

"You know, I do. I've recently come to the conclusion that mysterious things happen all the time, and the world is full of what some would call magic. And I don't mind it at all." I looked over at Michael and smiled. He sat next to me on the sofa sipping coffee.

"Why do I get the feeling you're turning down my offer?"

"That, Mr. Klein, is called a hunch. It's one of the mysteries. And it is absolutely right. But thank you very much for the offer."

"Well, if you ever change your mind about the offer, you know where to find me."

I got off the phone and turned to Michael.

"That felt good." I put my arms around him. "Now, what kind of trouble can we get into today?"

"I don't know," he said, "but if there's any around, I'm sure you'll find it."

ABOUT THE AUTHOR

Julie Leo

Julie Leo likes to make up stories and often writes them down. Educated in Anthropology/Archaeology and Law, she also writes fantasy and science fiction under the name Dawn Lyons. Fond of unreliable narrators and happy endings, her short fiction and poetry have appeared in magazines and anthologies, and she blogs about marketing for TechWeb. Originally from Washington, D.C., Julie currently lives in San Diego County where she raises miniature giraffes.

Visit her website:
julieleo.com

*　　　*　　　*

75293833R00139

Made in the USA
Columbia, SC
18 August 2017